# HANGING FIRE

# HANGING FIRE

## Jessica Mann

**ISIS**
**LARGE PRINT**
Oxford, England

First published in Great Britain 1997
by Constable and Company Ltd

Published in Large Print 1998 by ISIS Publishing Ltd,
7 Centremead, Osney Mead, Oxford OX2 0ES,
by arrangement with Constable and Company Ltd, London
and Lavinia Trevor

**British Library Cataloguing in Publication Data**
Mann, Jessica
 Hanging fire. – Large print ed.
 1. Detective and mystery stories 2. Large type books
 I. Title
 823.9'14 [F]

ISBN 0-7531-5890-6 (hb)
ISBN 0-7531-5915-5 (pb)

Printed and bound by MPG Books Ltd, Bodmin, Cornwall

# CHAPTER
# ONE

They had given up expecting the new proprietor by the time he finally appeared. Three months had gone by since the newspaper group passed into his ownership. For a while Argus House had been filled with anxious discussion. What changes would Mr Carne require? Who would be for the chop? Would it be sensible for journalists to jump before they were pushed?

But no announcement was made. Articles went on being commissioned, advertising space sold, opinions formed and promulgated. Christmas came and went. The daily, Sunday and weekly papers continued to appear as usual and the atmosphere in the office returned to its frenetic normality.

Tess Redpath, being sufficiently senior to have her own parking space, usually drove to work but that morning she came out into Arundel Gardens to find her snazzy little yellow Mazda had been vandalised, the windscreen smashed, and the radio stolen. It was not an uncommon happening in west London but that did not make it any easier to accept. Tess felt an almost solid lump of fury in her stomach, accompanied by a quick vision of revenge: capture, chastisement, castration, her own right hand clenched round a gleaming knife. Then, as usual, she coped.

Back upstairs in her flat she dialled and redialled until the garage answered at last, was put on hold, explained and held on again. Tweedly baroque whining assaulted her tone-deaf ear. She watched a man getting dressed in the flat across the road, listened to frantic hooting from a car blocked by a double parker, twitched some yellow-ed leaves off a cyclamen and reminded herself of a recent *Argus* leader with which, at the time, she agreed. It had argued that thieves were poor with deprived lives and victims rich in comparison, and minor street crime was a cheap price to pay for being allowed to store her most valuable possession in a public place.

At last Tess managed to arrange for the garage to tow the car away, changed her shoes for the wet walk to Notting Hill and went to work by tube. On the Dockland Light Railway platform at Bank station she met an old and friendly acquaintance called Archie Frazer, who was the crime correspondent of the daily paper. They sat together as the train ran along its elevated track past slums and business palaces. Tess was struck by her colleague's pessimistic view of a future in which the once magnificent office blocks would have crumbled into ruins and the River Thames would be bordered by banks of broken glass. What would archaeologists make of a society which built, on so massive and vulnerable a scale, monuments liable to demolition by a single destructive blast?

"Like the enterprise itself," he added. "What if Carne just shuts us down?"

"He couldn't do that," Tess protested.

"He can do any damn thing he likes, he owns it all."

"But why should he want to?"

"Mischief, malice, malevolence. I'm always nervous of loners."

"Why?"

"Years of experience on the crime beat. They are the ones who've never quite taken in that other people are real or relevant."

"Well, I don't see it myself, you might as well say you're scared of old Bert in the car-park," Tess said, realising she was prickled by Archie's words because she lived alone herself.

Conversations about Carne were still daily fare in the febrile atmosphere of the daily paper's news and editorial floors. By this time everyone knew the little there was to know about Ferdinand B. Came, even though the *Argus* itself had only printed a factual news announcement with a large photograph. Came, as he was always monosyllabically known, was dark-skinned and could be of Mediterranean or oriental descent. His large, staring eyes were very light brown, his mouth plump with large, perfect teeth. The top of his pointed head was as bald as a tonsure and he had a ruff of thick grey hair which brushed his collar and merged into a short pointed beard.

All the rival papers had been free to run profiles, mostly rude, and the *Argus* staff had pored over every word. Though he invested in the media Carne did not encourage media coverage of himself. Never formally interviewed, he had once let slip that he was interested in influencing the world "for the good" and those words had often been held against or for him. One writer pointed out that Carne was short, like those other tyrants Napoleon and Alexander the Great; and he too was a self-made man who had built up an empire of his own, but he had always been obsessively secretive and reclusive so nobody seemed to know quite how he had done it; he was a man from nowhere. But there were carefully phrased guesses at past criminal activities; gun running? drugs? international crime?

Archie Frazer said Carne was reported never to interfere with the running of any organisation he bought. He only concerned himself with the profits. All the same, Archie was not optimistic, having lived through Rupert Murdoch's reign of terror at Wapping and Max Hastings's putsch at the *Daily Telegraph*. "I'm getting a bit old for all this, there's no place for the over-forties on newspapers any more," he said.

Tess, who was only a year off forty herself, winced and he added kindly, "Of course you must be much younger, it's different for you." Passing the car-park entrance, both fumbled in their pockets. Bert was sitting there beside his trolley as usual, with a rusty black umbrella poked into its mesh but not quite keeping the rain off all his worldly goods.

"Thought you wasn't coming," he grunted, as Tess put the usual guilt money in his upturned cap.

"I'm sorry, I'm terribly late," she said, and repeated it to the security officer who guarded the lifts, and then to the nearest secretary as she emerged on to the fourteenth floor into the familiar organised chaos.

Up here, at the *Argus* weekly magazine, staff had

always been able to take things a little more calmly than did their colleagues who had to produce a paper every day. Nobody supposed a magazine revamp or relaunch would be the new owner's first priority, and when Moira, the long-time editor, had to be replaced from one day to the next, everyone assumed her successor Jason Spedding would carry on as before. What mattered was getting the magazine out, that week and every week. Today's panic was dealing with a rush job about the Bride of the Year, a story that had unexpectedly to be squeezed into a schedule determined weeks before.

The cover decided on by the weekly's former editor had been a shot of the scene of a cult massacre which had occurred exactly thirty years ago in Arizona. A famous aerial photograph showed the first sighting of the disaster, a circle of desolation and destruction isolated in the desert, black against yellow, seeming for a moment like an abstract work of art until the explanation turned it into a vision of horror. Tess Redpath had only just stopped herself reminiscing about the picture's first publication, when the horrific killings had seemed unprecedented; others had outdone it in horror since. But in this youthful environment it was better not to remind anyone that she had already been nine years old in 1965.

The new cover picture would naturally be the official engagement portrait of Petronella and her prince, the heir to one of Europe's smallest principalities, still nominally independent and, being a useful tax haven and money laundry, immeasurably rich. Petronella Williams was best known as the manageress from a soap opera called *Beauties* set in a health farm, so the picture desk had no trouble coming up with all her earlier publicity photos and the lead story was virtually ready to run, under the title "The Prince and the Showgirl". Meanwhile, as everyone in the building knew, one floor down in the broadsheet's editorial offices and news room, an inquest was being conducted. It could have been worse: over at some tabloid papers, heads were rolling.

Someone had blundered: where were the watchers when The Pet, in complete secret, met, went out with and got engaged to the richest young man in Europe? The engagement announcement had come as a complete surprise.

Tess Redpath considered it a triumph to have so speedily commissioned, taken delivery of and sub-edited the complete piece but the new editor of the *Argus* magazine was not satisfied.

"There isn't enough about Petsy's family," Jason complained, tweaking at his pin-striped lapel with manicured fingers. "Where's a proper pic of her mother? We need to see more than a bloody Barbour and headscarf."

"This was the best anyone could find."

"For God's sake, the woman isn't a savage who thinks photos steal her soul, there must be more."

"I've tried all the agencies . . ."

Tess turned back to her own corner of the room, feeling sorry for the picture editor whose life was hard enough as it was, with a sick mother-in-law living in her house and a toddler with learning difficulties. She would be blamed for having failed to come up with something better than this, the only known picture of The Pet's mother, which was a snap of a mumsy woman with a pleasant but unremarkable face, square cheekbones and chin and strongly marked eyebrows. She had been moving an open hand to shield herself from the camera as the shutter closed, so the picture was blurred. "They've promised official pix," Tess heard.

She switched her attention away to her own desk and screen. Unconsciously twiddling her hair around her forefinger, she thought how much she longed for something sweet.

"What wouldn't I give for a Mars bar or a chocolate raisin . . . even one toffee . . ."

She felt around at the back of her stationery drawer in case a slim stick of chewing gum was still lurking there under the jumbled papers.

Abbie, the inefficient but sweet-natured secretary, came by carrying two steaming mugs on an in-tray.

"Abbie, you are kind. Hey, wasn't it your test yesterday? Did you pass?"

"Failed on hand signals, bugger it, I've got another next month. Here, Tessie, have a biscuit, I got your favourites."

"Better not, thanks all the same." To remind herself why eating was out of the question, Tess hooked her thumb into the rather too close-fitting waistband of her skirt.

Tess had revamped her own appearance in the two months since Jason came into her life, making an effort to alter the emphasis of the plump pink cheeks and round, light blue eyes of her naturally Dutch-doll face with subtle cosmetics; she discarded the trusty leggings and designer knitwear which skimmed so tactfully over

7

her wide hips, and gave some of them away to her niece Lara. Instead she wore little fitted jackets and tight, short skirts. Tess had realised Jason noticed every detail, reading designer labels with an unnaturally X-ray eye. She supposed another man might be able to tell which Savile Row tailor had built Jason's powerful suits, or which designer had stitched the creamy silk shirts or woven his gaudy ties. To Tess, he simply looked like a City gent in the wrong place. All the same, he needed to be kept up if not competed with.

Tess missed Moira and her comfortable manners but doubted whether anyone else did. Nobody ever looked back on newspapers. Journalists and editors worked on the next issue and the one after that while those which had appeared were already forgotten, yesterday's news. People slipped equally easily from the memory, even Moira and the dreadful way she died.

Moira had been mugged. She had come in to catch up with some work on Boxing Day when nobody else was around, gone out to the deserted car-park and been attacked. Her body was found when daylight came, half concealed by her own car. Nobody had seen anything. Even Bert, who spent the icy night under the overhang of the loading bay, said nobody had come anywhere near except the usual. Pressed, he identified the night staff, the assistant editor, the proprietor. No intruders, no criminals.

There was a lot of fuss, of course, at the time of Moira's death, front page stories in the daily paper, a glitzy service at St Bride's in Fleet Street, but that was it. By now the only reminder was the increased security and intensified lighting in the car-park.

Tess was appalled for Moira, of whom she had been fond, and frightened for herself — it could have happened to her! She was terribly ashamed to realise that her next thought was of her own promotion.

She went to the office on 28th December expecting to take over as the magazine's new editor. There she found Jason Spedding already installed. He was bright, young, keen and new. His smile did not reach his round grey eyes. He put no value on experience. He despised frumps and fatties. So today Tess was wearing a new suit passed on by the fashion editor from a batch of samples, and her shortened and sharpened hair had been freshly trimmed.

"A bob, how sensible, you can shake and shape it at home," Jason had remarked knowledgeably when she came in with her bushy, bouncing curls shorn. Today he called across: "Good jacket, Tess. Jil Sander's just right for the larger woman."

Luckily, given how late she was, the regular columns Tess dealt with herself were ahead of schedule. Others were already commissioned for weeks in advance. She checked on the screen: the two diary pieces known in the office as "Country Mouse" and "Town Mouse", the horoscope, the holiday spot, the "knicker drawer" piece in which celebrities revealed the secrets of their wardrobes, all organised. She left some telephone messages, spoke to a future contributor and disputed with a stylist about his fee. Then she turned to Moira's "notions" file. Jason had not been interested in it, saying he had enough notions of his own thank you very much, but Tess was gradually working her way through Moira's screened and scribbled notes. She'd had good ideas even if they were no good for Jason. A few could still be used in the magazine, Tess believed. She particularly liked the Luisa Weiss idea which Moira had noted last summer when she looked through the list of the coming year's memorable dates. "Death of Luisa Weiss (feminist), 1970," it had said. Tess remembered her, having once, at thirteen, actually been in the same room. "Brilliant idea," she had told Moira, "she changed lives, that woman, I'm here to prove it." But Jason was not keen.

"I can never see what's so special about these suicidal females, Sylvia Plath, Ann Sexton, Luisa Weiss, Virginia Woolf, poor mad things every one of them, why does anyone care? Anyway, it's old, stale, there's nothing left to be said."

Surely, a quarter of a century on, women readers at least would think the story was worth a fresh look, especially because a final volume of her writings, edited by her husband, was to appear on the anniversary of her death. The computer file, which Tess sadly saw had the date of the day of Moira's death, was simply a list of possible writers for the story and the inquiry letter to a couple of libraries to ask if they had pictures.

That was all there was on the computer but the filing cabinet contained an old envelope addressed to the magazine on which was scrawled a name, Peter Slowe, and an outer London telephone number, in Moira's writing. Beside it was a doodle, or, perhaps, an unfinished game of Hangman — a notional scaffold, rope, and a hanging figure. Tess dialled the number, which was answered "Yes?" after three rings.

"Please can I speak to Peter Slowe?"

A gasp at the other end, and a pause. The husky female voice said, "Then you haven't heard."

"I'm sorry?"

"He's dead. My husband's dead. He was killed."

"Killed! How dreadful, what —?"

"It was New Year's Eve. Some drunk driver. Hit and run. They never found him."

"You have my deepest sympa —"

"Anyway, who are you? What did you want with Peter?"

"I'm working at the *Argus* magazine, your husband spoke to —"

"A reporter. He spoke to a reporter. Was that you?"

"No, it was a colleague of mine, I'm just dealing with a story she's . . . passed on to me."

"You'll know what Peter had to say then. I can't help you, I wasn't there, I've never even been to Cornwall and anyway we were only together for two years and now he's gone and left me alone, I don't know how I'm going to manage without him . . ." The congested words merged into sobs and incoherence. Tess made sympathetic sounds, but felt helpless and eventually put the receiver gently down. Poor woman, what an awful thing to happen, she thought, visualising widowhood and bereavement, momentarily wondering whether it was better to remain single and be spared such sudden loneliness.

She peered into the envelope and saw it was full of

**11**

notes and cuttings sent up from the library: book reviews, criticism, an obituary, a reassessment of Luisa made by a hostile old diehard when the women's movement was at its height in the late 1970s, a re-re-assessment by a post-feminist guru of the eighties.

She did make a difference, whatever it was, Tess thought. I wouldn't be in a job like this if it hadn't been for Luisa Weiss and the other seminal pioneers of women's liberation. But it was pointless to expect Jason to be interested, he was still at playgroup when Luisa died.

Tess felt her self-confidence lurch. Demonic thoughts were lurking, terrors of being middle-aged and left behind by younger, prettier, trendier, livelier competitors. She summoned her own thought-police, the mental block against ideas she did not want to have. "Tess is so nice," people always said. But she knew she wasn't nice, she just seemed it. Cruel, inimical visions were always waiting to enter her head. She hated herself for it. At an early age she developed a technique of substituting good thoughts for bad. "Be nice," her mother always said when she was little, and Tess had learnt how to be nice while always secretly knowing such niceness was without merit, because it was not natural and nasty thoughts lay under her nice actions. Self-taught at first, she had since read often enough that similar techniques were well known to psychotherapists, and knew self-reassurance worked — sometimes. She ran quickly through a familiar, often repeated litany.

"You're assistant editor of the *Argus* magazine," Tess told herself, "and you earn more than your father ever did in his whole working life in the clay pits. You've got Jacques."

Tess was waiting for Jacques to set himself free — when he left the navy, when all his children had gone to boarding school, when he left his wife. Tess had never met Sibyl, though she often pored over the photographs of the pretty little woman by Jacques's side at the kind of naval functions that were covered by news agencies. Tess tried not to hate her. It was all too easy to visualise car crashes or domestic disasters, Jacques summoned back from a foreign posting, the minimum decent interval and then . . .

Tess sometimes had vicious thoughts about Sibyl. She could run her over. She could send poisoned chocolates. She could hire a hit man. She could persuade Sibyl to leave. It must be awful being married to a man who doesn't care for you, surely Sibyl couldn't help feeling Jacques's impatience and boredom, she must notice he doesn't hurry back from work or home from his postings. Be nice, Tess.

"You've got your own home," Tess's litany went on. Tess passionately loved her flat, a nineteenth-century conversion whose mortgage she was paying off slowly but surely and where she had lived alone from the moment she started earning enough to do without the rent from a tenant.

Tess also loved her company car, a Japanese coupé designed for the female executive, and often stood admiring, almost gloating over the clothes, encased in plastic bags, which hung in ordered array in her walk-in closet.

*Cosmopolitan* magazine had even featured Tess three years previously in an article about women and self-determination. "You're doing all right," she whispered, making an unconscious preening movement of her shoulders and head. The she realised someone was standing close behind her and the room had become very quiet.

"This is the assistant editor, Tess Redpath, Mr Carne."

Tess sprang to her feet, almost colliding with Hamish Beck, the editor in chief, and sending her chair rolling backwards into the much smaller man at his side. A circle of courtiers surrounded them: Jason, and the picture editor, and Derek Simon, the editor of the Sunday newspaper who was Jason's boss, and hers, and behind them hovered a bevy of personal assistants.

"Ms Redpath." F.B. Carne held out his hand. His grasp was cool and smooth and when Tess's palm slipped away from his, hers was slightly tingling. He exuded a sweetish scent like vanilla. His feline eyes were almost hypnotic; Tess found herself gazing into them until the monitor within commanded, "Stop it at once, he'll think you've got a crush on him."

"And have you been here a long time, Ms Redpath?"

"Yes, since —"

"Tess has worked on the magazine since its first issue, Mr Carne," Hamish said. "She's the fount of all knowledge about it."

"How long does that make it? Thirteen, fourteen years?" F.B. Carne inquired.

"Getting on for seventeen, I'm afraid."

"Afraid? Why?"

"It's — it's just a figure of speech."

"Never fear," he said, unsmiling.

"No, Mr Carne."

"And what are you working on, Ms Redpath?" he asked, his accent softly transatlantic, his tone warm and encouraging.

"I'm looking into the Luisa Weiss suicide, what really made her —"

He said, soft and drawling, "That old story?" and Jason leapt in.

"It's Tess's pet project, F.B., though I have to say, in my judgement this is not a nineties story, it's been done to death by now."

"Not the best idea," he murmured, still smiling.

"It was one of Moira's ideas, but we both believed there could well be a new angle to Weiss's death, to what happened to her in 1970," Tess said. "There's quite a bit of investigation to do into it, because we thought the story told at the time was worth looking at again. Of course, if you don't want me —"

F.B. Carne wiped his forefinger along the top of the computer screen and looked at the slight smear of dust. He said, "Onwards."

Followed by an anxious retinue, he planted his small, shining shoes precisely in front of each other as he crossed the ultramarine expanse of carpet. His eyes rested briefly on the illicit pot plants and cardboard crates of papers, the dreggy cups concealed behind paper trays, the flickering screens with their fringes of post-it messages. He paused at the long table where this week's pages were laid out. "As you see, Mr Carne, we've managed to get a good coverage of the wedding arrangements," Jason said.

"Yes."

"And there's men's fashion week."

"Yes. And what's this?"

"It's a Pulitzer winner we've picked up from the United States about cult massacres." Tess watched as the proprietor looked from one dramatic picture to the next. When they came into the office they had caught the attention of the most experienced and blasé of the staff, a series of atmospheric images evoking deathly smells and shocked silences: the rows of corpses in a jungle clearing in Guyana when nearly one hundred and fifty cultists committed suicide in the Jonestown massacre; the bodies being carried out of Waco after the FBI bombardment of the secret compound; the charred, disastrous mess left at Tarrant's Crossing, where dozens of cult members and their guru perished without survivors. The proprietor's eye skimmed over the vivid, shocking words of the accompanying text.

"Whose responsibility is this?"

Tess saw Jason glance across at her, hesitation clearly written on her face. With obvious regret Jason said, "Actually this is one of Tess's, Mr Carne, she spotted a link between —"

"Onwards," he said again. They watched him traversing the low-ceilinged room. The home editor and sports writer sprang to their feet as he approached, making that anxious gesture which is not quite a bow. The beauty editor smiled and flicked her long hair. The fashion assistant pushed a rack of beach wear out of his path and

16

stood aside with a balletic gesture of welcome and respect. The proprietor disappeared into the middle distance, and Abbie, the personal assistant sighed:

"Gosh, isn't he gorgeous, those eyes, when he looked at me I went all weak at the knees."

"He's certainly charismatic," Tess said, her face burning at the new proprietor's implied rebuke.

"As charismatic as Petronella, and that's saying a lot," said Dave, the sports writer.

"I think he's a bit creepy," said Lee, the fashion editor.

Tess rubbed her finger over her computer. She said, "Look at this! Doesn't anyone clean this place?"

"Yes, but fancy him noticing!" said Abbie.

"He notices everything, he fixed us with his glittering eye," Lee said.

"That's what we called a white glove inspection in the air force," Dave said. "It's a way of showing who's boss, a demo of the commanding officer at his most commanding. Yes sir, no sir, my big toe sir. Jesus, if we start any of that crap round here I'll be off like a bat out of hell."

Jason strode back and Tess said, "What did you think of him, Jason?"

"I knew him already of course. He's a charmer and he's completely on the ball. A remarkable man."

"Did he say anything about his plans for the mag?" Lee asked.

Jason shook his head. "He said it was the jewel in his crown."

"Does that mean he's satisfied?"

"Seems to be."

Yes, Tess thought, then and every subsequent time she went over and over it in her mind, reliving the brief encounter, repeating the short dialogue, yes, F.B. Carne had seemed to be perfectly satisfied by his visitation, he hadn't given the slightest hint of criticism or impending changes.

Tess went into work the next morning, as she had done for nearly all her adult life. How many times? Twenty multiplied by three hundred and sixty-five minus weekends, minus holidays — she must have spent nearly five thousand days of her life in that office.

Her car not being ready she arrived late again, because the Dockland Light Railway came to a halt for half an hour between Shadwell and Limehouse. As she came in a messenger brought some packages and files for which Tess signed. There was a typed message in a sealed envelope on her desk, summoning her to see the editor in chief. She shoved the note and some of the papers into her large shoulder bag because Hamish Beck was famous for always running late, and she could get started on the work while waiting in his ante-room.

Stepping out of the lift Tess ran into Ilona Spivak. The two were good friends, having originally met at an exercise class, and when Tess knew the job as Carne's personal assistant was coming up she had encouraged Ilona, then working in a dull job in a travel agency, to apply for it. "Sorry," Tess said, bending to pick up the comb which had fallen from Ilona's uncontrollable sunburst of hair. "Goodness, you do look hassled."

Ilona pushed the gilt ornament at random into her

curls. "Oh Tess, gosh, well look, it's just — but anyway, I'm fine, it's just all too — sorry, can't talk now."

"Shall we have lunch later?"

"Maybe — another time — sorry, must rush," Ilona called behind her, trotting away down the corridor.

Tess reminded herself to call Ilona later in the morning and make sure there was nothing wrong. She pushed open the door into the editor's suite, smiled at the secretary, whom she did not know, and turned towards a chair, but the secretary told her to go right in.

Tess had no premonition. She had been friendly with Hamish, first when he arrived as a young leader writer straight from Oxford and later when he did a stint on the magazine. Then he went off to cover the Falklands war, his first fine hour, and came back in glory to the editorial staff of the daily paper.

Everyone knew Tess was sent invitations to Hamish's parties and received a personal, handwritten message on his printed Christmas cards. Sometimes other members of staff asked Tess to intercede with him, because they knew she was his friend.

Some friend.

Tess went up to the top floor expecting some simple or social request. She came down again having been "let go".

Derek Simon was in the room with Hamish. Tess realised later she should have been suspicious when Hamish came round his desk to shake her by the hand, his other hand on her shoulder, pressing her down into a low chair. But it was Derek who did the talking.

At first Tess didn't understand. She could not take in

what Derek was saying. Something about down-sizing and out-sourcing. Rationalisation, he said, and the target reader. They must aim at a younger target-market.

Tess thought he was asking her to soften up some other members of staff. For a moment she even supposed he was offering her promotion.

"Well, there it is, Tess, I regret it deeply, I can honestly say this hurts me as much as it hurts you," he lied, and added something about severance payment, out-placement consultants and pension plans.

Tess said, "Hamish?" But he had walked over to the window and stood with his back to her. She stared at the red braces and blue striped shirt, and said again, "Hamish, you can't . . ."

He turned, but his familiar gaze, black-fringed and more blue than nature had made it because he wore coloured contacts, slid away from hers.

She said, "After all this time —"

"I'm sorry," he muttered, and turned away again.

Derek repeated his spiel. He put his hand on her, turned her towards the door, pushed her gently out of the room.

Going down, Tess caught sight of her own face in the mirrors that lined the lift and saw she had gone an ugly, mottled red, emphasised by the scarlet of her second-hand Chanel jacket. Her face's maturity was emphasised by the harsh light, her eyes seemed round and blank with shock. Blindly she made her way to the cloakroom and shut herself into a cubicle. She was shaking and sweating. In the dim privacy her control let go. Tears poured from her eyes, dribble from her mouth.

She sat, knees splayed, head bowed, on the lavatory seat, her liquidised bowels voiding noisily. She felt sick, ill, bereaved. It's like someone dying, she thought. Or me dying.

After a while she said, "It's shock. I'm in shock."

She couldn't move or think or plan. There was a pain in her chest. She'd been stabbed to the heart. "My job, my life, everything I've worked for. Gone, all gone."

At last, gasping and panting, Tess pressed her knuckles painfully against her nose and eyes, forced herself to stop, to take deeper breaths, to relax her rigid muscles.

I can't believe this has happened to me, Tess thought. I can't deal with this.

But in the end she had to come out of the cubicle, mercifully to find nobody else standing at the row of wash-basins and mirrors. She splashed her wrists and forehead with cold water, combed her highlighted bob and reapplied make-up, smearing glitter on her eyelids and a scarlet slash on her trembling lips.

Don't let them see you care, she told herself, pretend you quit, make them think it was your own choice. Say you've found a better job somewhere else.

Tess walked past other desks to her own, realising from her colleagues' averted eyes and sudden silence that they already knew. She sat at her work station. The computer screen was blank and she pressed the switches to boot it up again but nothing happened. She tried again and yet again, before realising what had happened.

The shits. Bastards. I'll kill them! They had cut off her access, already, with brutal speed, in the brief period, twenty minutes at the outside, she was away from the desk.

She'd been in the middle of dealing with an article about women in Saudi Arabia by last year's Booker prize winner, and an exposé of adoption agencies, and a piece for next year on the anniversary of a women's college. There were all her own ideas and contacts list, her addresses, her personal memos and notes. She was barred from them all. It felt like having a limb amputated.

For a few minutes Tess sat shivering, her head down, eyes closed, like an animal under threat.

"Are you OK?" Abbie was standing beside her holding a cardboard cup of steaming coffee. "Here, drink this, you'll feel better." The girl's voice sounded motherly and concerned.

"Abbie." Tess cleared her throat and tried again. "Abbie, there's a problem with my screen, can I use yours?"

"I'm not supposed —"

"Don't ask Abbie that, it puts her in an awkward position." That was Jason. Creep. Slimeball. Scheming, manipulative, two-faced arsehole.

Fired with merciful indignation, Tess realised gratefully that she was going to shout not weep. At least it meant she'd go down with all guns firing. But it made no difference. Since the time, just after the paper went on line, that a sacked journalist had taken a swift revenge by inserting obscenities and libels into the next day's articles before he left the building for ever, it had been the invariable practice, occasionally enforced by Tess herself, that computer access was denied even before Form P45 was handed over, the cartons filled with the desk's long accumulation of junk, or the leaving gift presented. Tess was permitted a special concession. Under Jason's supervision, Abbie was instructed to print out the file containing Tess's personal documents. Abbie filled the embarrassing space with chatter as she did so, shrieking her incredulity around the office, volubly dismayed about what she called the "don't come Monday". Tess recognised the excitement, almost the glee, on her face. It was gossip-fodder. A happening.

There was a whispered, hissing murmur, a sibilance. "Tess Redpath, of all people." Lee came and uttered some sickly, insincere regrets. The others, embarrassed, failed to meet Tess's eyes.

Abbie handed her the pages and she folded them into her shoulder bag, stuffing them down into its muddle without looking what she was doing. She walked down the long room, between desks loaded with papers, flowers, pot plants, with their flickering monitors and corners of personality, where one worker had a mirror, another a mascot. Nobody looked at her. They were embarrassed and ashamed, as she had always been in similar circumstances. Behind her came Abbie, carrying one of the cardboard boxes.

As they waited for the lift to take Tess down, the door of another going up opened. Hamish got out, leaving the new proprietor standing in the lift. F.B. Carne's stare met Tess's without any gesture of recognition or word of farewell. Beside him were his team. A pink young man who was the personal assistant, the Canadian secretary

Miss Riordan, and Ilona Spivak. Ilona glanced at Tess and glanced quickly away, a flush flooding her cheeks and throat. She made a small mark in a notebook and the lift doors slid closed.

They had ordered a cab to take Tess home. On the *Argus* account, they said. To her own immediate and lasting regret, Tess actually thanked them.

# CHAPTER
# TWO

All those years.

Half a lifetime of rushing, scurrying, striving, scuttling from one urgent need to another, always a little late, never doing anything quite as well as it could have been done because there was still another thing on her list, the next obligation or deadline already overdue. And now, after all that — peace, quiet, freedom. Emptiness.

This must be the personal space and place Luisa Weiss had written about in her journals long before the words became a cliché. A place away from other people and a space without the insistent, repetitive demands of a woman's busy life.

I sometimes said I was longing for exactly this, Tess reflected, but the thought was bitter, now she was lonely and unoccupied in a silent and increasingly squalid flat. When Tess was busy she had kept her home in good order. Now the whole day was free for putting things away and cleaning the place up and somehow she just couldn't make herself get going on any of it.

Tess was still wearing the tattered old T-shirt she slept in. She had not cleared away her breakfast coffee or yesterday's dishes or made her bed or cleaned the bath. She had woken far earlier than was either necessary or desirable after a night interrupted by agonies of small hours angst. If she slept at all, it was to an accompaniment of disaster-dreams.

When she summoned up the energy to go downstairs for her newspapers she began to glance over the Situations Vacant. On Mondays the *Guardian* had pages of media and arts jobs listed. Tess marked three, telling herself she'd apply though she knew perfectly well there was not much point in wasting effort or a stamp on any of them. Anyway, she still felt so furiously resentful she could hardly bring herself to read the ads.

How could this have happened to her? Couldn't Hamish have slid her in somewhere else? Why did she need to go begging for a job?

With her eyes fixed on the hypnotic waving of a cobweb in the sun, Tess thought about that last encounter with Hamish Beck, the distant, silent man in his intimidating office. She'd expected him to ring that day, for his voice to be waiting on the answering machine when she stumbled into her flat from the *Argus*'s taxi. Or he'd come. They were friends, weren't they? They'd even been lovers. Not very long, never with love, but with pleasure; liking; a kind of loyalty. She had waited, pacing the floor, twiddling her hair, not daring to go out to the shops for fear of missing him, but he hadn't come and he hadn't rung.

Eventually she had broken, left messages for him. "You can't treat me this way, you can't do this to me . . ."

Four days later he rang back. Chilly, distant, as though they'd never rolled laughing on a bed together. He'd been such fun; not the great lover, not the most subtle ever known, but one of the most entertaining. A giggle a minute.

No longer. "I can't help you," he'd said. "I can't do anything about it."

"But Hamish, I don't understand, what did I do? Did I offend Derek Simon, or Jason Spedding, what happened?"

"It's the way things go. It's no use your asking, don't ring me any more, it's not in my power to take you back."

"You're the editor in chief!"

"It's out of my hands."

"Was it Mr Carne?"

"Don't even ask, Tess. Take my advice, forget it, forget him. For your own sake."

"I could sue, you know. Unfair dismissal. Sex discrimination."

"I wouldn't do that, Tess, not if you ever want to work in this town again."

"Is this all down to Carne? Did he take against me?"

"I can't discuss it."

"Or did I do something to annoy you? Surely you can give me some explanation!"

"Don't call me again, Tess. I'll try to have a word with someone on the *Independent* or the *Mail*, it might be possible to get them to take you on."

"When I'm not good enough for the *Argus* any more? Thanks a bunch, Hamish, I can just see it, one of that lot wanting your reject."

"Well, there it is."

There what is? Where was it? Tess hadn't the faintest idea. All she knew was that Hamish Beck's famous chill had frozen her. And now, nearly three weeks later, she had fully understood, as though she didn't already know it, that there was no place in newspapers or magazines for a woman not far off forty who had spent the whole of her career with the same employer and then been sacked.

What a mistake, Tess thought, remembering her former pride and devotion. Why didn't I listen? Tess's friend Sheila had always said she was making a mistake.

"You shouldn't have made a job the centre of your life." Tess found her body-language annoyingly smug. Sheila, having given up her partnership in a law firm to become a full-time mother, was certain that this, like every other decision she'd made since she and Tess became best friends at the age of eleven, was right for her and everyone else too.

Cassie, who had been a colleague on the *Argus* before sinking into a safe but unambitious job editing the house magazine of an oil company, was unbearably up-beat. Of course Tess would find a new job, a bigger and better one. It's always darkest before dawn. Everything would come good, Cassie insisted, who believed in the power of positive thinking, and added, "I can *feel* it."

It was even more depressing to talk to an ex-boyfriend, Neil, who at forty-seven had "taken early retirement" from a highly paid job in the City, and never found a new one. "Nobody wants people my age, I'm on the scrap heap. I've given up hope of ever working again."

As for Ilona — Tess grimaced in pain at the thought of

Ilona. Ilona did not return Tess's calls. She did not reply to her letters. A friendship lost. Then Tess saw her in the steam room at the Porchester baths.

Tess did not much enjoy a Turkish bath but believed it was good for her ever since a three-hour session banished flu one winter. But it was not to find well-being that she went there this time; as she took off her outer clothes, slowly, folding each garment, because she was not in a hurry any more and might never be again, she realised she had come to be cleansed. Somewhere deep inside she believed she had done something dreadful and losing her job was the punishment, Hamish Beck its agent.

Across the steamy room Ilona Spivak materialised into view as she scrubbed and scraped and preened her small, buxom body She squeaked at the sight of Tess, making a reflex grab at her towel as though hiding her flesh would hide her identity. Then she uttered some lame and inadequate inanities. She peered through the mist to see if anybody they knew was listening. Eventually she admitted she was afraid of getting the sack herself; contact with Tess would be regarded as disloyalty.

"But why? I don't understand. What am I supposed to have done?"

But Ilona only knew that Mr Carne had said Tess must go.

"Carne? Why? I never even — what does he think — there must be a mistake —"

No mistake. Ilona said, "I heard him telling Hamish to get rid of you."

"Didn't Hamish want to know why?"

"He did ask, but Mr Carne didn't say, he just gives orders, you know, it's like working for a dictator. He likes people to jump when he says jump, you can see he enjoys having us at his mercy so you don't dare ask questions."

"Are you frightened of him, Ilona?"

"Well, of course I am, he's bloody terrifying, those X-ray eyes, he can read my thoughts. You know I was lucky to get the job, God knows I'm not really qualified to be a PA, but as far as he's concerned I'm just for show."

"What's his secret then?"

"If only I knew," Ilona said, turning over in the moist heat. Sweat trickled down her round, pink buttocks and she scratched the tickle, saying, "I think he's, like, mesmerised me."

"You mean you actually fancy him?"

"God no, I wouldn't touch him with a long pole, thank you very much, but I'm under his spell, I suppose, but then everyone who comes into contact with him is."

"Is that how he got where he is today, do you think?"

"Well." Ilona made another of her hunted glances round the steamy room, but none of the towelled, dozy figures seemed to be listening to her whispered words and having overcome her initial fear she gossiped on. "I got into the wrong file one day, I'd be out on my ear if anyone found out. You know people say he's Canadian but I saw this list of . . . health farms, you've got to go to the Golden Door, it's out of this world. Hi, Daria, look who I ran into by accident, I was just telling Tess about that week in . . . Tess, you remember Daria, she's the travel editor on the *Sunday Argus*?"

After that, Ilona became incommunicado again. Tess was out in the cold and not even her oldest friends seemed to be any use in this fix. As for her former colleagues! The only one who had even telephoned was Archie Frazer, a sympathetic but businesslike call, as though he were ticking it off a list of duties. Otherwise, universal, unbroken silence, as though Tess had somehow dropped out of the universe into some kind of limbo.

Tess wondered whether it was her own fault. She had put other relationships second to Jacques so often during recent years, cancelling appointments when he turned up unexpectedly, as well as refusing the confidences which friendships need to keep them in repair. She had always kept her promise never to utter the slightest hint of his identity, and only Tess's sister knew even that she was having an affair with a married man.

Jacques was stationed two thousand miles away at NATO headquarters in Italy, though he often came back to the UK for meetings. He hadn't rung up. Where was he? If only he would come, now, this very minute. She imagined the sound of his key in the door, his voice in her ear, the comfort of his arms around her. Ages since the last time he was here, looking in on his way home to Oxfordshire from a government reception. He'd hardly got through the front door before he started stripping off his dress jacket and starched shirt, exposing his brown, muscular, spicy body. A gush of adoration and lust had swept over Tess. Her skin had been boiling hot, the

31

blood beating in her veins and at the back of her eyes. They were intimately familiar with each other's tastes and techniques, they knew how to please. They did please. They were pleased.

Afterwards, lying in his arms, breathing in the very essence of the man, imprinting his warmth and strength and masculinity on her skin, Tess willed him to fall asleep there, but too soon he said he must be going.

Jacques, Tess thought, Jacques, damn you, I need you, why don't you ring? Who do you expect me to talk to? What do you expect me to do?

The only person who seemed to be any use at all was, unexpectedly, Tess's ground-floor neighbour, Desmond. Up until now Tess had known him only as an acquaintance, polite but not intimate, who kept an art and curio shop nearby in the neighbourhood of the Portobello Road.

Desmond dressed in conventional tweed suits and sober ties, lived very quietly and, as far as Tess knew, alone. His demeanour was so restrained and uninformative that she would never have known he was gay if a picture of him marching in a Gay Pride rally had not appeared in the *Kensington Post* last summer. Not long afterwards Tess met him on the doorstep. He was collecting his milk, wearing silk pyjamas and dressing-gown. Tess had asked if he was all right. "You don't look at all well, can I get anything for you from the shops?" That was when he told her he was HIV positive. But he recovered from that bout of illness and since then they had passed, friendly but still distant, in the hall.

The previous day Tess had run into him in the Elgin

Crescent newsagent's and, in explaining why she was there in the middle of a weekday, blurted her troubles out. That evening he appeared at her door with smoked salmon and Chardonnay from the most expensive local delicatessen, and over them listened to the recital of her problems.

Desmond told Tess to stop using words like scrap heap. "Tell yourself you're the greatest, you've got to make yourself believe it. When the force chucked me out I wrote down what I could do and what I might learn and what I'd like, and that's exactly what you've got to do now. Make a list. Think positive."

The next morning Tess again twisted her lips at the idea. What was she supposed to think positive about? The pension scheme aborted, the company car repossessed, the status lost? The mortgage, threatening and unpaid? Bert the beggar, missing her daily alms? The weather, blustery and wet? Tess looked through the streaming window with distaste. The wind had torn the spring bulbs in her window box into tatters. Somebody's refuse bag had been blown open, scattering styrofoam and polythene over the pavement. A dog had crapped on the front steps.

Ten to twelve. The morning nearly gone. In the office they'd be coming out of the editorial meeting, making final decisions about this week's running order, ordering cabs to take them back into town, prinking for the business lunch.

Desmond had written Tess a memo. She scrabbled for it under the *Guardian*. At the top it said, "Things to

Remember. One, you're nice. Two, you're healthy. Three, you're clever."

Underneath came his suggestions — study, advertise, change direction. And again, a reminder that she was The Greatest.

I suppose I could study something, Tess thought. But a wave of uninterest flooded through her. There's nothing I want to learn about.

Tess's degree had been in general studies at Edinburgh University, but she wanted to start her real life instead of staying on for a fourth year and taking an honours degree. It didn't matter in those days. With an "ordinary BA" and a certificate in shorthand and typing she walked straight into a job at the *Argus*. During that period of boom and full employment things were easy for young people and even those who were not so young.

Tess's only contribution to Desmond's list consisted of describing her few qualifications. She knew how to use computers, edit copy, proof-read and commission articles. Nothing else.

"You never did much writing yourself?" Desmond asked.

"Hardly ever had the chance."

"You'd be good at it, you should try something like radio plays or short stories. Why don't you go on a course?"

"Perhaps. One day," Tess had said, more to make him stop going on about it than because she meant it. She'd seen enough of writers and their anguishes to have abandoned any desire to be one herself. Writers had blocks and were lonely, they sucked up to editors and committed suicide, like Luisa Weiss. Writers also drank.

Good idea. Tess picked up a bottle from the draining board. Empty. Get some clothes on, go and buy some booze. Where's my money? Tess stretched across the table for her shoulder bag, which turned upside down. Everything fell out.

Of course the bag was unzipped, it would be. Even inanimate objects are against me now, Tess thought.

She scrabbled on the grimy, crumb-strewn floor for her purse, and found herself holding some envelopes addressed to the assistant editor of the *Argus* magazine. It took her a little while to remember picking them up and shoving them into her capacious bag on the last day, just before she'd been summoned by Hamish. A picture of him sitting in his office flashed into her mind: overfed, almost bloated, his cheeks too pink. Please God let him have a heart attack. She did not add "Be nice, Tess" to the thought.

Slitting an envelope open Tess saw it was the type-script of a column by one of her most reliable country mice.

"I ought to let them know I've got this stuff," she said aloud. She grabbed the receiver and dialled the familiar number.

"Good morning, the *Argus*, how may I help you?"

Jason Spedding, please."

"May I say who's calling?"

"Say it's Tess."

After a long pause the same indifferent voice said, "Sorry, he's in a meeting."

Tess banged the receiver down.

How dare he? In a meeting indeed! Like hell he was. That was the euphemism for not wanting to speak to someone, the modern equivalent of Victorian butlers mendaciously telling callers that Madam was not at home.

The least that bastard could do is bloody speak to me!

Tess wondered whether to call one of the others instead. But what was the point? They'd probably forgotten her existence by now. She dialled again.

"Good morning, the *Argus*, how may I help you?"

"Tess Redpath, please."

"Sorry, who did you say?"

"Tess Redpath."

A long pause. Then, "She's not on my list."

"On the magazine."

"Nobody of that name working here, sorry."

"She was there a month ago."

"I'm sorry I can't help you."

That's how it goes, Tess thought, a month and I've been written out already.

Someone half Tess's age would be at her desk, talking to her writers, laying out her pages, checking the articles she had commissioned. Twenty years gone for nothing, lost without trace.

The telephone rang. That'll be them, she thought, how silly of me to think they wouldn't — "Hallo. Tess Redpath."

"Hi, it's Desmond."

For a moment she could not speak. Then anger with

herself for feeling disappointed restored her voice. "Sorry, Desmond, here I am."

"I just called to see how you're getting on."

"Badly, frankly. I'm still so — so absolutely bloody furious. I'd like to kill them."

"Don't get mad," Desmond said. "Get even."

"Believe me, I would if I could. If only I knew how."

"Well, dear, you know what they say."

"Do I?"

"Living well is the best revenge."

"Living well!" Her voice went high in mockery, and then she found herself blurting out a litany of self-pity. "How can I live well when I haven't got a job and my redundancy money won't last more than another three months and I've got a mortgage and my boyfriend's stationed two thousand miles away —"

"Tess. Stop. Listen, I've got a customer. I'll come in this evening."

He was a good friend, better than those who Tess had thought to be her real friends, who had condoled and consoled at first and hardly been heard from since. They had found her out, realised she was nasty, ugly, a failure, bitches the lot of them — stop it, Tess. Be nice.

Only Desmond, so recently a stranger living discreetly with his cats, early music and enticing cooking smells, seemed to understand what she was going through. Tess was ashamed to remember she had let Jacques call him a poofter.

She reached for the list Desmond had written, which was lying under the letters she'd inadvertently brought home from the office. What were they anyway? Nothing to do with me any more, Tess thought, I should simply readdress them and put them in the post box. Instead she began to open them.

Two more typescripts, one a commissioned piece, the other unsolicited. A press release, a book launch invitation, a sample of a new perfume. Copies of some pictures she had inquired about when she started planning the abortive article about Luisa Weiss. They had been sent from a private library in the West Country which specialised in feminist subjects.

Most of the pictures had been published before. Tess recognised them. Here was Luisa as a debutante in a low-cut black dress, wearing a single strand of graded pearls and an artificial smile. Raymond and Luisa Weiss, newly married in their wedding finery, going away on their honeymoon in a silver Rolls Royce, on a beach. Raymond looked like a young film star, with dark, wayward curls, a narrow nose, a generous, undulating mouth. Here he was gazing proudly down at Luisa, her hair smoothed into a bouffant style, wearing white lipstick, holding a lace-draped infant and being clutched around the white-booted knee by a curly-haired toddler. A clever-clever shot from July 1970's *Nova* magazine, showing Luisa behind bars to illustrate the subject of *Into Captivity*, the book which became a seminal feminist work. By the time that issue appeared, Luisa was dead.

Here was an unfamiliar photo, a fading colour snapshot. Luisa was standing with her arm round the shoulder of another girl. They had long straight hair, skimpy T-shirts and flared jeans, holding bottles of Coca Cola.

Were they on a beach? Was that the Stars and Stripes? Tess could not quite make out what the structures behind the girls were. Luisa looked voluptuous, or buxom, her figure admirable, no doubt, for her time but too substantial for modern tastes. Her companion was taller and skinny, with in-turned feet, looking at the camera slightly sideways from under her eyelashes. She had a clear-cut, square face, straight fair hair and a wide, low forehead.

I know that face, Tess thought. She must be in some of the other pictures of Luisa. She left the pictures scattered on the table to go to the lavatory. Then the telephone rang. It was Tess's sister in Cornwall. With the telephone wedged between her ear and shoulder, with occasional murmurs of "Really?" or "Oh dear" she pulled the duvet flat and threw an apple core out of the window down into the communal gardens, flung some clothes towards the overflowing laundry basket.

Tess had not confessed to being out of work to her family yet. They admired her career too warmly: hadn't the little girl from the clay pits done well. Tess's big sister Biddy had married an employee of English China Clays, and settled down in St Austell, at that time virtually a "company town". Malcolm Trevail had been doing all right then. Before he was laid off from the ailing industry he bought a four-bedroomed house on a modern estate, with a granny flat in which Lena Redpath lived. Now Lena had Alzheimer's and Malcolm sold burglar alarms on commission. Lara and Paul were at the local comprehensive, where Tess, welcomed back as a local girl made good, had once lectured to a leavers' class about her glamorous job. Biddy was surprised to find Tess answering her own telephone home on a weekday.

"I've got a cold," Tess said.

"You do sound a bit rough. We're all coughing and sneezing too, it's the weather, bucketing down as per usual."

"Everything all right though?"

"Yah, fine, but what have you been you up to, Tess? Some bloke was asking about you the other day, so casual he was, I just thought it might have been more than old times' sake. Have you got the tabloids after you?" Jacques, Tess thought. But not even Biddy knew who he was. She said quickly, "How's Mum?"

"About at her fifth birthday today," Biddy said. She took their mother's decline into her second childhood calmly, being used to senility from her work in a residential care home. Tess could not bear it, possibly, she realised, because she had always got on less well with their mother than Biddy. Biddy was the good sister; responsible, reliable, predictable. Tess had never conformed to the local or social mores of their class, never done what was expected of her, was always with the wrong boys, always in a dream of love. Then she'd left home and dragged herself into the middle classes. Lena had never been pleased for her. "What you need is a nice husband, my girl." The cheques Tess sent did not serve to alleviate her guilt and pure embarrassment. How could indomitable Lena, once so fierce and infuriating, have dwindled into *this*? Tess's thoughts twitched automatically away from the painful image.

40

"What were you going to say, Bids?"

"Lara thought she might crash out on your floor at half-term, would that be OK?"

Tess answered quickly, rejection amounting almost to revulsion surging into her mind. "Oh no, Biddy, that's not —"

"Oh Tess, she will be disappointed."

"I'm sorry." Tess loved Lara who looked punky but could not help behaving like a sunny-natured, considerate, good daughter. Biddy never needed to tell Lara to "be nice".

"You've always been so close to her, I only wish you had some children of your own. You know Tess," Biddy gabbled inexorably on, "how Mum always used to say nature had designed you to be a mum, with your hips, and so good with the children, I came across that photo of you and the kids on Newquay beach, back when you could still sit on your hair, d'you remember, before the first time you cut it, you looked so right and natural holding the baby, Mum used to say if you'd not got in with those lefty feminist types back at college you might have found . . ."

Quite unconsciously, Tess twiddled her shorn hair into a headful of corkscrews while Biddy was talking. It was a habit Jacques deplored. She guiltily began to untwist each lock.

"And what about your bloke, it must be about time he left that wife of his, all those years you've been hanging on for him, not that I ought to wish it on her, poor woman, I don't know what I'd do if Malcolm —"

"Biddy. Listen, that week Lara wants to come, I'll be

away, I've got a job to do for the — she'd better not be in London on her own."

"Oh, then why don't I come up too, we could both —"

Spurred by desperation, Tess said quickly, "I'm lending the house to a friend who'll be over from New York. Natalie, d'you remember me talking about her, the one who works on the *Washington Post*. Listen, Bids, I am sorry, really, but we'll fix it for another time . . ."

Lies, lies. That was mean of me, she thought, putting the receiver down. Why did I do that? I love the children and Biddy ought to be the first person I turn to in times of trouble now Mum's not all there. But they all think I'm such a success, Auntie Moneybags, arriving with trendy presents from posh shops, carrier bags from Gucci and Joseph, my posh luggage full of gear for them to marvel at, telling them gossip about the world they read about. Biddy's always envied me, I can't bear her to pity me instead.

"Pity you?" Desmond, who had looked in to check she was all right, said that evening. "Self-pity, more like. It won't do, Tess, believe me. I know."

Desmond had come out during a brief window of time when he wrongly supposed society was embracing liberalism in the early 1990s, but in the part of Surrey he lived in then even the few councillors on the police committee who had paid lip service to gay rights were not having any of that sort of thing in their constabulary. He had been dismissed immediately.

"Come on," he said. "Snap out of it. At least you've

42

still got Mr Right." Desmond's own Mr Right had run like a rabbit rather than join him in self-exposure.

"I hope I have," Tess said with a desperate smile. "I haven't heard from him for ages."

"I thought he was away in Italy?"

"That's what he said," Tess agreed, and did not voice the doubts which filled her mind. There were telephones in Italy, and faxes. He could even have asked her to go out there with him, now she was free. And hadn't there been something on the news about a changeover at the NATO headquarters?

Furiously twisting her hair round both forefingers at once, she reran their last night together in her mind. After making love they had settled down to eat, Jacques reading the *Evening Standard.* We're just like little old married people, Tess thought, waiting until they had started eating before she told him what had happened at the *Argus.* It had been only four days earlier, the wound was raw. Jacques said she'd find another job, no problem. Then Tess hinted at an alternative. Perhaps the time had come for Jacques to leave his wife at last? "If I could live with you all the time . . ." Watching his face, she saw him lower his eyes, his mouth narrow, the lines which ran from nose to chin deepen. He said something non-committal. And very soon afterwards he pushed back his chair and said he mustn't be late, better be on his way. Tess had not heard from Jacques since.

Desmond interrupted her thoughts. "Why don't you make a start by sending this lot back to the *Argus*, they'll only upset you." He picked the papers up to knock them into a neat pile.

"All right," Tess said.

"Who's this a picture of?"

"The dark one's Luisa Weiss as a young woman."

"I know the name."

"I'm sure you do. The feminist writer, you must have heard of *Into Captivity*."

"I remember. 'Any rabbit can be a mother,' wasn't that her line?"

"Only one of her lines, it sounds silly now, but she wasn't really."

"Is she the one who killed herself?"

"That's the only thing everyone remembers about her."

"Was there any doubt about the verdict? What sort of investigation did they —?"

"Desmond, stop. You aren't a copper any more."

"I could ask one of my old mates though."

"Listen, it was suicide, she hanged herself. Ugh, doesn't that sound awful? Even if she was in despair, I can't imagine being able to do that."

"Don't worry, Tess, when it's my turn I'll choose a less painful method. I shall fly to some distant shore where the sea is blue and warm, and I'll swim out until I can swim no further. I've got it all planned."

"Oh Desmond . . ."

"When you know the alternative it's a comforting idea, as a matter of fact, but hanging — that's agony and messy, awful for whoever finds you, a nightmare for your friends or family. Believe me, I know."

Looking at his sensitive, ravaged face, Tess realised

Desmond must have had friends who had taken that way out.

Desmond said, "It might hurt my family and friends less than the alternative. But other people . . . a young woman like that, she makes a wound nobody left behind ever recovers from because the suicide has gone away and the survivors are forever in the wrong. They can't forgive themselves. Never mind what the reason was, no matter how rational and even considerate the decision, we're left like the damned. We can never make amends. I knew a chap once . . . never mind."

"Desmond, I'm so sorry, I didn't know —" Tess began.

Desmond shook himself abruptly as though knocking a touch off his shoulder, and asked, "Who did Luisa Weiss leave behind?"

"Two baby daughters and a husband. Raymond Weiss."

"At the time she must have thought it would serve him right to realise she had been in such despair. Suicide is quite aggressive."

"But it wasn't Raymond who found her, it was the au pair girl."

"Even so," Desmond said. "Wasn't the idea that he drove her to it by being unsympathetic about her work and leaving her with the babies while he did what he wanted?"

"That's the politically correct line on it but we have — we had — to be careful about quoting it. Anyway, it might not be true."

"One never knows what really goes on behind other people's front doors."

"No," Tess agreed, "and the Weiss researchers saw private material, so they may have had a better idea. Something must have driven her to despair."

"Don't forget how different things were then," Desmond said. "You're talking about, what — twenty-five years ago? You can't blame a man for not being in advance of his times, and most men didn't get involved in babies and houses then."

Tess said, "I know, it's like blaming my old mother for not being a career woman. Anyway, I thought Raymond Weiss was awfully nice when I met him. Of course it was years later, he was part of a series we were doing on the *Argus*. He didn't seem at all the sort of man to bully a wife."

It had been in the mid-eighties. Tess had gone along to hold a photographer's hand. The series had been called "The Imperfect Husband" and covered about a dozen men whose wives had succeeded in spite of them. The men who had agreed to be featured were under the impression the subject was "Perfect Husbands", so Tess was there to make sure the photographer did not give the game away. Expecting to dislike him, Tess had got on very well with Raymond Weiss. Tall, thin and dark, he had an intense, enthusiastic air, waving his hands round as he spoke very fast and seldom finishing a sentence because he had moved on to the next thought before articulating the previous one. He was careful of his visitors' comfort, getting room service to bring them drinks on his bill, adjusting cushions and table lamps.

They talked, she remembered, about gardens. Raymond intended to replan the planting at Thalassa, the estate Luisa had inherited from her family and of which he was trustee for their daughters, Saffron and Scarlett. The place needed to become less labour intensive, but he was not sure whether he ought to make any alterations in the gardens Luisa described in the diaries he had edited and published after her death, because Luisa's fans still came to see it and touch the trees she had touched. Other admirers had decided Luisa's husband had destroyed her, and came to Thalassa only in order to deface any mention of Raymond and get rid of any memorial to Luisa's marriage. A while after Tess met Raymond she had read that Thalassa was no longer open to unauthorised visitors. But that day she had told him she remembered it, having made her own pilgrimage, and said how much seeing Thalassa had meant to her.

They were so absorbed in conversation that the photographer did his work and went while they were still talking. Raymond asked her to dinner but Tess suddenly realised that she should have met her current boyfriend at Covent Garden half an hour before, and left in a hurry. The next day she went through the copy for the "Imperfect Husbands" series. The writer had been catty, snide, supercilious, showing all the worst qualities of clever-clever journalism, and Tess persuaded Moira to spike the series.

Suddenly his memory seemed very clear in her mind, and Tess said, "I wonder what happened to Raymond, I don't even know whether he's married again. I don't really suppose he'd talk to me about Luisa."

Desmond said, "This photo was taken in the States, d'you see, that's a Howard Johnson's."

"Mmm, so it is."

"But it's the other face I was wondering about. She looks like that Mrs Williams, I thought the photo might be wanted for a piece about Petronella." He held it further away from his long-sighted eyes. "In fact, I'm pretty sure it is Jill Williams."

"How on earth do you —?"

"She sold me some of her watercolours."

"In the shop? Here, in London?"

"No, it was at one of those flea markets I go round to in the off season, I bought the lot cheap, gave her a cheque which is why I knew her name. Lots of amateurs make a bit of money selling their stuff that way and sometimes I pick up quite nice things, frame them up in matching mounts and you make a good profit. But it must be years ago now. Does it make a difference?"

"Oh Desmond, how unworldly you are, half the world's press is looking for info about Jill Williams. She's been keeping a low profile ever since the engagement was announced."

"Don't blame her," said Desmond, who had suffered from the attentions of reporters and photographers himself. "I wouldn't wish that on my worst enemy. Not even Councillor Widdecombe."

"Anyway, it can't be her, what would she be doing with Luisa Weiss?" Tess, who was short-sighted, held the picture within six inches of her eyes. "I can see what you mean though. Actually, I must have got . . ." She broke off to cross the room and leaf through the untidy pile of old newspapers which should have been taken for recycling weeks ago, and came back brandishing a copy of the *Argus* magazine. "I ought to keep this one as a historical document, it's the last to appear with my name in it. Now, where — here we are. The Prince's Pretty Pet."

"Ugh."

"Don't blame me. Look, this is the only picture we could come up with."

Together Tess and Desmond peered at the photograph of Jill Williams.

"It is her, you know," Desmond said. "See, the forehead, the eyebrows, the space between nose and mouth, the facial bones, they all correspond."

"I think you're right."

"This is your chance, Tess, it would make a good piece. Prince's mother-in-law childhood friend of famous feminist. Start your own writing career with a bang."

"You could do the same for yours. The watercolours you bought will be worth quite a bit to some tabloid."

"Nah, they're too soft. Nothing to say about them. Anyway, you can have first go. Your need, said he with a noble air, is greater than mine."

"But what can I say? I'd need to talk to Jill Williams, and if none of the pros can get her to it's hardly likely I will."

Desmond pushed his chair back. "Write and ask, I would. Promise not to mention Petronella at all. Just ask her about Luisa."

Tess knew he was right. But would she ever have the heart, the energy, the confidence, the simple get-up-and-go, to do any such thing? "What's wrong with me?" she asked herself. "Snap out of it."

But she was afflicted by a paralysing pessimism. Waking up late to another day without duties or appointments, she went to the lavatory but did not clean her teeth, pulled on a sweater but could not face getting dressed, and sat on the edge of her bed, head in her hands. She said aloud, "If I lie down, I might never get up again." Instead she shuffled out of the bedroom, picked up the few letters on the mat and poured hot water from the tap straight on to powdered coffee in yesterday's mug. Making a face at the tepid bitterness she thought she deserved no better. A bill. A circular. An invitation to a closing down sale. A typed letter from — "Oh, my God, it's a letter from Jacques." A card inside an envelope. Half a dozen words, he'd come tonight!

Tess leapt up to get tidying. Then the telephone rang.

"Tess? Turn on the TV, quick."

"Desmond? What —?"

"Just do it. A news flash. Hurry up."

He rang off and Tess reached for the remote control. The set warmed up and the sound came on, the solemn, elegaic tone of the newsreader's voice warned of some tragedy even before his actual words made sense.

# CHAPTER
# THREE

The television picture blurred into life with a shot of the Williams house enclosed in a fence of flimsy orange tape. An expressionless young policeman stood outside the closed front door as a wheeled stretcher carrying a shrouded passenger was pushed down the path and into an ambulance. Some photographers ran behind as it drove away, pointlessly holding their cameras high and flashing them at the blank windows.

Jill Williams had been in the wood and glass lean-to she used as a studio. She had been hanging from a crossbeam.

Hanging? Tess tensed herself for further details, but none were given.

Luisa Weiss had hanged herself. Was it a coincidence?

Jill Williams's dog had attracted the neighbours' attention. The long-haired red dachshund was found whining and scratching at the closed studio door.

The neighbour had been interviewed already.

"I couldn't believe it, she'd never leave that animal, not for a minute, she'd have taken him over to the kennels like always. They was always like tied together, inseparable." The camera took a long shot of the speaker, a fat, loose-skinned woman wearing a Royal

Wedding T-shirt and speaking with a Midlands accent. She explained how she had sent her teenaged son to investigate a bloody rumpus.

"I thought he were barking at the Jehovah's Witness, they were round here in the afternoon, but on and on it went so's we couldn't stand it so our Donny had to go over and take a look. The dog cut itself but it would have bit Don without that, always vicious with strangers it was, Mrs Williams got it so's she'd be warned of anyone coming by. But Donny had a peek through the window and there she was swinging, he was that sick . . ."

The reporter was from the local television station on the Isle of Man, a youth with a quiff and a slight lisp. Looking into the camera, he said the police were investigating but foul play was not suspected.

Desmond rushed in during the lunch hour. He was carrying the cardboard portfolio he had bought from Jill Williams. Hypersensitive to other people's moods, he said at once, "You look better."

"My boyfriend called, he's coming tonight."

"Oh good."

Desmond put the portfolio flat on Tess's table. "Do you want a look at Jill Williams's pictures?"

"That poor woman," Tess said. "I can't bear to think of it, she must have been in such despair. Poor Jill, poor Petronella."

"It seems shocking every time," Desmond said sadly. "But don't judge her till you know why she did it."

"I wonder whether they have found a note." Tess felt a sharp stab of misery at the thought that she would have known the details in advance of the general public if she were still at the *Argus*. What titbits had they heard, what line were they deciding to take? Tess felt as though she'd been turned out of doors to freeze to death pressing her face against a lighted window.

She switched the television on again. By this time the news room had assembled a more detailed report and package of comment, much of which was devoted to the effect of Jill Williams's death on her daughter's marriage. The princely family had already issued a formal message of sympathy. They were sorry, upset, shocked. Otherwise all was speculation but for the fact that the police had announced there was no suicide note.

The news reporting was mostly devoted to pictures of Petronella scurrying across a London pavement in dark glasses and a fur hat. But there was a close-up, lingering shot of her mother's home and an aerial view showing the surrounding houses and fields.

The house was a small stone cottage, two up two down at a guess, and probably built at the beginning of the century. It stood isolated from its neighbours on the outskirts of a rambling village.

"It's one of her pictures!" Desmond cried. "In summer, with clematis round the porch. Look."

A wall surmounted by a woven fence marked the boundary of the road, and enclosed a driveway just large enough to park one car, so nothing could be seen of the side and back gardens or the studio. The nearest neighbours were across a field on one side and separated by their own large garden on the other. At the front was a road, at the back, outside the fence, some scrub land leading to a small wood. The enlarged air photograph showed the lean-to studio-conservatory, one storey high, running along the back of the cottage. The oblong garden consisted of a trim lawn surrounded by burgeoning flower beds and a large bird table.

"Robins," Desmond said. "Here they are." Jill's watercolours were soft-edged and brightly coloured, as though the birds she had painted on her own bird table were imaginary, perfected examples.

The chilly clarity of the photograph on the screen showed a bleaker image. After Petronella's engagement a photographer had seized the brief chance to get an interior shot at a moment when someone had knocked the thick net drapes aside from the downstairs window. His snatched picture had been copied around the world and flashed up again now: a conventionally neutral sitting-room, its fireplace blocked up, with a three-piece suite and a jug of carnations on a coffee table.

Jill Williams had lived in Dunkloss for thirteen years, but other residents said she kept herself to herself. "She'd give you good morning" but there had been no socialising in the village, she never attended church or helped out at the annual fête. She did not even seem to go for walks. Presumably the little dog got enough exercise running round the garden.

Until two years ago Jill taught art at the comprehensive school in Douglas, driving herself the eleven miles to work in a small Renault. More recently she had supported herself by selling her watercolours to summer visitors.

Since the announcement of her daughter's engagement, every remembered and as many invented details of

Petronella's rare visits had been described both by those who knew her and those who did not. Petronella had not come to Dunkloss often. She had been educated at boarding school in Bristol and spent most of her holidays with her father's relations. The engagement had provoked catty speculation about the prince's reaction to his future mother-in-law's modest home. Some of those jibes were repeated now, with the implication that his contempt had driven Jill to despair.

The BBC's court correspondent was beginning an assessment of the impact of the news. "Speculation and guesswork," Desmond said crossly. "Mind if I turn off?"

"Let's have a look at the portfolio."

There were about three dozen watercolours, signed with the initials JW, all innocuous, pretty pictures of rustic subjects, realistically copied.

"You can sell these for a packet now," Tess said. "There's a terrific demand for anything which has been touched by a hand that touched a hand that . . . and so on *ad infinitum*."

"You make it sound like the apostolic succession," Desmond said.

"Human instinct, that's all."

"I thought her pictures were quite sweet before, but now they seem sort of, I don't know, sinister. Sad. Spoilt."

"The eye of the beholder," Tess said. She leafed through watery primulas, irises on blue tables in the sun, pottery coffee mugs full of nasturtiums, robins and roses. She said, "They'd make good book jackets for one of those 'there's honey still for tea' efforts."

She lifted a flap at the back of the folder. "Oh look, here's another. Wow, Desmond, this is something completely different." The large sheet of cartridge paper which had been folded into the back pocket of the portfolio case was clearly the work of the same artist, but was closely covered with tiny cartoon-like drawings, doodles or sketches of a liveliness and vigour lacking in the conventional, saleable watercolours. Two female figures appeared several times. Their faces had been left almost blank. Both had long lines of hair, one blacked in by heavy pencil strokes, the other sketched with light, spaced lines. One wore a flowing skirt, the other trousers with wide legs. They were running, crouching, standing behind a palm tree which was on fire. Palm trees. Cacti. A vista of spiky bushes, burning. In one corner of the page there was a long low building enclosed in a wall pierced with square holes. Flames were coming out of its roof. Between the scenes a face recurred; a bushy beard, wild hair, staring eyes.

"Pretty gruesome fantasies for a nice lady artist," Desmond said.

"Unless she was trying to do a comic book of some kind," Tess said.

"Action pix for illiterate adults, you mean," Desmond said.

"I wonder whether they are sketches for a book that did get published, that could explain why I seem to have seen bits before." Tess peered more closely at some of the minute drawings. "Some fantasy story, d'you think? The man looks like a wizard or warlock."

"Maybe I should ring the local force about these pictures, could be there's a clue here."

"Not a bad idea," Tess said.

The hectic flush which had surged into Desmond's face faded again, leaving his usual gaunt pallor. He said, "No, what am I talking about, it's a barmy idea, they'd only drag up all that business again. But you can use them, Tess."

Tess had already thought of that. "Can we talk about it tomorrow? I've got to clear up and do some shopping, this place is a tip."

Tess had a shower, made her bed with clean satin sheets and did the best she could with her hair. She threw out the irises Desmond had brought her ten days before. She plumped the ochre silk cushions on her dark green sofa, looped back the chic white curtains, wiped the table tops and straightened the row of lustre jugs on the mantelpiece. She dusted the whole room, even including the picture frames; her walls were decorated with a set of eighteenth-century prints of Cornish scenes. Tess had found a book of them in the Portobello Road, cut out each illustration and put them in wide, primary coloured mounts. Jacques said it was sacrilege. Tess didn't care; she liked being reminded of home.

Dishes had piled up on every kitchen surface. Tess washed and wiped, toiled downstairs with half a dozen bulging refuse sacks, and prepared the dinner, artichoke soup and venison casserole. She set a cinnamon and orange scented candle to burn on the mantelpiece.

But where was he? Late, making her wait, cruel when he had not been near her for so long and she needed him so badly. Be there now, Jacques, Tess willed, be parking your car this very moment, locking it, leaping up the front stairs . . . she saw it so clearly that renewed disappointment kept flooding over her when the sound of a key in her lock did not follow. But he came at last. Every time she saw him Tess was enchanted afresh by his aquiline looks. He wore a formal striped suit and a naval tie. She nestled her body into his embrace, reminded that he appreciated a substantial armful in comparison with Sibyl, a flimsy little creature who hardly came up to his shoulder. Tess raised her hand to undo his tie but he moved aside and said, "I've just got to make a phone call. Sibyl? How is she? Oh good, that's a relief. Tell her I'll be back as soon as I can."

"Oh Jacques, you aren't in a hurry, are you?" Tess protested as soon as he had replaced the receiver. "I've been so looking forward —"

"I can't stay long, Milly had a fall today, Sibyl had just got back from the hospital when I got there."

"Oh poor little thing, was it off her bike?"

"Her pony, but she's all right."

"Thank God for that. So put your troubles out of your mind for a while, it's been such ages since you last came. When did you get back? Tell me about Italy while we have dinner, I've made your favourite —"

"We might as well eat, Sibyl thinks I'm getting something at my meeting. But then I'll have to — ah, soup, excellent."

"Take your coat off first. Mmmm." Tess pushed her arms under his jacket, round his hard, strong body. "God, I've missed this."

58

He moved away to sit down. "What was that you were watching when I came in?"

"It was about Petronella Williams's mother, there's been nothing else on all day. Here, I got that Portuguese wine you liked last time, the Dao. Tell me what you've been doing." Tess stretched her hand out across the white cloth but Jacques's hands were busy buttering a roll.

"One of my chaps was talking about her not long ago," he remarked.

"About Jill Williams?"

"He knows Petronella and she was telling him about getting engaged, apparently it was all quite traumatic."

"Didn't they think she was good enough?"

"No no, not the prince's family, they took it in their stride, it was her own mother. Apparently Petronella always stayed with the Blagdens when she went to see her mother, they have a guest house over there, and she came back in floods of tears the day she told her mother. The Blagdens didn't know who she'd got engaged to at the time but she couldn't help letting it out that she was upset because her mother wasn't pleased. God knows why."

"Could that be why she . . . but I never heard anyone say Jill Williams wasn't pleased," Tess said.

Jacques raised his eyebrows. "You don't expect my young chap's people would talk to anyone from the media?"

"Why do you say it like that, so disdainfully? I've been in the media ever since you've known me."

"But you're well out of it now."

"What d'you mean?"

"Trivial, ephemeral, shallow — anyway, everyone knows how they distort things, when you know the facts you always find they are wrong. Honestly, Tess, what does working on the *Argus* magazine contribute?"

Later Tess was to wonder why she hadn't asked Jacques what the peace-time navy contributed to the world, or a wife who spent her time at the pony club or gym? At the time, she could not think of any reply, but gazed at him with wounded, tear-filled eyes.

"Doesn't matter what I think, though," he said. "It's your life."

She answered, "But my next job will concern you, won't it, Jacques. Have you told Sibyl yet?"

"As a matter of fact that's what I came to discuss. I couldn't very well leave it for a letter." He squared his shoulders and pulled his chin in, every inch an officer. But he didn't meet her eyes. "I don't know quite how to say this but the fact is, Tess, the time has come for us to part."

"Part? You and me? But Jacques, I thought — you've always said —"

"Things have changed now, you'd not be content any longer with occasional visits, and with my new posting in the bag I've got to be even more careful. They're doing another positive vetting and —"

"Oh, my sister said . . . I thought it was tabloids."

"Your line of work, it's not what you'd call secure. And then there's the children. And Sibyl. She trusts me implicitly, I can't hurt her."

"But you're hurting me."

"That's different."

"Why is it different? I love you, I've been loyal to you. Why should positive vetting make a difference? Whoever snoops and spies on me, they won't find anything wrong."

"All the same it's better if I don't . . . Look, Tess, we've had good times together, but it's not as if . . . things are different for career girls like you . . . Sibyl's lost without me . . . don't imagine this is easy for me, but . . ."

A dozen excuses later, Jacques had gone. For ever. He had dismissed Tess, if not with the efficiency of Hamish Beck at the *Argus* (who, no doubt, had more experience than Jacques of "letting people go"), none the less decisively and finally. She'd had the sack — again. Without going so far as to offer her the services of an out-placement bureau, Jacques had mouthed words of reassurance about Tess's future. "You'll find someone else," he said in the indifferent, official tone he would use to an unsatisfactory junior officer. This was merely another necessary duty, one which left him unemotional. Cold. He didn't care. He didn't give a damn. He didn't love her. He had turned his back and slammed the door, though not perhaps quite as cool as he seemed, since he had forgotten to pick up his overcoat from the hall chair.

Reduced to tears yet again — how much had she cried during these last weeks? — Tess wondered what she had left to lose. Her life? Would she end like Jill Williams or Luisa Weiss? A vision of ropes and beams flashed through her mind, of the scratchy fibres under her chin,

**61**

her clumsy fingers tying a knot, climbing up on a stool, kicking it away.

No, no. Absolutely not, never. Nothing would make me do that. Tess went to the sink and splashed cold water on her face and wrists, leant out of the window to draw in gulps of cold air. She saw Jacques had left a piece of paper on the table. A cheque? Redundancy pay? He couldn't have been so crass.

It was not a cheque, whose signature and payee could be identified by, for example, an indiscreet bank clerk or a jealous wife, but a draft on Credit Suisse for three thousand pounds payable to its bearer.

Did he know that had been exactly one month's pay?

Her hands were poised to tear the paper across and across. Then something stayed her hand. She said aloud, "Use it, don't lose it." Use it, show him, pay him back. Show the sods at the *Argus*. Make them all sorry.

Tess felt her cheeks burning, she almost felt the blood pouring through her veins; her hands were shaking and heart pounding. I won't, I'm damned if I'll let them destroy me, she thought, and dialled to invite Desmond to come up and share the rest of the dinner she had cooked for Jacques.

When he came in, Desmond cried, "You look like a new woman. I like the hair." Surprised, Tess put a hand to her head and found she had twiddled up a row of knotted coils. "If that's what a visit from the boyfriend does for you, then —"

"Not quite in the way you think," Tess said, hearing a crisp, businesslike tone in her voice that had been absent since the day she left the *Argus*. I'm not desolate, I'm furious, she realised with pride and surprise. Maybe I didn't love him either, really. She told Desmond what had happened.

A tight little smile wrinkled his neat features. "Good riddance to bad rubbish," he said.

They watched the midnight news together. The lead story was still Jill Williams's suicide. Tess said, "Do you think it means anything that she did the same as Luisa Weiss? She was found hanging in an outhouse too, did you know that?"

"Most people must know that, same as they know Sylvia Plath gassed herself."

"But can it just be a coincidence?"

"I expect it's where Jill Williams got the idea. She's not the first one, either, we always knew — *we!* what am I saying? I mean," he interposed bitterly, "*they*: the police. They always knew it's one of the favoured methods for female suicide."

"Why?"

"God knows, though there was one police surgeon who always quoted something about a girl who hanged herself from a green tree for love. Could be 'cos they don't own cars, can't get drugs, could be following some pattern. Could be what other people believe they might do — the power of suggestion."

"Or make them do?"

"That too. Murder looking like suicide. After all, what would you expect a girl to use to top herself? A rope and a rafter, like the famous Luisa Weiss. It's another connection for you, Tess. Like the photograph."

# CHAPTER
# FOUR

The day before she was due to go home Saffron Weiss, who had had a horrid time in London, found out why Scarlett had pressed her to come.

Saffron knew all along that Scarlett didn't really want her but their father made her go. "She rang up to ask you, Saffy, you know Scarlett never says things she doesn't mean."

"But I'll only get in the way and all her friends'll despise me."

"My darling girl, what nonsense, it'll be fun, you don't want to spend all your life down here with me. You need a bit of excitement."

"I hate excitement," Saffron muttered, and she certainly hated the kind of excitement Scarlett provided.

Scarlett had a basement studio flat in Islington. Her place was full even on the very first evening though Saffron did not know if it was a party or just what life was always like round here. Having not seen Scarlett for months she thought they might have had a cosy evening gossiping, but not a bit of it; strange, trendy people kept coming down the area steps armed with bottles and cans, and crammed themselves into the flat. Everyone shouted over the music and danced and snogged, breaking off to swig from cans of drink or smoke splifs. One man sat in a corner sucking at a bubbling glass bell.

Saffron tried not to look because she didn't want to know. All her fears were being confirmed. She cowered cross-legged on the mattress which she would presumably have to share with Scarlett later and watched other people gyrating and/or embracing. None of them seemed like anyone Saffron had ever even seen before, with their unlikely clothes and mysterious phraseology. A man with greasy dreadlocks and three ear-rings moved in on her so she edged away till the wall stopped her edging further and then put up her arms to ward him off. He terrified her, a big, strong, implacable orange man. Saffron saw everything in colour, days of the week, names, numbers, people, and had not realised until quite recently that not everybody did. There was even a name for Saffron's idiosyncracy. It was called synaesthesia.

She didn't need a fancy name to rely on her own perceptions. This orange man, whose skin, actually, was black, was bad; orange was always a bad colour. She let out a muffled sound of fear and misery. The words "I want to go home" wailed childishly through her head.

The man told her to relax. "Live a little."

He ran his fingers gently up the bare skin of her thin forearm, lifting the dark hairs against his roughened skin. Saffron shivered and pulled the sleeve of her T-shirt down as far as she could.

Another arm appeared over Saffron's shoulder, fair hairs mocking her own hirsute ugliness. Scarlett bleached her body hair but blackened the spikes of hair on her head. Her lips were a juicy fruit of stickiness, her face dead white. Her body had been pierced in a dozen places. She fizzed in Saffron's sight, the comforting vermilion of a familiar sister shot through with purple and orange streaks.

"Your sister doesn't like me," the man said.

"Oh, please, I never said —" Saffron stammered.

"The only man she's ever really liked is our dad."

"Scarlet, it's not true, how could you —" Saffron felt shaming tears at the back of her nose and eyes.

"Not much alike, are you?" the man said.

They certainly weren't. Saffron had long, limp hair with a long, straggling fringe and a meagre, concave body. She did not use make-up or jewellery and her jeans, nicely ironed by Mrs Trimble who "helped out" at home, and clean trainers looked completely out of place, to the extent that Scarlett's friends, unable to place her, either ignored her completely or were easily put off. Waking next morning, Saffron realised she had fallen asleep on the floor and been left there. A mound of dirty duvet rose and fell rhythmically on the mattress. The others had left, but empty bottles and full ashtrays were scattered everywhere, with damp patches on the carpet and, in the tiny cubicle of kitchen, a chaos.

Saffron leant over the mattress, which smelt of smoke and ashes and booze and sex and sweat, and nervously poked into the duvet.

"For Chrissake what time is it?"

"After ten."

"Christ, it's Sunday, why the fuck did you wake us up?"

A deeper voice came from under the bedding. Saffron

jumped back in alarm as a man sat up. Even unshaven, filthy and half asleep he was the most beautiful human being Saffron had ever seen, a cerulean blue, though his skin, hair and bleary eyes were the colour milky coffee would be if it were shiny, the lines and planes of his face all conforming, Saffron imprecisely thought, to some golden mean.

He was called Zak. He lived here. Zak and Scarlett were an item. Zak and Scarlett trailed Saffron round with them. Scarlett was impatient with Saffron's country-mousishness. Zak was kind when he remembered to be, though he treated her like a child instead of a woman of nearly twenty-five, which, Saffron acknowledged, was fair enough. She felt like a child amongst adults with her sister's friends and in her haunts.

Zak, after checking whether she was gay and learning that she was not, kept trying to fix Saffron up with a bloke. She was not a virgin, having been out with a boy from school for years, a doctor's son called Jonathon who wrote to her every week from university until one day he wrote that he had met someone else. Saffron had pined briefly before realising she felt lightened and relieved because now she would not have to face the conflict about where to live. Jonathon was never going to come back to work in west Cornwall, and Saffron never wanted to leave it. She wanted a husband who would come and live at Thalassa. She wanted a large family to grow up there. She did not want any of Zak's trendy friends.

Saffron moped through two days in London, pretending to Scarlett and Zak that she was going round art galleries or shops, but actually scared to set off into the bandit territory outside, lurking indoors when Scarlett left her alone and then following her to pubs and night-clubs in the evening, counting the minutes till she could get away from the noise and nosiness.

On Tuesday Scarlett and Zak took Saffron to supper in a neighbourhood restaurant called Café Flo, which they said was just like Paris. There were bare floorboards, bentwood chairs and zinc tables, clouds of cigarette smoke and cheerful bustling young waiters with starched aprons hitched under their ribs. They ordered steak and chips and house wine and then Scarlett said, "Right, so let's just run through what we're saying tomorrow."

Assuming she was talking to Zak, Saffron did not respond and Scarlett went on, "Saffron. For God's sake."

"Sorry, I didn't realise — what who's saying tomorrow?"

"Wake up. You and me, to the lawyers."

If Saffron had been told, she had not remembered it, but apparently there was an appointment for the two sisters to see their mother's lawyers, Wootton Hardman, who were also their trustees.

Saffron said she didn't know about the plan.

Scarlett said that was the whole point of her coming to London.

Saffron said she thought she'd come to see Scarlett.

Scarlett said, "Well, you have seen me. And you've been having fun. We've taken you everywhere."

"It's very kind of you," Saffron said humbly.

"And tomorrow we go and make the arrangements, another fortnight, I can't wait."

"Another fortnight?"

"Oh do sharpen up. Till your birthday, of course, you can hardly have forgotten it. Two weeks left till we bring that bloody trust to an end and get some money of our own. In any normal family it would have happened when you were eighteen, why it had to wait till you were twenty-five — anyway, now you are old enough we can realise the capital. At last."

"We're going to set up our own business," Zak explained, "we've got a stall licence in Portobello Market."

Scarlett lit a cigarette and breathed in deeply. "Clothes. Dresses, Vionnet, Worth, Chanel, we've been buying them up."

Saffron said, "But I don't understand, Daddy never said anything about —"

"What's it got to do with him? Thalassa's yours and mine, not his, and now we're free at last we can get rid of it."

"Get rid of — what are you talking about? We couldn't sell Thalassa."

"Why not? I don't want a half-share of that mausoleum, I've always hated it ever since I can remember, I can't wait to turn it into cash. Good riddance. We've got an appointment with Wootton Hardman tomorrow, they've got some family papers they want us to take away, which you can have —"

"Me?"

"Well, I don't want them, do I? More of Luisa's ghastly self-absorbed ramblings, no thanks. So we'll sign all the papers and get going with the sale instructions."

"But it's my home, and Daddy's home, we can't possibly leave Thalassa, I'd — I'd die."

"Don't be silly, it'll do you good to get away. Look at you, Saffy, you've got arrested development after being stuck there all your life, it's time you grew up, you should have got away at seventeen like I did."

Zak said, "Hey hey, cool it, Scally."

Neither sister was listening to him. Saffron was infused with the feelings of inadequacy and inability to hold her own in the dominating shadow of the assertive, vehement Scarlett which had pervaded all her childhood. She had forgotten what a relief it quite soon seemed, only a few days after Scarlett left for London at the age of seventeen. Saffron told herself she missed her at first but then she leant back into the gentle flow of life at home, no longer a reluctant conscript in the battle against it. But here she was feeling threatened and frightened again. The very idea of selling Thalassa was a nightmare.

"It's our family home," she said weakly. "Mummy inherited it."

"That's not much recommendation," Scarlett snapped. "I don't want anything to do with Luisa's family relics. God knows why you do, considering the example of family feeling she set us."

"But she loved us really, it's just she was so unhappy," Saffron said.

"She had no right to be unhappy, not with two little kids. She was just selfish, she didn't care about anyone else, she couldn't ever have killed herself if she gave a stuff for me. Or you, Saffy. We don't owe her anything."

70

"Everything all right for you?" a waiter inquired. Only Saffron bothered to reply.

"It's lovely, thank you very much."

"Think what you can do with your share of the loot, Saffron," Scarlett said. "You'll be rich."

"I don't want to be rich."

"Tough. I do."

"I won't do it, you can't make me!" Saffron surprised herself with her own fierce assertion. "I won't treat Daddy like that after he's slaved all these years to keep Thalassa going for us, and anyway I don't want to, I love it, it's my home, I'm going to live there."

"Cool it," Scarlett said, picking up a long, thin chip and nibbling it delicately. "You can live at Thalassa if you buy me out. We'll get it valued and you can give me half, how's that?"

"Give you — but I haven't got any money. There isn't any money."

"You see? That's the whole point. All the cash Luisa ever had went on death duties, that's why the only thing left is the place. But I want cash. Money. Lolly. And that's got to come from selling Thalassa. Anyway, Saffy, it'll be a liberation for you and Raymond too, no more scraping a living from those silly courses, no more worries about roofs blowing off and barns blowing down. It's time Dad lived his own life, he always claims he wanted to be a writer once."

"He's never had time."

"He's never had the talent, more like, he knew he was never going to be first rate so he filled his life up with other things so everyone would think he was a wasted genius."

"Scarlett, how can you talk like that?"

"Because I'm a realist. I'm fond of him but I can see he's an ineffectual, well-meaning guy who's been living off his wife's money and reputation for far too long. That argument won't wash with me, little sister."

"I hate you."

"No you don't, think what you can do with your share — it might be half a million."

Saffron thrust her lower lip out in a mutinous expression which had always infuriated her older sister. "There's hardly enough money coming in as it is, Daddy certainly hasn't got any more, so we can't buy your share, but we won't sell. I won't, I won't."

"I can't think how he's kept it going this long as it is."

"Him and me together, the holiday cottages and art courses are a joint venture, you know that. And there's the money from Mummy's books. Her poems and journals did very well."

"Eleven years ago."

"It's still selling."

"Not enough to make a difference."

"But Daddy's bringing out another one on the anniversary, he sent you the proofs. Didn't you read it?"

"It's not exactly best-seller material, I thought it was pretty boring if you want to know," Scarlett said disdainfully. "More dismal whinges about life, the universe and everything, self-absorbed and old-fashioned."

"People will buy it for Luisa Weiss's name," Zak said knowingly. "Like Tolkien."

"Well, from now on we're having half the profit, it's not all going into keeping that white elephant in Cornwall going."

"Scarlett, how can you?" Saffron moaned.

"Easily. All Luisa's estate was left in trust. Raymond got the income till the youngest of her children was twenty-five and then it becomes ours outright, the place, the copyrights, everything. I just wish I'd got my hands on it ten years ago when I left home, that's when I could really have done with it."

"Well, I think you're disgusting." Saffron stood up abruptly, knocking over her wineglass and the mineral water bottle. "I shan't stay with you a minute longer, Scarlett Weiss, I'm going home, I'll catch the night train. You can't make me give up Thalassa and I jolly well won't. Not ever."

# CHAPTER
# FIVE

Waking late after sharing with Desmond not only the spurned Dao but also both of the bottles of Sinfandel he had contributed, Tess found that being dumped by Jacques had not pushed her deeper into depression. Instead she had been shocked out of it. She visualised herself stuck in a puddle of deep, sticky mud; suddenly her feet, one by one, plopped out. Energetic and furious, she settled down to work. First she read the newspapers; Archie Frazer's *Argus* account of Jill Williams's suicide, as always, clearer, fuller and apparently more knowledgeable than his rivals on other papers.

She packed together in a parcel Jacques's silk dressing-gown, the copy of Philip Larkin's poems in which he had written "Tess, with eternal love", his razor, toothbrush and the spicy aftershave he had made up for him by a barber in Jermyn Street, along with a shirt marked by indelible lipstick she had never managed to wash off. She addressed the parcel to Jacques's and Sibyl's home.

Next she wrote a note to an acquaintance who worked for *Private Eye* and gave him enough clues to work out on which occasions Jacques had not been where he should have been, and that he had been with someone

74

other than his wife. "And it's no skin off my nose if you use my name," she added venomously.

I'll show Jacques what the media's really all about, she thought. Let him suffer.

But then she crumpled the letter up in her hand. It was a weapon to keep in reserve, not to use. She hesitated over the betraying package of Jacques's possessions, and put off deciding whether to send it. Meanwhile she must turn her mind to earning some money. The *Argus* would be paying her for three more months and by then she would need some other source of income.

Tess printed out three copies of her curriculum vitae and enclosed them with applications for the jobs advertised in Monday's *Guardian*. She composed handwritten letters to two editors she had met at meetings of Women in Journalism, to ask if they could employ her. She left a carefully thought-out telephone message for a former colleague now commissioning for *Hello!* magazine, and faxed off two proposals: an exclusive about Petronella to the *Argus*'s chief daily rival, and a story about Luisa Weiss to the features editor of the *Sentinel*, a woman who was much mocked in the trade rags for her old-fashioned commitment to right-on feminism.

She found the old apple crate into which she had always thrown newspaper cuttings that might come in useful — ideas for stories, *aides-mémoire*, addresses. Most of the scraps seemed pointless now. What had she been thinking of when she saved this or underlined that? She leafed through a profile of a prize-winning novelist, a recipe for Thai sauces and a series of drawings which showed wedding dresses and threw most of the contents of the box away, muttering, "I hate weddings."

Then, surprised, she paused, foot poised over the pedal bin. "Do I?" she asked. Tess took off the reading glasses which, at the office, she had never admitted to needing, and thought of her best friend at primary school. Mandy was pregnant at seventeen and "had to get married", as, twenty years ago, people still said. Mandy had the full works: white tulle, pink bridesmaids, church bells and tears. After that had come a flurry of weddings. "Always a bridesmaid never a bride," Tess's mother sorrowfully told her. Other relations put it more kindly. "Your turn soon," they said, or "Mr Right will come." But Tess insisted on staying at school for A levels. She didn't want to turn into a weary drudge before she was twenty. Tess's vision of her future had changed when she was thirteen and went to stay with Sheila's gran for half-term. It was February 1970.

Sheila's gran was not like other grans. She made Sheila and even Tess call her Maeve, dyed her hair, painted her withered cheeks with thick, vivid make-up, and dressed in the kind of mannish trouser-suits which had not been seen yet in St Austell. She lived in a tall, dust-caked rambling house in Oxford, where every wall was lined with books, and other books were piled on the stairs, leaving a narrow passage between them. She let the girls do whatever they liked so long as they did not touch her desk, on which papers stood in tottering piles around an ancient upright typewriter. She drove an ancient, upright car, in which she had met Sheila and Tess at the station. Between there and Rawlinson Road she had discovered that neither girl was learning Latin and Sheila couldn't do the nine times table, corrected their pronunciation, told them "Don't say pardon, say what" and promised them a Chinese takeaway — not yet a familiar concept back home in deepest Cornwall — for what she called dinner. "Not tea, dears, please. We have our tea at four o'clock."

Sheila and Tess spent the first two days gawping at Oxford's shops but told Maeve they had been to the museum and feigned agreement with her that the Indian miniatures alone were worth the journey from Cornwall.

On the Saturday Maeve said they must meet her at Ruskin College. "Do you know what feminism is?"

"Course we do, we did suffragettes at school," Sheila replied.

"Your own grandchildren will be learning about women's lib at school," she said in her high, posh voice.

So Tess went to the first ever women's liberation conference. The organisers had expected about a couple of dozen people. Instead, hundreds came.

Among them, Sheila Binyon and Tess Redpath, who found their way to Ruskin College by mid-morning. Maeve was not there, in fact there was nobody to be seen, but following the noise they came upon a large room full of babies, toddlers and shouting small children. A little to one side a sulky girl of nine or ten was ostentatiously reading with her fingers in her ears. The adults present were all men. Tess and Sheila stared at them in astonishment.

"You never seen a bloke holding the baby?" one said.
"No."

"You're in the wrong place then," he said, expertly plugging the infant's mouth with a bottle containing a pink liquid.

"Where is . . ."

"The Union. That's where the action is, there wasn't room here. Go with Ray, he's chickening out."

Ray was a desperate-looking man in corduroy, with long hair falling over his face and a thick beard, his features so obscured as to be invisible. He was holding a screaming toddler as though he had never done so before. "She'll have to take over. I can't cope," he called over his shoulder as the girls trotted behind him. "Look, that's where it's all happening, you can't miss it. Oh Scarlett, please for Chrissake stop that bloody rumpus, I'm going as fast as I can."

Other women were still making their way towards the Union. "They've only just started letting women in here at all," one said, marching in like a conqueror. Inside it was seething, buzzing, alive with women.

Most were young and had long wild hair dangling from centre partings and swirling coats down to their ankles. As Tess pushed open the swing doors a wave of noise came through them. Hundreds of females were trying to make their conversations heard.

More were arriving all the time, pushing up behind Tess and Sheila into the huge room. An upstairs gallery was crowded with chattering women; others were leaning over the balustrade and shouting to people below. Women peddled ideas and pamphlets from trestle tables set up as stalls. Posters and banners hung in gaudy profusion. Statues round the walls of the room were draped with shawls and scarves. Between them some slogans had been scrawled or sprayed, blood red paint dripping from the words.

Down with penis envy.

Women in labour keep capital in power.

Women need men like fish need bicycles.

End penile servitude.

The two girls giggled at the rude words on public display. Then Sheila said she was going to find her gran and would see Tess later. Tess felt abandoned and shy. The treacherous thought, I want my mum, surfaced in her mind. It was like her first day at comprehensive school, noisy and smelling of people, wanting to be part of the crowd but not knowing how to. Like a swimmer plunging into the surf, she pushed forward into the throng. Snatches of conversation rose above the clamour. Many women were holding babies. Small children ran around in a forest of legs. Tess found herself at the stairs and went up to the gallery where she edged forward to stand beside an immensely pregnant young woman in an Afghan coat and watch the pandemonium below.

She did not recognise anyone, but was interested in the clothes: a cossack coat trimmed with fur round the collar and edges like in the film of *Dr Zhivago*, flowery child-like clothes, sexless clothes; a jangling woman with strings of Nepalese temple bells wound round her arms; a pair of identical twins with feminist slogans embroidered on their dresses; a Valkyrie in a floor-length white fur coat before whom other women were queuing up for words or signatures. There was a television personality in bell-bottomed trousers and jangling necklaces. There was a leader of fashion in layers of toning fabrics, with two scarves wound round her orange hair. There was a phalanx of uncompromising females in dungarees and others in Chairman Mao suits. Things were more organised than had at first appeared. People found seats or went to attend fringe meetings in side rooms. Tannoy announcements were made:

"International Socialist Women meet in the lobby now."

"Anarchists group: upstairs at three o'clock please."

"Urgent message for Benjie's mother. Can she get to the crèche right away."

"Equal pay for equal work badges available at table D in the main hall now."

She had arrived during the coffee break, and when the formal programme was resumed, Tess stayed in the gallery and listened to snatches of impassioned speeches. Some were all right, but most she found boring. They were about socialism and women's liberation, state capitalism and women's liberation, housework, housewives and women's liberation. The acoustics were poor since the chamber had been planned for booming male orators, not for the more conversational style in which women preferred to speak, and they had to make themselves heard above the crying babies scattered through the room. Maoist women in work-suits went in and out to their co-ordinator in the hall and came back to follow their instructions. Every time the heavy doors swung open a freezing current of air flowed through the room.

Speakers introduced themselves: an Italian delegate from *Le Libere Donne*, a spokeswoman for the Peckham Women, a sororal participant from New York. The audience quietened down to hear Audrey Wise, the MP for Coventry, speak about women working in industry. Then a middle-aged woman with a cutglass voice said women should not be working at all.

"Work oppresses women," she shouted.

"I suppose your daddy's working to keep you, is he?" someone called, and another voice yelled, "What do you know about going hungry?"

"Yeah, or seeing your kids hungry?" asked another. The posh lady was booed from the stage.

A lesbian was both clapped and hissed when she waved her personal banner. One woman stood up from the middle of the hall to make a lucid, formal plea for legislation. "What we need is an Equal Pay and Equal Opportunities Act." Silence. Then the meeting closed round her again and went on discussing how best to support the revolutionary left.

Tess wandered out of the main hall and found fringe meetings going on elsewhere. In one room someone was talking about housework, in another the subject was contraception. Tess wanted to hear that but was embarrassed so went on to another room where she found a fiery speaker in full flow. She was a tall, mountainously pregnant young woman, with a fall of glossy, waved hair, dark, flashing eyes, a clear complexion. No men were in the room, but the child called Scarlett had been offloaded and was clinging to her mother's knees as she spoke about the book she had written called *Into*

*Captivity*. She gave an outline of its liberationist message, and the vision of the future as Luisa Weiss insisted it should be, and could be, struck the adolescent Tess Redpath like an arrow in the gold. Make your own decisions, be your own mistress, determine your own life. Ambition seized Tess. She wanted to look like Luisa, sound like her (confident, inspired, inspiring) live at the centre of things, wear lovely clothes, write a book, be free. That was what Luisa Weiss did.

Tess could never remember the actual words Luisa said. She was too dazzled to take in anything except the intonation and tone of a deep, musical voice, a fresh scent, like the earliest narcissi,, and an aura of glamour and almost literally of warmth, so that when the small child began to whimper and someone came back to fetch Luisa for lunch, Tess felt literally encouraged: courage for her own grown-up life had been poured into her.

Six weeks later Luisa Weiss's baby, a second daughter, was born. Her book appeared with widespread publicity at the beginning of May. Not long afterwards she was dead.

Worn out by the demands of two small children Luisa hanged herself from the rafters of an outhouse in the grounds of Thalassa, the estate inherited from Luisa's family, where the Weisses lived. Tess did not hear of it at the time, for she seldom read papers or looked at the news and nobody in her home would have been interested. It was later, in the sixth form sociology class, that she learnt about Luisa's dying and for a long time after that Tess was haunted by Luisa, first as she had seen her, vibrant and charismatic, and then as she imagined her, reduced and weakened, creeping in tears out of the house to kill herself while her husband, the hirsute Ray, and the small Scarlett were out together in Penzance.

The baby, Saffron, was found howling on the out-house floor, mercifully too young to recognise or remember what was swinging silently above: her mother, a fine strong rope knotted round her neck, an overturned stool kicked away from her feet.

That was what marriage and motherhood did for you, Tess had thought. She would stay free to have lovers and fun.

And so, for years, it had been.

Tess remembered a mild crisis in her late twenties when suddenly everyone she knew, except herself, seemed to be pregnant. But she had a niece and nephew, there was an extended family back home in Corn-wall, she always seemed to have a boyfriend. Tess's life was enviable. She was happy as she was, there would be plenty of time later to settle down.

But at some point, without noticing it, she had stopped liking weddings and taken to averting her eyes and thoughts from them as automatically as she quickly turn-ed any page on which there was a picture of a snake or worm, protecting herself from uncomfortable thoughts.

Was it too late?

Tess got up from her work table and went through to her bedroom. The long mirror showed her a mess. Since leaving the *Argus* Tess had eaten too much of the wrong food. She had spots and her jeans were held together with a safety pin. Her hair had not been trimmed or touched up. The incipient shadows by her nose and faint lines on her forehead betrayed her age. What had ever made her suppose Jacques would want to chuck everything up just for her?

There was a bottle of sleeping pills on the dressing-table. I don't have to go on, she thought. Then she wheeled her internal monitors into action and said aloud, "Pull yourself together this minute, Theresa Marie Redpath, you're not a hysterical novelist or poet, you're not a hypersensitive aesthete, and you don't have post-natal depression."

Luisa Weiss and all those other vulnerable women may have killed themselves, but not people like Tess Redpath. She remembered what the out-placement adviser had said after a wasted morning of multiple-choice personality tests. The adviser was paid for by the *Argus* as part of Tess's "severance package" and so Tess had not been surprised nor believed it when he concluded Tess should never have been an editor in the first place. He said she was tenacious and conscientious, people-orientated, well organised. "If I'd been advising you at the start of your career I might have thought of social work or nursing but I'd never have come up with working on a paper. Writing, manipulating words — have you felt yourself it was your true metier, be honest now?"

Tess had primly insisted that the job suited her, though admitted she had never wanted to write. Then she left his consulting room, an attic in Harley Street of all places, clutching a sheaf of leaflets about late entry to professions she loathed the idea of such as teaching or social work. She deposited the lot in a litter bin. But some of the psychologist's assessments were more acceptable. Tess didn't need him to tell her she was tenacious.

If at first you don't succeed, try, try, try again, she thought, and went to ring the editors she had faxed that morning. She offered some inside information about exclusives to be covered by the *Argus* coupled with libels about its staff and proprietor.

"Have you met him? What's he like?"

"He's a creep," Tess said. "It must have been him that told Hamish to get rid of me, God knows why, but I can't think of any other explanation. He wanted to be rid of me."

"Any hint of his background?"

Tess tried to sound knowledgeable and worldly as she repeated all the stale old gossip she could think of. F.B. Carne might have made his fortune through arms deals, drug smuggling or money laundering. No wife was in the picture but he'd had three, seven, or possibly none. He was by birth an American Jew really called Cahn; another story had him growing up in Afghanistan, enriched by gun running and changing the spelling of his name from Khan. But everyone agreed he was a bad person to cross.

Then, using a voice that she hoped sounded careless rather than pleading, Tess said she had new material about Luisa Weiss. "I'll need a commission," she said. "Are you interested? Because if you're not I know Chris is quite keen."

"I might be," said the high, indifferent voice. "Have you really come up with a new line? Because we're all bored with the heroine worship bit, and the frustrated feminism. We've got past all that."

Tess said she had. And she'd look into Luisa's effect on other women. Had it been healthy? Speaking off the top of her head and the tip of her tongue, Tess realised this was the first time it had ever crossed her mind that Luisa's influence might have been anything other than beneficial.

The commission was the reverse of generous and Tess hesitated.

"That's what we pay writers who aren't established," the editor said in a take-it-or-leave-it voice.

Tess took it. She needed to if she was to keep her flat, and the thought spurred a mini-resurgence of the satisfaction she had habitually felt in her achievement.

I got all this, alone I did it, she thought. I'm not bloody letting it go.

She made notes for the two possible articles, one about Jill Williams and her relationship with her daughter, the other on the anniversary of Luisa Weiss's death. In doing so, Tess noticed the telephone number Moira had noted down and remembered the unsatisfactory conversation with the widow of Peter Slowe. It might well be worth following up, Tess thought, tapping out the numbers again.

Could she come and see Mrs Slowe? Oh, great, today? This afternoon? Great, fantastic, perfect, Tess enthused, much relieved, on hearing the address, to find it was no further away than Turnham Green.

A final riffle through her cuttings box revealed what she had been looking for in the first place, a publicity hand-out the Argus travel editor passed on months before. It advertised art courses which took place at Thalassa, organised by the Weiss Trust. Tess filled in the form. She walked with it to the letter box on the corner and went on to pay Jacques's bank draft into her account before going down to the hairdresser's in Kensington Church Street. Trevor lifted sections of her lank hair in disgust and told her a bob needed trimming every six weeks. As he reached for the scissors Tess changed her mind. "Don't trim it, I'm going back to the other style, is it long enough to perm again?" She had had a bushy frizz for years and it had been far less trouble than a bob. Anyway, she missed the soft cushion between her head and a chairback or pillow.

"Are you sure, Tess? It's not very *now*."

She was sure. How had being trendy helped? "Perm it," she said firmly. The tight curls seemed to lend their spring to her feet and even her heart. I'm cured, she thought. At the travel agency she booked an air ticket to the Isle of Man, and then took her parcel to the post office, where she paused, weighing it in her hand. She could see dear little innocent Sibyl unwrapping it, disclosing Jacques's possessions, wondering where they had come from, finding the lipstick stains, wrinkling her snub nose at a strange scent as understanding slowly dawned. How miserable she'd be. Serve her right.

Be nice, Tess. She heard her mother's voice in her head: Nobody will love you if you aren't nice.

She hesitated still. The Notting Hill Housing Trust shop was on the other side of the road. How elegantly Jacques's Fortnum and Mason dressing-gown would decorate its window. His shirt would lend tone to the rail crowded with dreary garments.

No, Sibyl could damn well take some of the pain.

The moment Tess left the post office she was overcome with shame. How could I? she wondered. That was a dreadful thing to do! Be honest if you can't be nice, Jacques was right, you didn't truly love him, not like a wife, you always liked keeping your freedom. But I miss him, something wailed in her mind. No you don't, the severe internal critic said. You miss having a lover, you don't miss Jacques himself, you didn't need to punish poor Sibyl.

Too late now; there was no way to get the parcel back from the Royal Mail. Tess crossed the road to the Notting Hill Housing Trust shop and went in to make a donation larger than she could afford. Conscience money. She was shamed by the thanks of the two helpers; they remembered Tess from the Christmas soup kitchen she had served at. What was she doing these days? Might she have time to help out at the shop some time?

Her own vague promises followed her out of the shop. The right bus was right there, stuck in a traffic jam, but its doors were closed. I might write a light piece about London buses, Tess thought, making a note in her Filofax while she waited at the bus stop; would the *Evening Standard* take an article saying leaping on a London bus at the lights was a human right?

Mrs Slowe — "call me Amanda" — was mid-brown with bloodshot dark eyes, drooping grey clothes and down-at-heel shoes. She looked cold and miserable and although she invited Tess in, it was clearly not to be for a long visit, for no food or drink was offered and they went into a room so strewn with toys, clothes, cardboard cartons and scattered ornaments that there was nowhere to sit down.

"I'm leaving this week," Amanda said; she spoke in a hoarse monotone as though she had been crying for weeks. Tess voiced all the necessary sympathy before wrapping her query up in gentle tact: what was it that Peter Slowe had told Moira?

Amanda kept saying she didn't know much. It had all started last December, when Peter had been reading the new, January issue of some magazine. There had been a list of dates to look out for in 1995 and one of them had been the anniversary of the death of Luisa Weiss. Amanda Slowe said, "I'd never even heard of her, and when Pete explained I couldn't understand why he was interested in some raving feminist — a macho bloke like him. But he wasn't interested, as it turned out, or any road, only in her dying. He'd got keen about being an author, it all began with getting paid for letters to mags, and then he went on short time and we were that skint — he thought there might be more money in doing things for papers."

"So he suggested a piece to the *Argus*?"

"Yeah, well, it said that was what paid best in some writers' handbook he looked at in the library. So he rang up in Christmas week, he had a few days off from the works, and that woman he spoke to was keen, he was going to do her — what did he call it?"

"An outline?"

"Mmm. An outline, about what he knew."

"You don't happen to have it here?" Tess asked.

"Funny you should ask, 'cos I was looking for it the other day but I couldn't find it. But so many things went missing — we had a break-in, you wouldn't believe it, while we were at his funeral. They knew the place would be empty."

More expressions of sympathy; and then Tess asked if Amanda could remember what the outline had been about.

"It was something about when Peter was staying with his grandad in Cornwall, it was the day Luisa Weiss killed herself and Peter saw something, he was only a kid at the time, but it made him realise later she might not have done it herself, he thought she'd been murdered."

"What did he see?" Tess asked eagerly.

"I just can't tell you, I'm ever so sorry. I can't even remember if Pete told me. And I can't find what he wrote either."

"Never mind, that's enormously helpful all the same." But the disappointment sounded in her voice, and Amanda Slowe said she'd send it on if it ever turned up.

Even without further details, Tess realised, it's a whole new ball-game if someone else was involved. A good story — my story, she thought, possibilities rushing through her mind. She felt energised and excited. "With two good exclusives you're really on your way," she told herself, and hailed a taxi to get back to Notting Hill. There was one last item to be ticked off her list before the shops closed. Tess went to the shop which had a do-it-yourself printing machine and made herself a variety of visiting cards. In only one version did she describe herself as a journalist.

Then she walked up the hill back to her flat where, on opening the door, she realised she had forgotten to pack Jacques's coat in with his other belongings. Tutting at herself, she picked it up and noticed there was something hard in the pocket; a computer diskette. Idly curious, she tried it in her own AppleMac, but it was incompatible and she found only the "systems error" message. I bet it's top secret, she thought. I could pass it to someone. I could get him into trouble for being so careless. I could probably sell it. That would serve him right.

Be nice, Tess. She hung the coat up again, and went into her bedroom to pack.

# CHAPTER
# SIX

The Blagdens were listed in a small, exclusive directory of guest houses called *Cranmers At Home.*

Cranmers specialised in homes whose owners "extended their hospitality to a few carefully chosen guests". Each entry enthused about the cuisine, chosen, supervised or made by Mrs or in several instances Lady so-and-so; it mentioned every welcoming touch: real log fires, fresh flowers, a decanter of sherry in each room. Exclusivity was implied with every word.

The Blagdens' "welcoming interior designed home pervaded with family atmosphere" was called Holly Lodge. Tess had called to book one of the two rooms on offer, explaining she was planning to move to the Isle of Man and did not want to live in an impersonal hotel while she house-hunted. "Am I speaking to Mr Blagden?"

"You are indeed, Miss Redpath, and we'll look forward to seeing you. And how long will you be staying?" Tess was beginning to say she was not sure yet, when she heard a woman shouting in the background. "Ah, Miss Redpath. Slight hitch. My wife reminds me we may not have a room free later in the week. But come tomorrow as ever is, and we'll pass the parcel if needs be. We're friendly folk here on the island, it's all for one and one for all as you'll find out soon enough."

The same could almost be said of Tess's fellow passengers on the little aeroplane who sat knocking back the miniatures of spirits and gossiping. She recognised some former colleagues but none seemed to remember her, and at Douglas airport she was left behind in the scramble for the hire car desks as experienced journalists pushed to be first in the queue. Tess had prudently reserved a car, and once at the wheel of the small Fiat set off southwards across the island.

The landscape seemed at once strange and familiar. In patches it was so like Cornwall that Tess felt herself to be at home, and relaxed into absent-minded enjoyment of homely features she missed in London like the grassy dry-stone walls and the windblown gorse. When gorse is in bloom kissing's in season, she thought, and then said aloud, "Huh, much good that'll do me." But she sounded quite cheerful, and was. A new start, she thought, I'm over Jacques. Perhaps I'm over love. But she did not believe it, because ever since she could remember Tess had always been in love. When, in her twenties, she had read that Cyril Connolly said, "Life without love is like an operation without an anaesthetic," she'd realised it was a description of her own feelings. The gaps between love-objects were always bleak and painful.

I'm getting on for forty, she thought. Perhaps I can do without it? Perhaps I'll have to do without it.

She drew in lung-expanding breaths of the damp sea

air. Soon she came to alien features: houses whose corner stones had been picked out in black, as she had seen in Ireland; gaudy Bretonstyle villas with first-floor entrances and wrought-iron galleries above garages and stores dug in below ground level; the three-legged logo of the ancient kingdom. The air was sweet and at every field gate came a glimpse of vivid sea.

Negotiating the tight turns of the narrow, high-hedged roads, Tess followed signposts to Dunkloss. Approaching the village she saw again some of the men who had been shown on the aeroplane, talking on their mobile telephones as they peered uselessly into the curtained windows of the Williams house. There was obviously nothing to see that had not already been on the screen. Tess had driven this way out of curiosity, no more, and for the same reason stopped at the larger of the village pubs. Roaring trade was being done and as he poured the strong drinks, the publican was repeating a practised line about Petronella and her reclusive mother. At the other end of the bar a younger man was talking to a little knot of customers.

"Nah, couldn't have been anyone else did it, she was all alone there. No foul play suspected, that's what they're giving out 'cos it's obvious, she topped herself, got a rope and slung it over a beam in that shed. She called it her studio. You could see it through the window, there was a crack in the shutters, and so we broke the window and went in. Dangling like a wax dummy. Not swinging round — funny, I'd always thought they'd twist on the end of the rope, don't know why, but she wasn't, just hanging there quite still with her toes pointed like a ballet dancer or something. Her hands and face and legs was all purple and bulging, like they'd been puffed up, didn't look like skin at all. And shit on the floor. We couldn't hardly cut through that old rope, nasty blue unbreakable cord. Billy said we ought to try the kiss of life, but she was stone dead, eyes all bulging and her tongue swollen up like a balloon and sticking out like she . . ."

Tess, unable to swallow the drink she had ordered, went out and took in deep breaths of the chilly air. Disgusting, she thought, obscene. Did Luisa look like that? How the young man had been enjoying it. Jill Williams's pitiful death was probably the most exciting thing that had ever happened to him.

It could not be more than five miles from here to Holly Lodge, but Tess was soon hopelessly lost, finding that she had first driven round in circles and then off at a smart pace in the wrong direction. At dusk she stopped at a telephone box in Castletown to say she was still on her way.

"Don't worry, that's all right, dinner's ready when you are," said a comfortable contralto voice.

Some time later Tess parked on the gravel sweep at the foot of some wide, shallow steps. Light spilled out of a wide open front door from which a burly giant bounded, followed by an equally enthusiastic and sizeable dog.

"Courage, Tess, it isn't going to bite," she muttered and opened the car door. The dog stood itself up against her, its wet nose almost in her face.

"Rumpelstiltskin Blagden, get down at once. I say, Miss Redpath, I do hope you don't mind dogs. How d'you do? I'm thine host, Vic Blagden's the name. And here's Vicky. Don't worry, I know it's muddling, our respective parents had the same idea about names, some years apart I may say. Rumpy. Down, I said. Down. How d'you know our guest likes dogs?"

"It's quite all right," Tess forced herself to say, and put out a cringing hand to pat the animal's head. Her host grabbed its collar and heaved. Then he held out his free hand and enclosed Tess's in it.

"I'm afraid I'm terribly late, I got completely lost."

"No matter, no matter, come away in now and relax."

She followed him up the steps. "Rumpelstiltskin, did you call it?"

"Our daughter's idea. It was her turn to do the christening. Our boys got the cat and the goats. Vicky, here's Miss Redpath."

"Oh, please do call me Tess."

She followed both the Blagdens, one vast and the other substantial, through a warmly lit entrance hall, up wide stairs covered with thick rust-coloured carpet, and along an arched passage.

"Here you are. Light switch, light switch, here's where the electric blanket turns on, bathroom through here, mind the towel rail, it gets boiling hot, anything you want just give us a shout. If you'd like to sort yourself out then there's drinks in the drawing room."

"Thank you very much, I'll be right down."

Left alone, Tess opened the drawers and cupboard, pulled the flowered curtains aside to find she could see nothing outside, and used the lavatory. The room was full of hand-crafted decorations. There were crocheted mats on the tables, embroidered cushions on the arm-chair, a needlework rug by the bed. The curtains on both window and bed head were ruched and tucked, the walls in this room, like those in the hall and passage, were ragged or dragged, with a stencilled border and dado. Knitted covers fitted over the lavatory seat and the spare roll of paper. Broderie anglaise covers enclosed paper tissues and a container of spare toiletries. Shampoo and bath essence had been decanted into hand-painted jars. Dried flowers stood in a rough pottery jug, and a tray, table and sewing box were made of découpage.

When she entered the drawing-room she saw that it too was decorated, as her mother would have said when she could still say anything, within an inch of its life, with frills and ornaments and a dazzle of colour and pattern.

"There you are, come you in, we're on our own tonight. Vicky will be with us in a moment, she's bent double over a hot Aga," Vic Blagden boomed. "Dry sherry suit you?"

"Lovely, thank you," said Tess, who disliked the mouth-puckering taste just about as much as she disliked being leapt on by large dogs. "What a gorgeous house and how beautiful you've made it all, I really love the way it's all in toning shades," Tess said, advancing towards the fire. Above it hung a still life whose colours had evidently been copied in the interior design; it showed a woven basket full of peaches, oranges, apricots and yellow plums.

"Glad you like it."

The mantelpiece was decorated with a row of photographs in silver frames; three were of a young man in naval uniform, a girl in academic dress, another man on skis. "Your family?"

"Guilty as charged! But they've all flown the nest now. That was when we started having guests, must have some excuse for staying in a house this size."

"Your sons are very like you."

"Don't let them hear you say so."

Tess ran her eye along the other pictures, three of elderly people and one, signed across the corner, of Petronella Williams. Tess did not allow recognition to show in her face. Moving away to a chair she said, "I can't get over how pretty this is, it's so cosy and —" She remembered the adjective the House and Home editor at the *Argus* often used. "Eclectic, isn't that the word?"

"Vicky does it all."

"She's very talented, in that case."

The Blagdens and Tess had dinner in a formal dining-room, with lace mats on gleaming mahogany, candles burning in silver sticks and family portraits on the yellow walls, and ate fish mousse and beef in a pastry crust, followed by pears in chocolate sauce. The conversation was a nicely judged combination of friendliness and impersonality; the Blagdens had made a fine art of treating customers as guests. They talked about the island, what sort of house Tess might look at, and how much she would enjoy living there. Although they did not ask, she took the chance of telling them about the unthreatening, unwordly past she had borrowed from an acquaintance.

Tess had prepared a legend: she had turned herself into a theoretical psychotherapist who had held an academic post at one of London's former polytechnics. In the last round of education funding cuts she was made redundant, and the university offered generous terms to staff who agreed to steal quietly away. Tess said she was going to finish a book she had been working on for years, a study of non-chemical treatment of post-natal depression. She told the Blagdens her book was to be for a general, non-academic market, using anonymous case histories and some named and well-known sufferers such as the Princess of Wales and Luisa Weiss as examples. Tess was hunting, she said, for a cottage or flat; she had always dreamt of moving to the island after a holiday there in her teens.

As she spoke, Tess was mentally cursing Petronella's absence. She'd been shown on the news, coming out of the police station in Douglas. She must have been here earlier in the week. Surely she'd be back?

But then, if Petronella had been here the Blagdens might well have told Tess they had no room available. Now at least she had a chance to make herself seem friendly and trustworthy, so they would let her stay on even when Petronella returned, as she surely must for her mother's funeral. And if not? Tess reminded herself of her alternative plan. She had equipped herself with listening gear, bought at an electronics shop in Hounslow on the way to the airport. If the Blagdens turned her out before the inquest and funeral, their walls would have ears.

Tess's requirements were twofold. She wanted to find out whether Petronella could explain the photograph of Luisa Weiss with Jill Williams; but the big money would be made from intimate titbits about Petronella's relationship with her mother. And the *Argus* was not going to get either story.

Arranging her belongings in her room that evening, Tess set out tokens of intellectual seriousness, a novel by Iris Murdoch and a biography of Gladstone, on the dressing-table beside copies of the *Times Literary Supplement* and the *Literary Review*. By the bed she placed two feminist pamphlets about Luisa Weiss and her file of notes and cuttings, from which she had removed the photograph showing Jill Williams. She had not brought a portable radio because it was important to seem like someone who took little interest in current affairs. Magazines would be too frivolous for her assumed persona.

After picking up the hired car at the airport she had stopped in to a couple of estate agencies, and now laid their lists beside her other props, which consisted of a tapestry cushion cover she had begun years ago and never got very far with and a paperback guide to the wild flowers of the west coast. In it she stuck a visiting card which read "Miss Theresa Redpath, Faculty of English and Social Studies, University of West London".

Tess sat up in the very comfortable bed and opened her battered edition of the Weiss memorabilia. The diary wasn't poetic or historic, just a painfully candid record of real life in an era when women were still mealy mouthed about it; orgasm, menstruation, contraception, childbirth. Luisa recorded privacies and her husband had edited some of them and published the first instalment on the anniversary of her death. Another volume was due on the twenty-fifth anniversary of her death.

Presumably it consisted of dregs, the final scrapings of a long since emptied barrel. Tess wondered how painful it was for the daughters to read, as adults, their mother's lament.

It was not news any more that motherhood was a hard grind. Two decades of feminist writing had shattered any sentimental illusions society retained. But when Luisa became a mother she had expected a rosy glow of maternal fulfilment. Exhaustion, physical discomfort and boredom took her by surprise. It was the raw, fresh, undisguised experience she had set down on paper and distilled into argument in *Into Captivity*.

Leafing through notes she had made so far on the known facts about Luisa Weiss, Tess realised for the first time that nothing was ever said about the admittedly short period between school and art college, the months later generations called "the gap".

The formal details of Luisa's earlier years were known: brought up between her reclusive Cornish father and her remarried mother who lived in London, Luisa had been a bright pupil at a fiercely academic school, gone to art school, married Raymond, borne him two daughters, written her books and died.

But at some stage she had been in America. Tess had paid a photographer to blow up and try to sharpen the image of Luisa with Jill Williams. It became possible to discern that the girls were standing in a car-park in front of a Howard Johnson's drive-in. There was a long low car with big fins and a neon sign behind them. Why had no American trip ever been mentioned by Luisa's biographers?

It poured with rain the next day, and the next, and the one after. Tess put off the awful necessity of going out as long as possible. She washed her underwear and hung it over the bath. She did the crossword in the *Daily Telegraph.* She rang her own number to check for messages. Biddy, for a chat. The flat freeholder warning of a call from the cockroach exterminator. Jacques's voice. Don't be moved by it, she thought, keep cool. It was not difficult, as all he'd said was, "I left my coat, please send it to my office soonest." Then came Ilona. She wanted to be rung back. I'll let her stew, Tess thought resentfully.

At last she had to go out and go through the motions of looking at properties for sale, holiday flats, stone cottages, modern bungalows. She gave herself lunch in pubs and cafés, and over dinner in Holly Lodge discussed the merits and possibilities of the homes she had seen. Neither she nor the Blagdens mentioned the island's local drama, and when, on the second evening, an American golfer who had stopped in for one night asked which direction Dunkloss would be from here, Tess made no sign of knowing the name. But she followed the news stories about Jill Williams. Anybody who had ever spoken to her seemed to be telling a tale, but always the same one. She had lived an isolated, apparently friendless life, without visitors. Nobody ever even knocked at her door, said the neighbour, practised with the media by now, her hair newly set and her eyes made up. "I never liked to go round there myself, she let you know when you weren't wanted. I even warned the Mormons not to waste their breath on her."

On the fourth morning, Vicky Blagden came into the dining-room where Tess was drinking coffee on her own. She said, "Sorry to press you, Tess, but how many nights were you thinking of staying?"

"As long as it takes, Vicky, if I may."

"I'm not sure, your room may be needed for —"

She's coming, Tess thought gleefully, and said, "Oh, that is a disappointment. It's so nice here, I'd love to stay on if it's at all possible."

"The thing is, we have a bit of a problem —"

"I was just thinking how lucky I was to find you, your son was quite right, it's really —"

"My son? Which one?"

"I never heard his first name, he was in the navy."

"That's Tim."

"It was at dinner with some people in Hampstead and he was talking about his home and how lovely it is staying here. That's what brought me in the first place."

"If you know Tim that's a bit — I'll go and look at the bookings again."

The sideboard was near the serving hatch. Tess went across to it and picked up the coffee pot from the hot-plate. She could just make out Vicky's low voice. "I'd have thought it would be OK, Vic, she's ever so quiet and unworldly, she'd never give Petsy away."

"I'm not sure, Vicky, we promised Petronella —"

"Yes, I know, but honestly, Tess is so quiet, and not a bit nosy, she's obviously nothing to do with the press and it's the only long booking we've had since September. We really oughtn't to . . ." Their voices faded, as the Blagdens moved out of earshot, and when Vicky and Vic came back to the dining-room together, Tess was demurely buttering some toast. She looked up and said, "A deputation! Are you going to turn me out into the snow?"

"No, please do stay on, but the thing is, there's something we'd have to ask you to promise."

Their friend Petronella, they said, had stayed with the Blagdens for years, ever since she started work and could afford to visit her mother without having to share her small and uncomfortable house. "We met her first through Dan, our eldest, he brought her here one New Year, but she's more like a member of the family these days. And now of course, she's having such a difficult time, we're terribly anxious for her not to have any —"

"Petronella . . . did you say Williams? I do know the name, but I can't quite . . ." Tess said.

"Didn't you read about her engagement? It's been all over the news."

"Oh yes, I'm afraid I haven't been following it, you'll probably think I'm stupidly unworldly, but —"

"Her mother lived over here, but she's . . . passed away, and Petronella has to see to things over here."

"Poor girl, of course, what a shame," Tess burbled.

"At Holly Lodge she can be sure of being safe from prying eyes, she knows nobody will give anything away. But we're certain you wouldn't, Tess."

104

Trying not to overdo the slightly spinsterish image she had adopted, Tess assured the Blagdens she was not capable of such treachery. "I'm afraid I'm a complete ignoramus about the popular press, I sometimes think I should take more notice but I've never really been very interested in gossip."

"If only more people were like you, the poor girl gets so dreadfully pestered."

"I won't pester her, Vicky, honestly. Believe me, I never would."

Tess spent another day poking her nose into other people's homes, each less appealing, more damp and undesirable, than the last. She wondered whether she was going to excessive lengths to maintain her cover, as she pretended to consider a flat designed for summer visitors, with damp, mould-speckled walls and no central heating. But on Sunday the estate agencies were mercifully closed.

Tess began the day walking on a cool but temporarily sunny beach. Then the rain began. She drove into Douglas and bought all the Sunday papers, filling in the day by reading them cover to cover: the news, the comment, the reviews, even of ballet which bored her and concerts to which she was deaf. Unaffordable travel, unwearable fashion, unbearable advice. The colour supplements. Tess counted the times each dippy girl columnist used the word "I". Then she made herself read the extracts from a politician's memoirs until at last she thought it was late enough to return to Holly Lodge. When she turned in at the drive, in the late afternoon, a smart little French car was parked by the steps. In the drawing-room, Tess's quarry was sitting with her tea.

# CHAPTER
# SEVEN

Petronella Williams sat curled in the corner of the large sofa. She was wearing a black top, miniskirt and tights, and held a small, comatose dog on her lap. Open beside her on the sofa was a large, shabby leather suitcase full of papers.

Petronella's appearance and mannerisms were so familiar, even to someone like Tess who hated the soap opera she appeared in, that seeing her in the flesh was like meeting an intimate. Every inch of those irregular features, the tiny nose, the monochrome skin, the cloud of conker-coloured hair, the compelling eyes, amber yellow with a darker edge round the iris, all had been discussed to death. Even relaxing in privacy, without make-up or jewellery except for the famous emerald engagement ring, Petronella looked glossy and expensive, as though she bathed three times a day and did not know the meaning of the expression "dirty knickers". Beside her Tess would have felt shabby even if she were not in her unthreatening disguise. Perhaps, she thought, the women princes marry are a different species after all. This one will accept curtseys and courtesies as her natural due.

Petronella glanced at one of the papers in her case,

crumpled it up and lobbed it into the fire. Rumpelstiltskin was pacing jealously up and down, repeatedly pushing his nose into the smaller animal, being pushed away by Petronella, pacing huffily away and coming back all over again. Tess came forward from the door and managed to say without cringing, "Hallo, Rumpy, good boy. All right, that's enough, get down. Get down, I said."

"He's just too big, isn't he," said Petronella, in a high and breathy voice. "It's all too much for Beano."

Beano, Tess now saw, had a shaved patch on his forehead with two strips of sticking plaster across it. "Poor little chap, what happened to him?"

"He cut himself, the vet said he probably ran into something terribly sharp."

"You must have felt awful about it."

"I wasn't there, he was my mother's dog." Petronella looked up at Tess, who, without giving Petronella a chance to make any permissive gesture, sat firmly down on an antique elbow chair, put on her spinsterish spectacles and appeared to be concentrating on matching wools as she held a pink and purple strand up to the light. "My mother died recently," Petronella added. "That's why I'm looking through her papers."

It was a challenge; implicit in her voice was the accusation that Tess knew all about it and was gasping to know more.

Tess did not try to pretend ignorance. She said warmly, "I know, you poor thing, Vicky told me. I'm so sorry."

"I'm here for the inquest and funeral."

"Oh dear, that's awful for you. An inquest!"

Petronella said no more, but picked up the remote control to turn on the television. Tess went on calmly stitching the rather unpleasing design, begun many years before when she had been laid up with a sprained ankle. Her sympathy was sincere; but it was overlaid by an innate suspicion of the public faces that beautiful or prominent people invariably assume. During Tess's time at the *Argus*, the magazine's policy had veered between *Hello!* style adulation and *Private Eye* style sneering. Tess had come to understand that neither was ever entirely justified. Somewhere underneath Petronella's veneer was a bereaved if invisible mourner.

Vic came in and made a bowing gesture towards Petronella. His words were avuncular but his tone a courtier's, as he invited her to come in to dinner.

"I'll be right with you," Tess said, slowly folding her canvas and putting it into the bag. With one eye on Petronella's back, as she crossed the hall carrying one dog and followed by the other, Tess bent to the open caseful of documents, and lifted the top layer. Underneath lay a faded blue folder marked "USA 1965". Bingo.

"Tess, dinner's ready," Vic called.

"I'm coming," she said.

Over dinner the conversation stayed on local island politics and Vic's experiences on his boat in the last round-Britain race. Petronella nodded and smiled and interjected encouragement. Was she interested? It was impossible to tell.

After dinner Tess excused herself and went up to her

room. When she heard the others come up to bed she switched off her own lights, and heard a whisper from someone passing her door. "Sssh, she's asleep already."

She heard lavatories flushing, a bath running out, a radio playing softly and then turned off, coughs, sighs, a subdued bark. About two hours later, after a long period of silence broken only by distant snores, she put on a dressing-gown and slippers, opened her door and by the moonlight coming in through the landing window, crept downstairs. She went into the drawing-room and turned the light on. Paying guests are entitled to wander round if they can't sleep, she told herself, I have every right to be in here and in a minute I'll go in the kitchen and make some tea.

She crossed the room to the sofa by the fire, where the suitcase of papers still lay. A faded, blurred image with an indistinguishable background showing, presumably, Jill Williams with, more clearly, a fair-haired, blue-eyed, fresh-faced, cheerful chap in a shirt with rolled sleeves and an open neck. Petronella herself, a dumpling on a pony, another in ballet gear on points. A straight-up, uncomplicated bourgeoise, now almost completely transmogrified into an icon.

School reports: Petronella Williams, spring term, summer term . . . a teacher's round, regular handwriting. A cutting showing a primary school nativity play. And here was the folder labelled "USA 1965".

Tess eased the flap back. It was full of newspaper cuttings. Articles torn or cut from English language papers bulged out of the cardboard: *New York Times*, *Washington Post*, *Cincinnati Inquirer*. It was hard to discern a theme; they were news stories and comment columns about affairs then current and now forgotten. Car crashes, shootings, deaths, massacres.

Suddenly Tess heard herself gasp almost before she registered what had made her do so. It was the dog Rumpelstiltskin, which had padded silently into the room and pushed its cold, wet nose into her behind. "It's all right, it's only me, good dog," she whispered. It was wagging its tail, but would not back off. And there was a footstep on the stairs. Tess pushed the papers back into the file and grabbed a book from the table and when Vic came in seemed to be looking at it. She looked up, smiling, and said, "Sorry, did I disturb you? I was looking for something to read, I simply couldn't get to sleep."

Prophetic or descriptive: Tess spent the rest of the night tossing and turning, eventually putting on the bedside light and returning to Luisa's writings. She murmured the words of a poem aloud under her breath. It was about fires and the terror of them, and odd images came back to Tess in the course of the next day. Flames leapt like dolphins from the water. Fire rustled like a snake. Heat put fetters of terror round the poet's body.

Tess spent some time asleep in her hired car in a lay-by the next day, instead of pointlessly trudging round another undesirable residence. In the evening Vic and Vicky went out to a vital protest meeting about plans for a new supermarket. Back in the drawing-room with Petronella and watching television, Tess could not plausibly pretend not to recognise her face when it was flashed up behind the news headlines. "Suicide verdict on Petronella Williams's mother Mrs Jill Williams, government defeat predicted on —"

Petronella snapped the sound off, and Tess said, "Did you have to be there? I'd have thought it a pretty nasty experience for you, and with all those people watching you, that can't have helped."

"I'm used to cameras. They don't pester me so much if my fiancé's not there, but of course I'm pretty secure these days — we've got protection, if you know what I mean."

"I meant that it must have hurt to hear what they said about your mother, to be told she was so dreadfully unhappy."

"Unhappy!" Petronella put the little dog on the hearth-rug and began to walk restlessly around the room, followed by Rumpelstiltskin. The day's experiences had left her less cool than before. "I should worry!"

Tess, sitting demurely with her needlework, kept her eyes lowered to hide her satisfaction. Gotcha. She's desperate to talk and I'm elected, she thought.

"You're some sort of therapist, aren't you? You wouldn't pass on anything I told you?"

"No, of course not, you can trust me as though this were a professional encounter. Absolute discretion."

So Petronella told Tess all about it.

"We were never close, my mother and I," she began. Then she paused and shot a suspicious look at Tess. "Are you sure you're not a reporter?"

"Do I look like a reporter? Honestly!"

"No. No, I suppose not. Anyway, one simply has to

**111**

trust somebody, or what's the point? Were you close to your own mother?"

"She always disapproved of me intensely," Tess said truthfully. "We fought all through my teens and she was bitterly disappointed when I had a proper career because all she wanted was for me to settle down in a conventional house with a conventional husband and provide her with grandchildren."

"That's the exact opposite of what my mother wanted, but she was never what you'd call maternal."

Petronella was born in 1966, eight months after her father's death in a car crash in the United States. "They were travelling around, just a couple of kids, Ma was only twenty. They'd met out there and fallen in love and got married and then he died and she came home pregnant. Well, that was all right as it turned out because my grandparents, my father's parents that is, they were thrilled, they thought a baby would make up for losing him. And then Ma got really bad post-natal depression so his family took me in while she was in a clinic for about two years. Then I lived with her for a bit, not that I can remember it, but when I was four she gave me back so I sometimes lived with my uncle or aunt and otherwise with my grandparents in Herefordshire."

"It sounds rather unsettling."

"No, I learnt to be very adaptable, I always fit in. And I saw Ma too. She moved round a lot, never seemed to settle until she came here and getting to the island takes ages and there never really seemed to be much room for me in her house, but as soon as I could afford to I started staying here. The Blagdens have been wonderful to me."

112

"They are the salt of the earth," Tess agreed primly.

"I went out with Dan at one time. They've treated me like family."

"Was your mother happy about you staying here, instead of with her?"

"I think she was relieved. You see, it was always . . ." Petronella slid down to sit on the hearthrug, hugging her knees and staring into the gentle flames. She spoke in a low voice, almost to herself. Tess had a tiny tape recorder concealed in her needlework bag, but she did not dare to make even the slightest sound of turning on and tried instead to take every word into her own memory, as with many hesitations and pauses, Petronella Williams spoke about her mother.

"I came to realise there was something missing. Whether it had never been there, or maybe it was the effect of Ma's two years in hospital when I was a baby . . . I sometimes wondered what had happened to her in the crash that killed my father, but she wouldn't talk about it. It was exactly as if something had got frozen up in her, so she couldn't love people. She never loved me, I used to wonder if it was 'cos I didn't look like her or my dad, but really she didn't care for anyone, it was like she was running away or hiding or something, always suspicious, unsociable, kind of separate from life."

With Petronella's back turned to the silent screen, Tess could take in the pictures being shown on another news programme: there was Jill Williams again, and Petronella herself, walking, head down, into the coroner's court.

"We never did the things mothers do with daughters. She just wasn't interested in any of the things I liked. Clothes, music, acting, having some fun. All she wanted was to be a recluse and when I turned up it was just like an interruption. And she got furious about the smallest things. Once when I came here I brought my camera, Gran had given it to me for my birthday and I took it when we went for a walk on the cliffs over at Jurby, I was playing round with it, snapping things the way you do if you've never had one before, and she snatched the camera away from me and threw it in the sea. Just like that. It was so sudden, such unexpected violence . . . I was too scared to say a word. But that was the kind of thing she'd do, be perfectly all right, just quiet and nervous like she always was and then she'd suddenly flip. Gran said she was like the mouse in that poem, a wee cowrin' timorous beastie."

A reporter's face faded into a computer generated diagram: a wooden beam, a rope with a noose at the end, a three-legged stool fallen on to its side. A dangling female figure.

"Needless to say Gran was never there when Ma went nuclear. Like she did when I came to tell her about getting engaged. I mean, you know who I'm getting married to, it was pretty exciting, other mothers would be thrilled. Not Ma though.

"I waited till the evening, we'd had supper, all shut up together in her little house with the doors locked and curtains tightly drawn like they always were, she had this thing about people being able to see in, as though there was anyone who'd have been interested! Or would

114

have been, before I started going out with . . . well, you know. So I tried to break it to her gently, leading up to it sort of in a roundabout way. I told her about my boyfriend and eventually I said we were going to get married. It was good news, I thought. I mean, she might have pretended to be pleased.

"She just sat there looking across at me, like I was some stranger or something, and she said, her voice was all little, fierce, sort of hard, she just said, 'Petronella, you cannot do this thing to me.'

"That was a laugh. To her! What was I doing to her, for God's sake? I was doing it to me, to myself, not to her.

"And then I told her about the wedding, and I tried to make her take an interest in the dress and bridesmaids and all the things other mothers get so hooked on. And she just wouldn't. No, no, no, she kept saying, you can't do it.

"But I had to get her to talk about it, she couldn't just opt out of my life this time, not like when she never came to anything at my school and left it all to Gran, this time she was going to have to meet the in-laws and show her face in public and bloody well look pleased.

"Then she went on with the same old tune, wasn't it better to earn my own living and be independent and not sacrifice my life to some man, the same boring stuff, I'd heard it all before, you know? And I said I didn't bloody want to be a merchant banker or prime minister, I don't care about being a famous actress, I just want to make my husband happy and share his life and bring up my family. I'm going to have lots of children."

Another shot of Petronella closed the news bulletin; it had been taken about a month ago. She was walking with her fiancé and her future in-laws. She was smiling widely, swinging a little bag, prancing along on spike heels like a circus horse, waving to well-wishers.

"And then before I left to come back here, I asked her just once more. 'Aren't you happy for me, Mum?' I said. I was begging her, just one word, that's all I wanted, one little word. D'you know what she answered?"

"Tell me," Tess said softly.

"'This will be the death of me, Petronella. This will be the death of me.' That's what she said." The girl wiped tears off her cheeks with the back of her hands and sniffed juicily. "And she made bloody sure it was, didn't she? Bloody hanged herself, that's all, better be dead than have her daughter happily married. She punished me. I'll never forgive her. Never."

"That's so sad," Tess said sincerely. She sat in silence listening to Petronella's gulps and sobs, her hand resting on the girl's heaving shoulder. She felt like crying herself, partly in sympathy and partly in self-pity because she had realised she was never going to be able to use this story, which would have made her rich. Tess was visualising herself telling it and selling it, the words she would use, the praise she would receive, and at the same time she was getting her mind round the idea that she couldn't do it; she wouldn't be able to live with herself if she repeated the intimate confidence of a desperate girl.

After a while she heaved a great, final sigh of acceptance, disappointment and pity, and said, "Petronella, I want to ask you something about your mother. Do you mind?"

"Ask me about my — why?" The girl grabbed the tiny dog and sprang to her feet, clutching it like some kind of shield. "You're a reporter!"

"No, honestly, it's nothing to do with your mother herself, or with you, it's just that it's such an opportunity, meeting you unexpectedly like this, because of the book I'm working on."

"Vicky said you were writing about —"

"Post-natal depression, but not in connection with your mother, I never even knew she'd suffered from it, though it's so common it isn't at all surprising. The statistics show that more than a quarter of all new mothers get it," Tess asserted, guessing wildly at a figure. She went on hastily, "One of my subjects is Luisa Weiss."

"I know the name. Did we do one of her short stories for GCSE?"

"Your mother never mentioned her?"

"My mother? No, I'm sure she didn't, should she have?"

"Luisa wrote a book called *Into Captivity* which —"

"Oh yes, I know about that, one of our teachers was always talking about it. I tried to read it, but it all seemed so old-fashioned. I remember now, funny you should mention it, because I brought it over here to Ma's place one weekend and she threw it on the fire."

"Why?"

"Some temper tantrum or other, I never knew what was going to set her off, she was just like that."

"Had she read it already then?"

"That isn't the kind of book Ma read, she liked thrillers."

But Jill must have read, if not Luisa's book, then at least about her death, Tess thought, for she seemed to have copied its method exactly. Jill did know about her. She knew her. Tess said, "Petronella, take a look at this photo if you wouldn't mind. That's Luisa on the left, with dark hair."

"Oh yes, I've seen pictures of her in — wait a minute. Who's that with her?"

"What do you think?"

"It's Ma, isn't it? That's my mother before I — where did you get this? I've never —"

"Then you do believe it is a photograph of your mother?"

"It certainly is. And what's more it's one of the only photos I've ever seen of her apart from the ones people tried to catch after the engagement. She never let anyone take her picture, she had a real thing about it."

"Didn't her own people —?" Tess asked.

"She didn't have any really, which is why she didn't know what to do with me, at least that's what I always thought."

"No family at all?"

"She'd been fostered and hated her foster family, that's all she ever said. Her own relations were killed at the end of the war," Petronella said. She peered at the photograph. "This must have been in the States, there's a Howard Johnson's. She met my father in America, she went there for a vacation from art school."

"Luisa was at art school too."

"I suppose they met up there. It might even have been my father that took this picture."

"Your mother never said anything about Luisa?"

"No."

Tess laid her embroidery on the stool and drew closer to Petronella. She did not warm to the girl, even unguarded as she had been this evening; there was still a chill of self-absorption about her. And I'm jealous, Tess recognised. Once Petronella's got over this hurdle she can put her mother's death behind her and the rest of her life will be so rich and privileged.

Be nice, Tess. She put her hand on the girl's back, trying to send some sort of comfort through the contact to neutralise the cruelty of what she had to say. "Listen, Petronella, I know it's not my business, but I've got to mention it. Your mother must have known quite a bit about Luisa Weiss because she — I'm sorry, I'm really sorry — she copied her exactly when she — there are so many similarities in the method — when she took her own life, I mean."

"My mother hanged herself with the rope of a clothes line," Petronella said in a clear, hard voice.

"In an outhouse, from a beam, as Luisa did. And there's another parallel too, the —"

Petronella sprang to her feet. "Listen, Miss Redpath, I really don't want to hear this. Not meaning to be rude or anything, but lots of suicides hang themselves, just because you happen to have come across two, twenty-five years apart, doesn't mean anything. I should prefer to change the subject," she added.

Tess gathered her belongings, the liking she had begun to feel for Petronella dissipated in a moment by her proleptically assumed regality. This girl didn't really care. Now she had got it off her chest she would be free with a bound, onwards and upwards to the glories awaiting her, unencumbered by memories of a discarded, discarding mother. Tess did not need to like her. What had liking to do with a good story? This woman would be the prey of paparazzi and stalkers for the rest of her life. It was part of the status she had chosen, the name of the game. Wasn't it?

Tess said, "I must go to bed in any case, I have an early start tomorrow. I'll send you a copy of this photograph as soon as I have one done. But just let me confirm, if it was taken in America, it must have been not long before you were born."

"I was born in April 1966."

"Right. That helps."

Tess wrote carefully on the back of the photograph: "Jill Williams and Luisa, somewhere in America, summer 1965."

# CHAPTER
# EIGHT

But Luisa Weiss did not seem to have been in America, not in 1965, not ever. No such visit was mentioned in any of the material. How could Tess interest a commissioning editor in the story?

"Could you just say you know Petronella's mum wasn't best pleased?" Desmond asked.

"It's not enough for anyone to pay for, not unless I can tell them how I know."

All night and all the previous day during the journey back to London Tess had been battling with her own better nature.

There was a fortune riding on Petronella's outburst. Tess could see the banner headlines. She could write every word of the media-psychiatrist's analysis of Petronella's problems. She knew which columnists would use them as a peg for a thousand words and what line — superior, sympathetic or supercilious — each would take. She even guessed which publisher would offer a lump sum for a rapid, book-length blow-up of the unguarded conversation, full of pop-psychological analysis of the effects of a fatherless childhood, lacking in mother-love, and the worldly ambitions such deprivation had engendered.

It's every woman for herself, Tess thought. Nobody's looking after me, why should I look after Petronella?

Tess's conscience fought with her need. She argued with herself all morning, as she carefully washed and scrunch-dried her hair, applied cosmetics, put on and took off her smarter clothes. What was the right image? Should she look as though she was desperate for work, or as though other editors were queuing to commission her? In the end there was not much choice, because she had put on too much weight since leaving the *Argus* to be able to do up anything but a second-hand Farhi she had never much liked.

She thought, If I've got to do what it takes to be a freelance journalist it's not my fault. Don't blame me, it's not what I ever wanted. It's Hamish to blame, not me. Hamish and his toad of a proprietor.

I'd pay him back if I could.

The automatic corollary of the thought came — Be nice, Tess — and was banished. Why should I be nice? she thought, the words in her head in the high, petulant whine of her childhood. Biddy could be the nice one if she wanted, though it was not often Lena Redpath had to tell her to. "I'm not nice, I'm Tess," she'd said once, aged three, to be quoted ever after.

Tess had learnt to seem nice. But not this time. If she could get her hands on F.B. Carne . . . but there he was, more of a monarch than Petronella's in-laws, if you measured it by power and wealth. Won't Carne kick himself if there's a scoop in a rival paper with my by-line on it, Tess thought, he might even kick Hamish out. Anyway, why shouldn't I make a living out of Petronella and the prince? Plenty of other people do.

Do they? Not the kind of people Tess was. Had been. Should be.

This isn't the real me, Tess thought, peering at the bulky figure in the mirror. This isn't the person I am in my head. What happened to that Tess? She's meant to be loving and funny and warm, full of laughter and generosity.

And what have I turned into? the internal voice went on, nagging, accusatory, self-pitying. She simultaneously despised the self who had asked the question, and mentally answered it. A lonely woman in a scruffy, small flat in a part of town called trendy when Tess had mortgaged her soul to buy it, but which, considered dispassionately, was still as dirty and dangerous as it had ever been. And a lunch date with someone I once did the favours to. Something screamed inside Tess's head, "I don't want to be grateful, I want other people to thank me!"

"Kind of you to spare the time," she said to her hostess, a commissioning editor who had started as an office junior on the *Argus*. In those days she had looked up to Tess, who now suddenly realised that this lunch was probably intended as a final pay-off. Valerie Michaels would give her champagne and sympathy and then delete her name from the address files.

They met in the fifth-floor restaurant of Harvey Nichols in Knightsbridge, perching on chairs which looked better than they felt, and picking at food of which much the same could be said. They were surrounded by sharply dressed women from public relations or advertising firms, some of whom Tess recognised from the days when it was her they needed to win over. I may never have had much power, she thought, but it was power of a sort. I could give them publicity or refuse it. They depended on me then. I could make myself valuable again. They'll all want me if I tell what I know.

Three women who failed to recognise Tess stopped by the table to greet Valerie as soon as she sat down.

Tess knew the rule: the higher the status of the guest, the later business talk is introduced over the working meal. So she was not surprised when Valerie made Tess's place in an editor's esteem immediately clear over the starters.

"So, Tess, what sort of story have you got for me? Something spicy about Petsy, you said."

Tess hesitated. She made a show of sipping the wine and tasting the fish, and was relieved when the manager came by to hover and compliment and ask whether everything was all right.

What to say to Valerie? This was the moment of truth. Had Tess got what it takes to make a decent living as a freelance?

"Well, Valerie, as I told you, I went up to the Isle of Man."

"On spec, of course," Valerie said sharply. But Tess had not really expected to get her expenses paid, unless . . . suddenly inspiration struck.

"I found out something about Jill Williams's death."

"Her suicide."

"Yes, but it's interesting. Following up the Williams/

Weiss relationship I've found a useful connection there."

"I know that, they both hanged themselves. But Jill Williams wouldn't be the first neurotic woman to copy Luisa Weiss. You even commissioned a piece saying so back when I was at the *Argus*."

"There was more than the method in common," Tess said.

"Go on."

"Do you remember, the alarm was sounded at the Williams house by her dog whining and scratching at the door of her studio — but did you know the dog had an injury? A deep cut, cross-shaped, on its forehead. The vet thought it had run against the chain link rabbit fence in the garden, but of course nobody ever bothered to check if there was blood on it."

"It sounds perfectly likely though, poor little creature, why did you have to tell me, I'd so much rather not know, I really can't bear to hear of animals suffering," Valerie said, cutting a slice off her *vitello tonnato*.

"Did you know something similar happened when Luisa Weiss died?"

"I don't remember anything about a dog," Valerie said sharply.

"Not a dog. A baby."

At the time of her death Luisa Weiss had a daughter of two, who had been taken out for the afternoon by Raymond, and a baby only a few weeks old. Tess said, "It was because of the baby yelling that they found Luisa so soon, the body wasn't even cold. The baby was lying in the barn where she hanged herself, wrapped up in all its shawls and swaddling, bleeding from a cut on its forehead. It was mentioned in some papers, but not much was said about it. The suggestion was that Luisa had thought of killing the baby as well, and changed her mind. It just seems like a bit of a coincidence, that's all. Worth mentioning, do you think?"

Valerie had taken a bulging Filofax from her bag and was making a tiny entry. "I was hoping for something juicier than that," she said.

Tess did not reply. Shall I tell her? Shan't I? In a croaking, reluctant voice she began, "The last evening I was there, on the Isle of —"

Valerie was not listening. She gestured to the waiter for the bill, snapped her file together, slotted the pen into it.

"I'm running late, Tess. That's not bad about Luisa Weiss, do me a story on it."

"OK, that's great, I'll —"

"Eight hundred by noon tomorrow, all right? Good, that's fine, bye . . ." With a waft of swathing scarves and Patou's Joy, she was gone.

Tess delivered her eight hundred words on the dot. It meant staying up all night to write them, agonising over every word, rearranging, cutting, polishing. She had heard her own contributors say the easier a piece read the more difficult it was to write, and painfully discovered the truth of it. What to put in? What to omit? Should she mention Luisa and Jill might have known each other, or just suggest Jill had been, like so many other people, a fan, and like a few people, a disciple so

126

devoted as to have copied Luisa's actions in ending her own life?

But Tess still had not worked out where and how Luisa had met Jill Williams. What were they doing, standing there smiling in a car-park? Had they been in America together in 1965? Tess had looked up the almanac. Might there be some clue as to what brought them together in the events of that year, about which Jill Williams had saved newspaper cuttings for the rest of her life?

Tornadoes killed sixty people in Mississippi and Alabama; a black activist was shot on a civil rights march; there were race riots in the Watts district of Alabama, in Chicago and in Cleveland; US forces were built up in Vietnam; a man walked in space; immolation at Tarrant's Crossing; mass murder in Austin, Texas, when a student opened fire from the twenty-fourth floor of the university tower; the *New York Herald Tribune* folded.

Perhaps Jill Williams had been part of the civil rights movement, as so many young people were in those politicised days. Or the anti-war movement?

By the time the deadline was upon her Tess could not tell whether she had written an unpublishable, turgid piece of prose or a snappy, saleable story. Once it was irrevocably faxed, she stayed by the telephone on tenter-hooks. Surely Valerie would ring to say whether the article was all right, or ask for changes, or at least send a message? In the old days Tess herself had always put her freelances out of their misery quickly.

But no; Valerie used the black hole method of editing,

and no comment was made, either favourable or otherwise, though two days later most of the article appeared on an inside page. It had been fiercely cut, there were three misprints and the punch-line had been sub-edited out, but the main details of the story were there, and so was Tess's by-line.

"New claims have been made that Jill Williams copied Luisa Weiss's suicide method when she took her own life on the Isle of Man on March 21st. Mrs Williams, mother of Petronella, had a link with the feminist writer dating back to their student years . . ."

Tess immediately faxed an invoice. Then she totted up her income and outgoings. A modest fee promised for the Luisa story, maybe later on a better paid piece for a colour supplement. A radio spin-off? The rest of the redundancy money. And then it would be the dole, unless she found a new job. None of the applications she had sent off before leaving for the Isle of Man had even been acknowledged.

This is not an economical proposition, she thought, it isn't enough to keep me going. But then she listed the alternatives. There had been no job offers, either temporary or permanent, and she had not been summoned to any interview. Tess had no favours left to call in.

What am I going to do?

Tess had never really expected to have a solitary middle age. Though she had adored her work and liked her own company, she could not call herself a high-flyer. Competent, capable, loyal, she knew she was essentially a second-rater, in professional terms at least, but never cared, because the final satisfactions of her life were going to be emotional. Tess was always in love, passionately but not necessarily for ever. Even at the height of an affair, she had sometimes been aware of a different, undefined figure looming in the future, a lover, husband, soulmate with whose life hers would be blended. Then in the last few years there had been Jacques. Now, loveless and unloved, she felt naked, painfully forced to realise she was alone and might stay that way. There was not one single person in the world to whom Tess mattered more than anyone else.

Even Mum, Tess thought, even if she weren't gaga, she'd always liked Biddy best. And as for asking Biddy for money . . . I couldn't. Anyway, she hasn't got any. Tess's mind recoiled again from the idea of letting Biddy know of her failure.

In the end, as before, there was only Desmond. It was one of his bad days. Sweat gleamed on his bald head, but he was shivering and his hand felt clammy. He had shaved and dressed in a yellow cashmere jersey with a polka-dotted blue cravat and white trousers, but Tess exclaimed, "You look very poorly, oughtn't you to be in bed?"

"I'm all right in here. This too will pass." His sitting-room, identical in shape to Tess's, seemed only half the size because it was so crammed with pictures, objects and furniture he had picked up in bad condition and restored himself. The impression was light, glowing and warm and only emphasised Desmond's pallor and attenuation. Tess dismissed the notion that the vibrant room was draining vitality out of its owner.

"I saw your name in the paper. Well done," he said.

Tess felt a gush of concern and affection for Desmond, who had, so recently, been little more than a stranger. She said, "I think it's wonderful, the way you never complain or explain."

"You learn to be self-reliant. Needs must when the devil drives, as they say."

"All the same, there must be something I could do, can't I get you anything?"

"Your company. My own thoughts are as repetitive as the television."

"Why don't I bring supper down?"

Tess went upstairs and found her answering machine flashing. Jacques, sounding chilly, indifferent, indefinably frightening. "You have still got something belonging to me. I need it now." That's rich, from him, Tess thought. He can whistle for his blasted coat.

Then Hamish. He wanted to talk to her. Saw her name in the rival rag. Had a suggestion. Would ring soon. Mystified, Tess left a return message for him. She wondered if he was going to offer her another job. And why? Surely not because she'd written a short news piece. Had anything changed since whatever it was that provoked her sacking in the first place? She could not stop herself niggling at the old question again. Perhaps the processes too undefined and buried even to describe by the word "thought" would produce an explanation. But in a way Tess didn't really care any more. She realised she had moved on. "Good on you, girl," she muttered.

The next message was unidentified. A woman's voice, high and posh with modern Estuary English overtones.

"Don't think you can get away with it, don't you dare publish anything." Petronella? It must be Petronella, recognising Tess's by-line, realising she was a journalist after all. But it didn't sound quite like her. Perhaps it was Sibyl, terrified that squeaky clean Jacques, in his new, important post and vulnerable to blackmail, gossip or indiscretion, would be exposed as a long-term adulterer. Tess did not know what Sibyl's voice was like, the two women had never spoken.

What do they think I am? she thought indignantly. Then she set off to take a bus to the Marks and Spencer in the Whiteleys Centre because the dear little yellow car had never come home from the repair shop, but had been repossessed by the *Argus*. Tess had been forced to take a taxi to collect the box of motoring gear now uselessly stored in the hall cupboard. When would she ever earn enough again to be able to buy another car? It might be better just to throw away the atlas and first aid kit.

She bought some pasta and a bottle of the German white wine she knew Desmond liked, and picked up a bunch of scented lilies before it occurred to her that they might seem tactlessly funereal, and substituted some gaudy parrot tulips. When she got back, Desmond had laid his cherrywood table with starched linen mats and blue Bristol glass. They sat opposite one another in restful, uncompetitive cosiness, like little old married people, Tess thought.

Desmond always refused to discuss his future, although Tess knew he had lost several friends to Aids. She wondered how he could make himself care, or even seem to care, about her problems, when his own must overshadow everything. But he would not talk about himself. Instead he encouraged Tess. "You ought to get really stuck into the Luisa Weiss story now you've made such a good start."

The sharp crack of something breaking sounded elsewhere in the building.

"My God, what's that? Should I —" Tess began, springing to her feet.

"Don't worry, it'll be the people moving in upstairs, did you know it's got new tenants?"

"Not again? Nobody stays there more than five minutes."

"It's a couple, middle-aged, I think they are Spanish, with a cat. Look, they've got a self-drive van out there."

"Thank goodness for small mercies. I couldn't stand French students again, do you remember the last lot?"

Desmond took a small sprig of grapes and began, very delicately, to peel one. "So you'll be going to see the Weisses at Thalassa then?"

"Softly softly, though, because I can't just barge in and ask about Luisa. Her family's famous for giving researchers hell."

"You'd have thought they'd be pleased she's still remembered."

"Oh no, it's not like that at all, some people have written awful things, you can't blame them for being cautious. Luisa's been elevated into some kind of feminist martyr and Raymond's been made into a murderer, so selfish he drove Luisa to her death."

"That's the trouble with dying for a cause, it has to mean someone else killed them," Desmond said, and added, so softly that Tess could hardly hear the words, "Or God did." Before Tess could react, he hastily said, "And they'd want to protect her privacy even though she's dead."

"Do the dead have a right to privacy?" Tess asked, thinking of Jill Williams.

Desmond said, "There was a man I knew, completely obsessed by the human rights he'd lose by dying. He seemed to think he'd be lying under the sod, giving a damn. He said something that always stuck in my mind, "The dead lose all rights from the very first second of death." The poor guy led a very rackety life and dreaded it being exposed, so he started frantically collecting up any letter he'd ever written so as to burn it while he could. He thought there ought to be a law against libelling the dead, because he knew his privacy was going to be invaded with his love letters and photos published and laughed at. But I think what he really minded was that nothing would belong to him any longer. He had a very possessive nature."

"I suppose he didn't have children."

"Hardly," Desmond said drily, making a camp little gesture with his hands. He poured some wine into Tess's glass, and she noticed he had hardly even tasted his own. His hands were unsteady, and a drop spilled on to the table. "Don't move, Tess, I'll use my handkerchief. Tell me your next move. You'll need to tackle Luisa's family somehow."

"They run residential courses down at Thalassa so I did plan to sneak in that way, but now I'm not sure."

133

"It's a good idea. You could get a commission for a travel article while you're about it."

"Better not, as they are so neurotic about journalists. I feel bad enough about sneaking in to nose things out about Luisa."

"I'd have thought that was all part of a journo's job."

Tess poked her forefinger urgently into her fringe and began to twiddle a strand of hair into a knot. She said, "I wouldn't have thought twice about it before, but from out here it feels sort of underhand."

"You're developing scruples."

"I keep thinking how nice Raymond Weiss was that time, and how well we got on, and wondering what he'd think of me if he knew I was cheating him. Now I'm away from the everyday rush in the office, it all seems sort of different. I might just go to Thalassa as a holiday after all."

"I'm thinking of going away myself later on," Desmond said casually.

"Good idea, you look as though you could do with some sunshine," Tess said. "Where will you go?"

"The Seychelles . . . The Bahamas . . . I'm not sure yet. It depends on the time of year."

Tess began to tell him about a freebie to the Cayman Islands she had been given a few years earlier. Desmond showed her some holiday snaps from happier times. His companion, bronzed and gleaming in swimming trunks, holding a newly caught fish, had been dead for two years.

It was about half an hour later when Tess finally said good-night to Desmond. Carrying a tray piled with the left-overs of a meal of which he had eaten miserably little, she heard footsteps drumming down the stairs and stood aside to let a man pass. She saw his black legs and training shoes, black sleeves and tanned hands grasping a burden which obscured his face and chest, a computer balanced on a green canvas suitcase which was just like one of Tess's own and also like thousands of other identical pieces of chain store luggage. There was a whiff of petrol as he went by.

Tess called "Good-night" and as she passed the open door of the first-floor flat, peered in at the mess of half-unpacked boxes. It was not until starting up the second flight of stairs that it occurred to Tess to wonder why her new neighbour had been carrying belongings out of the house, not into it.

Reaching the top floor, she saw her own front door was open. It had been forced off its hinges.

For a moment Tess stood there without understanding what she saw. Her door was impregnable, surely? Then she remembered not bothering to use the Banham security lock when she went out, because she would only be downstairs at Desmond's. She put the tray on the floor of the landing, shivering. It's too much, she thought. I can't go in. I'll call the police from Desmond's telephone, he might come up with me, God knows what's in there now. Or who.

Only then did she realise she had seen the burglar. That had been her computer, her own case full of her own belongings.

"And I said good-night to him!" she exclaimed aloud, and stepped into the flat.

The man had left his petroly smell behind. A tap was noisily running. The lights were on, so she could see at once that the place had been turned upside down. In the bedroom the mattress had been slashed. The contents of all the drawers had been emptied on to the floor. A pillow had been saturated with some liquid. The bathroom cabinet's packets and potions were in the bath. The cistern lid had been taken off. The contents of kitchen cupboards and cabinets had been poured out.

There was similar devastation in the sitting-room. Tess's knees were trembling so much she could hardly stand. But there was nowhere to sit. The sofa and the yellow cushions had been slashed, papers scattered on the floor, ornaments swept from the flat surfaces, tables overturned. Tess felt her back sliding down against the wall until she was squatting against it. She lowered her head between her knees and took deep breaths. Her own body smelt acrid, as though she were sweating the essence of fear; and underlying it the smell of petrol — at that moment the pillow on the bedroom floor burst into roaring flames.

The curious numbness in Tess's mind gave way to furious understanding. The bedding had been soaked with petrol, why hadn't she realised that when she smelt it? Why hadn't she seen the tiny flame creeping along a wick towards its goal? As she thought, she was leaping to the door, stumbling over the supper tray, kicking it aside and rushing, slithering down the stairs, shouting, "Fire. Fire, there's a fire, Desmond, dial 999, hurry, hurry."

A man and woman ran out of the first-floor flat and

cannoned into Tess, who called, "The house is on fire, quick, get help!" and rushed on downwards. Desmond was in the hall holding a small red extinguisher. "It's too small, we need a fire engine," Tess gasped.

"I've rung already."

They stood out on the pavement waiting for the rescue services. Desmond was shaking with cold and shock. Tess felt herself to be blazing like the fire itself, with an energetic fury. She repeated over and over again, "I saw him, I said good-night to him!"

She heard screams as the new tenant had hysterics about her treasures. Even here and now she was immaculate in high heels and gold jewellery, her glossy hair in a round chignon, a Hermès scarf thrown round her head like a mantilla. Her lamentations were soon joined by other exclamations and complaints as neighbours ran out into the street, carrying children or shouting behind them for others to hurry up. Several raced to their cars, pushed the family in and drove off to safety.

Smoke and flames could be seen behind the top-floor windows. Then the glass broke with a loud bang, and the flames leapt outwards into the night. A gasping groan rose from the crowd. By this time there must have been hundreds of people in the street, as every house had been converted for multiple occupancy.

A fire engine raced up followed by a small red car whose occupants jumped out and began to move all the residents away up the pavement, out of danger. The road was narrowed, as always at night round here, by double-parked cars, and the fire engine could not get between them to the house until a crane-lorry arrived. Two men, one in pyjamas, began rocking one of the parked cars to try to shift it. The siren sound of its security alarm joined the wailing of smoke alarms from Tess's own building.

Tess started to apologise. "I'm so sorry, I'm sorry, it's in my flat, it started there, I'm so sorry . . ." After a while Desmond took her wrist in his two hands and twisted the skin till the pain made Tess stop.

They stood in a group of neighbours. Some already had slung over their shoulders the blankets which accompany every emergency, and two photographers were already there snapping their flash bulbs.

"My things, my furniture, my precious precious things," the new tenant was moaning, watching water poured on to the roof of their house and into Tess's rooms. She had introduced herself as Consuelo Esteban and her husband as Juan Pedro, and told anyone who would listen that this was a cursed day. After a while Juan Pedro said, "I think it will be OK, look, it's dying down."

As the fire was gradually put out, and the neighbouring householders gradually realised their own belongings were safe, the atmosphere relaxed. Children too large to sleep in their parents' arms were released and began to run around, excited by the night's strangeness. Two dogs, let go by their owners, fought briefly and were dragged apart. A cat slunk by and into the shadows. A woman in a pink dressing-gown and slippers went round with a tray of steaming mugs. Another elderly resident whispered a discreet invitation to each of the women in turn. "You're welcome to use my facilities."

The street consisted of stucco houses, with high sash windows and formal frontages. Silhouetted against the restless sky, their slated roofs and rows of oblong chimneys seemed to be moving, windblown like the clouds.

A murmur of conversation started up. When would they be allowed to go back, the children had school tomorrow, they needed their sleep. There were whispers of blame or attribution. Had Tess been smoking? Had her television set exploded?

Tess had apologised to everyone individually and severally, explaining what had happened. "They ought to be strung up, castration's too good for them," the moustachioed ex-officer from the modern flats on the corner barked. Another man said the country was going to the dogs. The new neighbours had already introduced themselves all round: Juan Pedro and Consuelo were deep in conversation about an export contract with a chance acquaintance. Incredibly, they seemed to be doing a deal.

The house had been converted into flats in the 1970s, at a time when fire regulations required thick insulation between the floors and walls, so when at last all the authorities agreed it was safe to reoccupy the middle and ground floors, it turned out that the neighbouring houses on either side, through the party walls, had been unaffected and the worst damage to the flat below Tess's had come from leaked liquid and scorch marks just above their outsize bed.

For the couple of hours left of the night, Tess bedded down on Desmond's sofa. But she did not sleep. She kept smelling the acrid smoke and chemical foam, and the same thoughts followed each other round in her mind in unalterable procession.

Insurance: she was under-insured. Replacement: she would not be able to afford it. Who, why, what for? Was it me, she wondered, Tess Redpath, or would any vulnerable householder have done as well? And back to insurance again.

When daylight began to seep between the curtains, Tess felt she was at rock bottom. Job, lover, car, self-esteem and home. What have I got left to lose? As the room lightened, she reminded herself, "At least nobody was hurt."

Hours later she picked her way through the disgusting remains, under the weary, accustomed eye of a woman police constable. Tess could hardly bear to look or touch. She longed to get rid of it all, now, immediately, never to see anything of this again. "There's quite a bit you can salvage," the girl said.

"God no. I couldn't bear to."

"A lot of people say that."

"D'you mean this happens often? Burglars leaving things to burn?"

"There's domestic fires all the time, even if they weren't started deliberately. The fire officer said there was no doubt about arson here though."

"That's what I said, I told you what happened, the man I saw . . ." Tess told her story again without imagining it would do any good. That man would never be found. He had emptied the contents of her desk and filing cabinet into her own suitcase, taken her computer and spare floppy disks and set fire to the flat. Presumably he thought she was out for the evening and would come home to find a burnt-out ruin.

"Did you say you're a journalist?" the policewoman asked. "Maybe someone wanted to stop you writing about them."

"That's incredibly unlikely, nobody could possibly have cared about anything I'm writing, believe me."

"Nothing scandalous? There wouldn't be anyone wanting to stop you telling their secrets?"

"I don't really think . . ." Tess's voice trailed away. Was it conceivable that Petronella or her fiancé had sent the heavies after her? Memories of countless thrillers and spy stories sent a cold shiver of terror down her spine.

"Or perhaps you had some information you didn't realise was valuable, notes, memos, floppies — yes? Did you think of something?"

Tess did not reply. Jacques's diskette. She had never found out what was on it. Suppose it was top security, state secrets . . . suppose it wasn't anything as important as that, but enough to lose him his promotion if it got out that he'd been so careless. No, she thought, not Jacques. No.

The policewoman said, "Sometimes it's a jealous lover, or someone jealous of him. Anyone like that in your life?"

Jacques wouldn't. Couldn't. Tess would not believe him capable of it. Could Sibyl have done it? Was this her revenge on Tess for sending that parcel of Jacques's telltale belongings? No, surely not, so disproportionate, especially now she's got him back, all for herself. No,

**141**

no, it's impossible, she thought, and said aloud, "I can't stop seeing the man I met on the stairs. Suppose he comes back?"

"We'll be offering you trauma counselling, and don't hesitate to dial the emergency services if you're worried. We take this kind of crime very seriously indeed. Arson is a serious offence," the young woman said.

Taking refuge again in Desmond's flat, Tess told him what the constable had said. "I'm supposed to get in touch with a Detective Inspector Rogerson if I think of anything he might have been looking for, but what could there be? I'm scared. It feels like there's someone out there watching me and I don't know who. Lurking, looming, threatening. Faceless. It makes me feel all jumpy and nervous."

"The force will pull out all the stops, you know. Nobody takes arson lightly."

"If only I could think what it was all for. It can't just have been a casual burglary —"

"Casual b
urglars don't leave fire bombs."

"Anyway, how could anyone sell my files? There must have been something specific, but God knows what, I certainly don't."

"It's all there, in your head," Desmond said.

"But what is? Which bit? If I knew something I shouldn't know, what was it about?"

"Funny you were burglarised immediately after that mention of your name and research in the *Sentinel*. Makes you think, after what happened to Jill Williams. Except you weren't found dead."

"What are you talking about?"

"Just the coincidence. If I was still in the force I'd think it was a suspicious circumstance. Here are you two women, both leading ordinary private lives until suddenly you're in the newspapers, and then something nasty happens to you."

"I'd hardly equate a burglary in a London flat with committing suicide," Tess snapped. But then she went on thoughtfully, "except of course, it happened to Luisa Weiss too. Nobody had ever heard of her till she wrote that book, and then she got masses of publicity and within weeks she was dead."

"I always knew publicity was a curse," Desmond said. "Look what happened to me when I got in the papers. Just take care of yourself, Tess, eh? We don't want anything happening to you."

# CHAPTER
# NINE

Some people are colour blind. Some have no sense of smell. And now Tess had become incapable of appreciating poetry. Admitting this failing to an *Argus* contributor, a professional novelist and academic, she was told the job had made her learn to read too fast. "You have to take poems in slowly, savouring and pondering and above all, pausing."

Tess could never make herself do so. She was too impatient, too keen to find out what happened next. When she read novels she looked at the end before reaching it. But she knew he was right, indeed remembered that he was from her student days, but now only odd lines remained with her, all sad, elegies for lost loves and hope and homes, distant childhood, regrets for wasted affection. Jacques, or rather Jacques's absence, still haunted Tess when she was off guard or at idle moments. He did love me once, she thought, remembering her English teacher saying those were the saddest words in the language. Or perhaps Jacques had never loved her. Like Ophelia, Tess "was the more deceived'. Unlike Ophelia, Tess had always picked herself up, dusted herself off and gone off and found someone else. Being in love was her natural state. Am I mutating, she wondered, shall I in the second half of my life not be in love any more? Perhaps it's a consummation devoutly to be wished. Or not; for life without love would not be life at all. She lay in bed trying to believe another love would come.

Tess was sleeping badly, and did not enjoy the thoughts which came in the dark. But she was staying with Biddy and did not want to wake the family by going down to the kitchen to make tea. Dear Biddy; so supportive and big-sisterly, treating Tess much as she treated Lara, always more maternal than their mother had been. Lena Redpath, a harried and irritable mother, hard to love, caused Tess more guilt than grief as she sank inexorably into inhumanity. It wasn't fair that Biddy bore the full burden, but Biddy did not complain and took it all calmly, while Tess, deeply ashamed though she was, had to use the utmost self-control to make herself stay in the same room.

Tess sat up and switched on the light. Think about something else, she told herself. She scanned Lara's book shelf, untempted by the row of tattered textbooks it contained. Eventually she took out the volume of Luisa Weiss's posthumously published diary extracts and poems, which was of very mixed quality. The advance notice in the *Literary Review* of the new volume which was due out next month made it clear that it was of uniform quality: bad. The reviewer could not see any reason for foisting these fragments and remnants on Luisa Weiss's fans, and had written a whimsical paragraph about the vital necessity of keeping dead best-sellers' families in the state of life to which they had grown accustomed.

Tess propped herself up uncomfortably on Lara's narrow futon and forced her eyes down the pages of broken lines and inscrutable phrases. Luisa's had been the kind of poetry which neither scans nor rhymes. It did not evoke a garden of bright images, it did not concern love or motherhood. Luisa's images were of slaughter, destruction and above all of fire.

Luisa's fear of fire had become one of the well-known details of her doomed personality; she had never allowed a naked flame in her home. In these verses the horror was expressed in words.

Tess made herself read them over and over again, her lips moving as she mouthed the words. Why was this evocative or emotional? Tess couldn't see it. Yet these scant lines, published after Luisa's death, had become standard texts, although, as far as Tess could understand, the lines did no more than obscurely describe a vision of fires raging, trees bursting into flames like giant gas jets, people running or dying, which would have been more clearly evoked by prose.

Lara came in to fetch some clothes and told Tess her teacher's view: that it didn't matter. He always insisted that whether art was created by the poetic imagination or the autobiographical impulse was only a matter for gossip. "He says we shouldn't ever read authors' biographies 'cos they tarnish the freshness of our response to what they wrote," Lara quoted, giggling. "Pompous old fart. He didn't even want us to go to Shakespeare's birthplace on the school trip."

"So I don't suppose you'll be hanging round Poets' Corner when you're in London either."

"I might have done, if they'd planted Luisa there," Lara said. "Funny, but her stuff always gets me right there." She rubbed her hand on her flat stomach and then zipped her jeans over it. Tess remembered an article about schoolgirls and suicidal role-models. The critic, suggesting it was unwise to use Sylvia Plath or Luisa Weiss's work as set books for teenagers, had written about the romantic alienation of the authors, and girls feeling that the words about romantic alienation, about specifically female problems and emotions, were addressed directly to them. A feminine version of *The Sorrows of Young Werther*, he had suggested, hardly gave the right message to impressionable young women.

Well, Lara was safely past the dangerous stage, Tess thought. At seventeen she had not succumbed to anorexia or substance abuse, but had passed her exams and made ambitious plans for her future.

Lara said, "I probably first liked her because of being Cornish."

"Me too." Aunt and niece smiled at each other with familiar complicity.

"I got Mum to drive me over there once, just to look. I used to wish like anything she was still around to go and talk to," Lara said.

"So sad, her suicide."

"D'you think it was?"

"Well, of course," Tess said.

"Maybe her old man topped her."

"Raymond! Goodness, Lara, what an idea, why ever did you —?"

"Sort of thing husbands do when they've got rich wives, isn't it?"

"On TV, sure, but not in real life, Lara. There is a difference."

"Boring," Lara intoned, her intimate gaze cancelling out any impertinence. Even Tess could see the likeness other people always remarked on. Lara, like Tess, was tall and sturdily built and often bemoaned her high colour and the unfashionable shape which always looked wrong in her preferred gear of tatters and leather. She wanted to be flimsy and exotic, not an English rose. Tess, not particularly proud of her own appearance, thought Lara's enchanting.

"Pass me the envelope over there and you can have a look at what they said at the time." Desmond had handed it to Tess just as she was leaving. He had been ill since the fire, wheezing and sweating, although he insisted it was only a touch of bronchitis brought on by breathing smoke and there was no need to worry about him. But Tess did worry, as well as worrying about her flat, and who had set fire to it, and whether it had really been random vandalism as the police suggested, or, as she couldn't help fearing, an attack on herself, personally.

She had racked her brains to think who might have taken such action.

Jacques was undergoing positive vetting. Jacques had forgotten his coat. In his coat pocket was a diskette. Could he have sent someone to make sure nobody could find it there? Steal the computer equipment, destroy any hiding places? No, Tess kept thinking, not that, please not that. She would rather think the security services had broken in. They might even have thought she had wormed secrets out of Jacques and passed them on. But stealing the computer was one thing, setting fire to the flat a different kind of crime.

Sibyl could have wanted to do that, could even have hired a gangster to do so. But what would she have wanted the files for? Jacques would surely not have mentioned the forgotten diskette to his wife.

Or had it been the mysterious protectors of Petronella and her prince? Were they willing to frighten off any possible investigators? But then, think how many of them there were, all the reporters and paparazzi. Perhaps The Pet had taken fright at what she'd told Tess, confessed her indiscretion to the prince and been promised they'd take care of it. Could that be it?

I could write and promise never to pass it on, Tess thought. But they might not believe me. I'm not entirely certain even I believe me.

It always came back to the same point. Tess, having sketched out to the police her inchoate thoughts about some possible enemies, could not bring herself to mention Jacques to them. She had been assured she need not worry, they would be keeping an eye on things and her flat would no longer be under threat now that her files, both on paper and computer, had gone. "They won't get away with it, don't worry, this isn't just your normal break-in, you know," Inspector Rogerson had promised.

He had told Tess there was no reason why she should

not let Biddy go to London with Lara while Tess was in Cornwall. Meanwhile Tess, just in case anyone was after her personally, would be safe and untraced in remote Thalassa. As it turned out, Cornwall felt entirely removed in psychic as well as geographical terms from inner London, so it was harder to feel anxious here. Perhaps everything would be OK after all.

Tess dragged her thoughts back from the unproductive repetitive worry and opened the envelope Desmond had given her. He hadn't kissed her goodbye. She rather thought he disliked the touch of women and knew better than to raise her cheek to his, but she had thanked him with sincere affection and stopped the taxi on the way to Paddington to send him a case of wine with a note saying he'd saved her life by his kindness in the last weeks.

His leaving present to her had been this contemporary police report on Luisa's death. "I'm still owed the odd favour by old mates in the force," he'd explained.

Tess had read the documents in the train, and now pulled them out again to show Lara. "They got lots of statements, nobody took anything for granted. She was all alone that afternoon, the others had gone out and left her with the baby to get a bit of rest. There was no sign of anyone being there, no fingerprints or footprints, and nobody saw anything. It had to be suicide."

"How do you hang yourself anyway?" Lara asked.

"I can't imagine being able to, but I suppose you'd knot a noose round your neck and climb up on a — hey, hold it, it's not exactly a suitable pre-breakfast topic," Tess exclaimed, suddenly remembering how many teenagers died every year after experiments with ropes and nooses.

"I suppose you could do it out of boredom," Lara said. "Sometimes I get so bored here I could willingly top myself and poor Luisa was bored to sobs."

She picked up the volume from the bed and leafed through it till she found the right page. "Remember, she wrote about it in her diary. 'Having achieved in every particular every blessing women pray for, wealth, health, husband, adorable children, worldly success and a supremely beautiful home, I wish I could understand why it is that I am so frustrated by my daily life and bored by its incidents that I sometimes feel like screaming and running mad through the valley with straws threaded in my hair.'"

Lara stroked her hand over the much marked page. "I always remember that bit because I can understand it so well. It's living here. Look, do you remember this? 'Every prospect pleases from these windows. They are the very prospects which so delighted me when I visited my father, the landscapes and seascapes of my dreams. But beauty is not enough. Where is life, excitement, variety, stimulation, competition? Not here. Here are Raymond, Scarlett, Saffron and tedium.' You see, she needed to get away like I do."

"But it is lovely here."

"That's not enough, Tess, you never thought it was either, don't pretend you didn't get away as quick as you could yourself."

It was just as well that Biddy called at that moment, "Hurry up, Lara, get a move on, we'll miss the train," and Tess could say to Lara, "Never mind, at least you're having a break this week."

It had been Biddy's own idea that she should see to the flat for Tess. "We'll enjoy it, me and Lara," she had insisted. "She's hanging round like a wet rag now the exams are finished and I'm due some time off from the rest home, all the overtime I had to do when there was that flu epidemic, we'll crash out on the floor while you keep an eye on Mum." Biddy's and Tess's mother had only just moved into the residential home where Biddy worked. She had complained, but didn't really know what she was complaining about. "She isn't with it," Biddy said sadly. Tess noticed her mother was with it enough, at least for about five minutes, to recognise Tess and to scold her for not being married. It was quite a relief when her mind wandered off again.

Tess had protested unconvincingly. There was no reason, she said, why Biddy should have to put up with workmen.

"We'll have a ball. London! It'll be a treat for me too," Biddy insisted.

Tess could not pretend she was keen on watching workmen demolish what was left of her domestic arrangements, or that she had much heart for supervising the rebuilding to follow. Having spent three weeks fighting with her insurers and wheedling contractors, she wanted nothing so much as to get away, even if it was to the company of her senile mother and her boring brother-in-law.

"Malcolm'll be out most of the time," Biddy added,

sensing her sister's thoughts. "He's got to go to a crash course on some new kind of heat sensors in Plymouth."

So Tess arrived in Cornwall on a Saturday. On Sunday she saw Biddy and Lara off at the station. On Monday she delivered Paul to a week's training for the Ten Tors Climb for the Duke of Edinburgh's Award Scheme. On Tuesday she looked in on her mother, who did not recognise her, and then set off in the old banger Lara had been given when she passed the driving test, to Thalassa.

# CHAPTER
# TEN

Thalassa, the Greek word for the sea, was what Luisa's grandfather, Louis Considine, had chosen to call the valley instead of the original Cornish name by which it was known when he bought the estate just before the First World War. An enthusiast for the verities and simplicities propounded by such sages as William Morris or Bertrand Russell, he set himself to create a perfect environment. He caused the original mansion, a granite box, to be pulled down and replaced by an arty-crafty house designed by Ernest Gimson. He had plans for the village and estate cottages, and for the spiritual conversion to a life of truth and beauty of the workers who lived in them, but everything was postponed when war broke out. Considine died in the flu epidemic of 1919, leaving a young son as his heir.

Oliver Considine did not inherit any interest in man-made niceties. He spent a wild and lonely childhood at Thalassa, relieved by occasional visits to members of the Bloomsbury Group. On holiday near St Ives they would invite his mother over to messy meals which, in her imagination and the tales she later told biographers and literary critics, were inflated into orgies of intellectual conversation.

When Oliver came back from the Second World War with a lame leg and impaired hearing, he found his wife Imogen had been running Thalassa as a refugees' sanctuary. But all he wanted was peace, quiet and nature. He turned the lodgers and visitors out, Luisa was born in 1946, and within two years Imogen had taken the child and moved in with a film producer in west London.

Luisa's childhood alternated between the fierce intellectualism of a highly academic day school and the gabby, colourful life her mother presided over in Hammersmith Terrace, and silent stays for two weeks a year with her father in Cornwall. His time and attention were entirely concentrated on recording every species of plant and creature to be found in his miniature kingdom, a rewarding task, since Thalassa was almost the first landfall for birds migrating from the south.

Thalassa, formerly called Cobban Cove, had sloping sides which narrowed down towards a small sandy beach and enclosed a stepped bottom. It was the closest to Land's End of a series of valleys dividing the small fields and gorse patches of the furthermost corner of Britain. When Louis Considine first saw it in 1907, he arrived in a pony and trap and the journey had taken two hours from Penzance. It was a journey cars could do in twenty minutes and Thalassa had become accessible. But the atmosphere of isolation survived. Visitors would always exclaim that it was "out of this world".

The lane from the main road was too narrow for two cars to pass, and large lorries could not negotiate it. In 1968, when Luisa and Raymond moved in, their new beds and armchairs from Peter Jones had to be offloaded from the vans on to farm trailers. Now Raymond had a pick-up truck of his own to convey regular deliveries of coal and Calor gas and occasional heavy purchases from the parking space by the main road. Mains electricity had come in after the war, and the spring had never run dry. By the time Raymond initiated the painting courses at Thalassa the brochure could accurately claim that the accommodation had all modern conveniences. Most of the time, they even worked.

Raymond Weiss tried not to let mechanical vagaries get him down. If the lavatory in Rose Cottage had been left blocked by the previous occupier, or the roof of Stable Block was leaking, it should all be in the day's work to get the repairs done before the next batch of students was installed.

But sometimes it all seemed too much. Standing in the garden of Thatched Cottage and observing a gash in the straw that was going to mean an expensive visit from the thatcher before autumn's gales, Raymond remembered how simple everything had suddenly felt when Luisa inherited Thalassa and they made the decision to live there instead of selling it.

It was the year after they were married and Raymond was working in a merchant bank. He did not much enjoy the work but was resigned to it as a way of earning a decent living. They lived in a tiny, heavily mortgaged house in a row of other dwarfish boxes undergoing (as it was called then) gentrification. Luisa was housebound, for they could not afford help with the baby, and she was miserably bored and frustrated. Although Raymond did not know it, she had started writing her diatribe against the expectations society had of young mothers, but by the time *Into Captivity* was published they had already moved down to Thalassa.

Luisa and Raymond brimmed with ideas for making the place pay for itself. They would let all the cottages, most of which Oliver had allowed to fall into disrepair, some to holidaymakers, others on long leases to writers and artists. They planned to create a self-sufficient community in which everyone would grow their own vegetables, eat their own eggs, give their children a healthy, free environment and live happy ever after. Raymond's father, a chartered accountant, was dismayed at their determination to "knit their own spinach" but they were in the vanguard of fashion, back in the 1960s before the expression "The Good Life" had even become a cliché.

Raymond read Luisa's book for the first time when it was in proof and managed not to take it personally, although his own family and many of their old friends did and considered he had been mocked and mortified by his wife's attitudes. On the contrary, Raymond rather enjoyed the ensuing fuss. Having transformed himself from a pin-striped City gent, if not quite into the guise of a flower child then at least into a corduroy-clad quasi-hippie, he threw himself into the role of what was not yet called "new man" and took his share of domestic chores and child minding. That was why he had not been at home on that dreadful day. She was alone because he'd got Scarlett out of her hair with the specific intention of giving Luisa a bit of peace and quiet. The baby was less than two months old and she was naturally tired. Not depressed. She had never seemed to be suffering from depression. If she had he would have known better than to leave her on her own.

Because he still lived in the same place and saw every day the sights they had seen together, he had never managed to put Luisa's death out of his mind for a single day. He did try.

"Stop it, don't think about it," he told himself, waving to Bettina and Leslie, who came over from Sennen once a week on changeover day to clean the cottages. They dragged their gear out of Miller's Cot and waved back. "Cheer up, it may never happen," Bettina called and hurried on down the hill to Honeysuckle. All the accommodation had to be clean by five o'clock when the new lot would begin to arrive.

Raymond wondered what Luisa would think of Thalassa now. Would she be pleased with the way he had kept the place going for the girls and think he'd done the right thing? Or wouldn't she give a damn, any more than she had at the moment when she'd ducked out of it all and left him to cope on his own with her place and problems?

How could she have done it? How could she abandon Scarlett and Saffron and Raymond?

The images were so familiar that mentally reciting the tale of his wife's death was as much a ritual as the rosary had been before he lost his faith.

Luisa stood in his mind's eye holding the bundle that was Saffron, shawl-swaddled in a white cocoon because the monthly nurse insisted babies were only comfortable when immobilised. But the nurse had left two days before, confident that all was well with mother and child. So was Raymond, when he took Scarlett with him to collect a parcel from Penzance station; an official had rung up that morning to say he'd have to sign for it.

It was Wednesday, 27th May 1970. Luisa had come out into the sunshine and waited in the drive while Raymond fetched their car, a white Renault 4. Her glossy head was framed against the high wall of long-established rhododendrons, crimson blossoms against the dark green leaves. She'd kissed the little girl, and kissed Raymond, who said anxiously, "You're sure you'll have a rest now, go and put your feet up."

"Don't fuss, Ray, we'll be fine, we might go for a little walk, it's a lovely day. Bring Mummy something nice from Penzance, Scarlett." She'd kissed the older child and untucked Saffron's tiny hand to move it to and fro. "Look, the baby's saying bye-bye."

Her last words.

Happy words. Loving words.

And within an hour she was dead.

Everything had been so many times remembered, relived, reconsidered, reassessed.

She'd seemed happy but she'd been miserable. The doctor had used the image of a storm, when a clear summer sky is suddenly covered with dark cloud. Luisa probably was happy when she said goodbye. Suicidal depression had swept over her like a hurricane. Raymond couldn't have guessed, he couldn't have known.

Luisa's fans thought he should. They were sure it was all his fault and said so in articles, television programmes, poems and in a book which the American author had chosen to call *Out Of Captivity*. The thesis was that Luisa had released herself from the chains of marriage into the freedom of death.

For a long time Raymond refused to believe that his effervescent, charismatic, life-enhancing Luisa could have been sad unto death without him having the least idea of it. But there was no pretending that Luisa could have been hanged by accident. Which left only murder.

That was a suggestion to which the police had given little serious consideration. He did not think they had made the inquiries needed and which, over the subsequent months, he made himself.

He had never been able to imagine who could have done it, and how. Did he really believe that ancient Joel and his wife Ada, family retainers who had died themselves not long after, could have had anything to do with Luisa's death? No. Nor could the dizzy girl students on holiday in Thatched Cottage — who had in any case been at the Minack theatre watching *Kiss Me Kate* that afternoon — or either of the fishermen who still lived in the valley, all known to be at sea at the time. It was the week after the May bank holiday. Only one of the holiday cottages was still let. The nucleus of their creative commune, all potters, woodworkers and poets, had spent the winter falling into hate and love with each other, quarrelled, fought and moved back to London before Easter.

Raymond had given the fishermen's wives a lift into Penzance with him and Scarlett. Their children were to be bused home from St Just later on. Meanwhile, Luisa was alone in the valley with her baby, deaf Ada and lame Joel.

He had invented so many other possible callers. A wandering psychopath, the postman, a tramp, a rambler, the bible basher who had called the day before while Luisa was upstairs bathing the baby. Raymond had wrangled enjoyably with him about the Apocrypha and accepted a leaflet about salvation. There were gypsies camped in a quarry inland from Thalassa, there was a campsite two miles away. Anyone could have come. But he had no evidence that anyone had done so. And there was the other, incontrovertible fact: Luisa, dangling and dead.

"Dad." Raymond blinked and returned to the present day. "Stop it, Dad." Saffron. "You're thinking about Luisa again, I know that face. It's because of the anniversary."

"Twenty-five years next week. I can't believe it."

"Which makes me quarter of a century old."

"Incredible." To her father Saffron still looked like a schoolgirl, unlike Scarlett who had looked thirty since she was fifteen, and was never seen except in black, with her hair dyed and gelled into black spikes. Saffron as usual wore jeans, with a skimpy grey T-shirt and her fine brown hair pulled back into an elastic band, revealing the faint scar that had been on her forehead since the day Luisa died. Saffron was thin and very narrow-hipped, with pimple breasts and turned-out toes; not conventionally pretty or voluptuous, and as far as Raymond could tell, not particularly sexy. If he thought about it, he supposed she'd had other boyfriends since the schoolboy she had gone out with for years, though he did not know of any, but his mind slid away from the idea. He relied on Scarlett, two years older in years but aeons in experience and self-confidence, to give Saffron advice about her private life. Scarlett herself had never needed it. She had grown up knowing exactly what she wanted in life, which was money, excitement and independence. She left school at seventeen to get a job in London and at twenty-seven was a trendy townie who reluctantly came to Thalassa for one brief, dutiful visit a year.

"Dad," Saffron said.

"What, darling?"

"I had a letter from the lawyers." That was not unusual. The trust of which Scarlett and Saffron were beneficiaries had been wound up on the younger girl's twenty-fifth birthday in March and there seemed to have been non-stop document signing ever since. "There's a box of Luisa's papers in their office, did you know?"

"About the Considine estate?"

"They say it's personal papers. They asked Scarlett to take them away when she went to see them but she didn't want to."

"No, I don't expect she did," Raymond agreed. Scarlett had never disguised the fact that she was not interested in Luisa's life or work. Raymond knew she had never forgiven her mother for deserting her.

"I said I didn't want to go and get them."

"Wouldn't you like to go and stay with Scarlett again? I can manage here."

"Dad, really, you couldn't possibly, not with the course starting and anyway, I hate staying with Scarlett,

162

I absolutely hate it. It's horrid there. You don't know what it's like, Daddy, she's got so hard."

"I know you quarrelled about something last time, Saffy, but you always quarrel and make it up again, all your lives."

"Well, there's no time to think about it now, they'll start arriving soon."

Only seven people had booked for the first course of the season, which meant it would just about cover its costs without making any profit.

Father and daughter looked at the list together. The course tutor was Alfred Rutter, who came over by the day from St Ives, a burly, voracious man who, as a much younger Saffron had once made the mistake of telling him, seemed to her like dark green velvet. He then made and gave her a very ugly fabric collage which she felt honour bound to hang on her bedroom wall.

There were two couples, one married, one lesbian, who had come every year since the painting courses began, still without any of them having sold a single canvas but ever hopeful and committed. They worked all day and then retreated to their own self-catering cottages and were not seen again until the next morning. Another was an American who had written that he wanted peace, quiet and a retreat, and wished to be accommodated in Lookout Cottage and excused any communal meals. A woman called Ilona Spivak was a last-minute booking. And the last was a woman who had taken early retirement from some high-powered London executive job and needed a new direction for her life. Her name was Theresa Trevail.

# CHAPTER
# ELEVEN

Cornwall always seemed much larger when Tess was a child. Going from the industrial starkness of her inland village near St Austell to the seaside had been a serious expedition then, undertaken hardly more often than if the Redpaths had to travel a hundred miles. Such excursions would be prepared for with great pains, as though the bus were to take its passengers to a strange and foreign place. Indeed London, or even Plymouth, hardly seemed less outlandish than Peru, and to some of their neighbours was more foreign, for there were men living in the row of stone cottages who had worked as miners in the Americas, Antipodes and Africa without ever travelling east of the Tamar in their lives.

So Tess was almost surprised by the abbreviated drive from Biddy's home to west Cornwall. Having expected the main road, the A30, still to be "the longest country lane in Europe", she found herself on a modern dual carriageway with a central reservation and trimmed verges instead. Only on the far side of Penzance did she rediscover the bushy lanes of memory. The weather might not be up to much, but the May flowers burgeoned punctually none the less in their stridently green leaves. A hillside, stony grey to an absent-minded glance, suddenly revealed itself to be swathed in bluebells; tangles of cow parsley and ragged robin lined the verges, trees were weighted with curdles of blossom, and still blooming in the springing grass, cowslips and primroses were backed by the heavy, vibrant yellow of banks of gorse.

Tess pulled Lara's little car into a lay-by. She had intended to check her make-up and straighten her hair, but was distracted by the prettiness of her surroundings. She said aloud, "It's lovely here," surprised by her own reaction. Tess had rather disliked the country for as long as she could remember, being ill at ease with animals and much preferring to see the signs of human interference in the landscape. She liked vistas of roofs and towers, lights and traffic and tame London parks, where the growth was ordered and arranged for her pleasure. Out of the rear windows of her flat in Arundel Gardens she overlooked the communal gardens shared by the residents of the two long terraces backing on to them. At the same level as the higher branches of oaks and sycamores, far above the laburnums and flowering cherries, she could watch squirrels, dogs, children and any rowdy trespassers who scaled the iron railings, safely removed from the threat any of them presented. Threat? she thought, catching her own mental use of the word.

Tess remembered how baffling London seemed when she first went there after university. In those days she had been optimistic and determined to turn herself into a middle-class sophisticate. She *would* make her way, she *would not* give in, though some evenings it had been an almost irresistible temptation to stay in and watch other people having fun on television, instead of making herself go out. But she had learnt to go to pubs and clubs on her own until she knew other people to go with. She forced herself to know the underground system without looking at a map, to learn short cuts and find familiar faces even if at first they were only those of the man who sat begging beside the cash machine and the newspaper vendor outside the tube station.

It was years since Tess had marvelled at herself for being at home in London. It just was home, she was a Londoner. But in Cornwall, temporarily displaced into a world at once so different and so innately her own, Tess felt a mixture of delight and fear. This was where she might have spent her life if it hadn't been for Luisa and the other feminists pushing her out into the big wide world to fend for herself. Pushing her out, Tess thought for the first time, while keeping all this; Luisa had stayed here, been married, borne children. Do what I say, don't do what I do, had been Luisa's message. Perhaps, Tess thought, it was all a giant con trick. Perhaps this is where I really belonged all the time.

Nonsense, she said aloud, shaking herself free of subversive thoughts, I couldn't possibly live so far from town. How could I manage without . . . what? The theatre? But it must be two years since she had been to the live theatre. Being tone-deaf she never went to concerts. Art galleries, then. Of course I go to exhibitions, she thought uneasily, but couldn't quite remember which and when. Biddy's voice came into her mind. "I don't know how you can bear to spend your life somewhere people rob and set fire to your home." They had been sitting in the bay window of Biddy's sitting-room, and Tess had insisted it could happen anywhere, saying, "Even Cornwall isn't safe any more." But the clean uniformity of the post-war housing development on the edge of St Austell looked immutable and Tess didn't believe her words as she said them.

She had been sitting still and quiet long enough to become part of the landscape. A bird alighted on the bonnet of the car and a small, thin fox sidled out of the gorse bush and crossed the road. When Tess moved the animal slid into hiding.

She was not due for another hour or so and must be nearly there, so she had time to fill in and today's *Argus* and *Sentinel* to fill it in with. She had taken to reading both and noting with glee the stories which the *Argus* had a day later than its rival, or the typos and howlers in columns which, pre-Carne, had been impeccably correct. No doubt many sub-editors had rashly been purged, sacked, like Tess.

Europe, fishing quotas, reshuffles. Boring, boring. Tess read some advice about dressing for the country in floaty chiffon and floppy hats and an article about late onset epilepsy. Then she found another Petronella piece, this time an interview with her great-aunt, describing what a consolation it had been to the mourning grandparents when they realised their lost boy had left Jill pregnant. Their relief, their excitement, their welcome to the widow and then to her baby, their generous assumption of responsibility when the child's mother was unable to care for her. "They felt it was their boy come back to them, especially when the baby grew to be so sweet and winning in her little ways. No child has ever been such a godsend as that little girl."

Yes, one could see she would have been, Tess thought, but wondered whether Jill Williams might have been a more affectionate mother if she had been left alone with the baby. It sounded from this as though the grandparents had grabbed her.

Tess tore that piece out and folded it into her bag. Then she drove on to the next village, and saw there was a telephone box. Not because she needed to check in, but because she had the impulse to ground herself in real life instead of this momentary fantasy of rusticity, Tess called her own number.

"Lara, hello, is everything all right, are you managing?"

"Hi, Tessie, yeah, we're doing brilliantly, but your friend in the ground-floor flat —"

"Desmond."

"Mum said he looked like death, so we did his shopping, he's ever so nice."

"Send him my love, won't you? And Lara, can you and your mum really stand the smell?"

"No, honestly, I quite like it, it's no worse than a bonfire, anyway it's great to be in London. We're going to Harrods and the King's Road today."

"Can you find everything you need in that disgusting mess?"

"Yeah, sure, we're fine. Only one thing . . ."

"What?"

"I couldn't find your music centre. Did that get thrown out after the fire too?"

"Darling, silly girl, what would I do with a music centre? But listen, Lara, do get one for the flat, you'll use it when you stay with me, I'll give you my credit card number. Really, I'd like you to."

"No, it's cool, I'll use the radio."

"Well, feel free to change your mind."

"Anyway, Tessie, how are you? Are you liking being in Cornwall?"

"It's wonderful, as a matter of fact, I hadn't realised how much I'd been missing it. But I went to see Gran."

"Oh dear. Was it a bad day?"

"It's so sad, I felt really awful. You know, Lara, I always thought we'd get close one day, Gran and me, I had this idea she'd suddenly start thinking I was wonderful. But now she won't ever think anything again and it's too late."

"She always used to speak about you very proudly, Tess."

"Nice of you to say so, Lara, even if I know it's not quite true. Oh well, there we are, I can't do anything about it now."

"Give yourself a nice holiday, OK? Mum said you looked knackered when you arrived."

"Anyone ring for me?"

"Someone called Sheila called about some drinks party so I said she should ring you in Cornwall, and a woman called something like Lola or Mona —"

"Ilona?"

"Could be. She wanted to know where you were so I told her, and there was a man who talked so fast he never gave me a chance to say I wasn't you, he asked if you'd stopped working on Luisa Weiss, so I said no, because there was exciting new evidence about her death and he rang off before I could say anything else. Was that OK? I mean, you are still, aren't you?"

"Certainly am, I'm on my way to Thalassa now."

"I bet it looks lovely down there, this time of year."

"Are you homesick, Lara?"

"No way." The girl's voice sounded bright and optimistic. "We're having a ball, Mum says we can go to Ikea this afternoon and get you a whole lot of new things and then we're going to one of those trendy restaurants in Kensington Park Road and tomorrow I'm going to hang out in Portobello. I thought I'd get you a memento of our visit on one of the stalls."

"I'd love that, darling, thanks. Really, thanks very much, it was a good idea for us to swap places for a few days. Send Biddy my love."

I must be nearly there, Tess thought, crawling along the narrow road behind a tractor and trailer. She was strongly aware of driving towards a terminus. To the south and west she could see the sea. Land's End was ahead. That was Europe's limit, nothing else before America except the dots of the Scilly archipelago and open sea. It was indefinably exciting. Tess felt at once liberated by the emptiness ahead, and secure in the comforting landscape whose high, overgrown hedges enclosed and directed her onwards, westwards.

The signpost read Cobban Cove, but an engraved slate plaque set into a dry-stone wall said Thalassa. Turning left, Tess was faced by the shining expanse of water below and beyond. Her eyes were caught by it, and, moving at a slow snail's pace, she scraped the car lightly against a boulder. Curses. Take more care with Lara's precious banger, she rebuked herself, and concentrating hard, drove down the narrow lane. It reminded her of a slot machine game at a funfair, when she'd had to steer a metal nib along a quickly turning image of a road, with a loud buzz when she missed her aim.

Then the road widened into a parking place. Beyond it an unpaved track continued downwards and she wondered whether she was supposed to go right down to the sea.

Tess was reaching for the map she had been sent when someone knocked on the side window.

"Hello, you must be Theresa."

"Tess," she said automatically, turning the engine off and opening the door to greet Raymond Weiss.

She recognised him at once, although he was thinner than ever and had gone completely grey. His curly hair, cut quite short but still unruly, blew round his long, tanned, creased face and his blue eyes disappeared into slits when he smiled. Good teeth too, she thought. As she pushed the door shut her hand brushed against his, skin against skin. She snatched her hand back. But the little shock had not come from the unearthed metal.

He said, "Hallo, haven't we met before?"

Tess had been certain he wouldn't remember her from that alien context so many years before, so had not prepared a story to go with Biddy's surname. In the time it might take to draw breath her mind had flickered over and rejected a variety of mendacious responses. She could simply say she didn't remember, she could pretend it was . . . but no. He looked too nice. It was such beautiful weather, the clear bright light, the fresh, salt-scented breeze were so — the word innocent flashed into her mind. Don't spoil it. She said, "Yes, I believe . . ."

"I can't think where. Never mind, it'll come back to me. You're in the house, as you asked." The form had a space for preferences: vegetarian, vegan, self-catering, isolation in a cottage, company in the house. "If you take your stuff up there you'll find my daughter."

Tess idiotically felt like a snubbed child as Raymond turned away from her and walked down towards the sea followed by a silent black mongrel which had looked at but not moved towards her. Lugging her stuff up a gravelled path, she heard a whine in her head saying, "I want him to like me."

"Hello, I'm Saffron Weiss." A tall, droopy-looking girl, not a bit like either of her parents, with a soft, tentative voice which had raised itself to a question at the end of her short statement. Limp, clammy hands with bitten nails, skimpy white T-shirt, floppy flowered skirt, dirty canvas shoes. But she was competent enough, showing Tess along a corridor and into her room and saying there would be supper at seven preceded by a show-round at six, once everyone had arrived. Meanwhile go anywhere you like but be careful of the tide, it was coming in and it was easy to be cut off if you didn't keep a look-out.

Left alone Tess looked round at the small, neat room. It was bare but complete, with a narrow bed built into the alcove between a narrow wardrobe and chest of drawers that doubled as a dressing-table. The walls were whitewashed, the furniture unvarnished pine, the blind, bed-spread and cotton rug all a strong, marine blue. There were no pictures, though a notice about meal times hung on the back of the door, but the view was a decoration in itself, with a shocking-pink azalea in a big mound in the foreground and in the distance the endless, empty sea.

It's fine, Tess thought, absolutely everything one needs and actually I quite like the lack of frills, it's rather restful. She hung up the few clothes she had brought and laid her newly acquired artist's materials out on the chest. It'll be fun, she told herself, even if I can't find a single titbit to use in an article it doesn't matter. I've been saying for years I wanted to draw and paint again and now's my chance. But there was a chill in her heart. Catching sight of her face in the small square of mirror, she saw the corners of her mouth turned down. How dejected I look. What's wrong with me? I felt so cheerful on the way here, too.

A gust of loneliness shook her like a strong wind. Wrapping her arms round herself she thought, I want . . . who do I want? Not Jacques. Someone.

"You've got Biddy and Lara," Tess's own, sensible, managing voice said in her mind's ear. "And how can you be depressed here when it's so beautiful? Be nice, Tess. Smile." She leant forward to her reflection and made the rictus of a smile, and the hurricane of misery passed as quickly as it had come. Tess had edited an article last year which claimed that the physical motion of smiling released a chemical into the bloodstream that actually made one feel like smiling. Drawing a smiling curve with her forefinger in the steamed-up glass she thought, if I believed in ghosts or manifestations I'd think that was a whiff of Luisa's despair.

Tess found her way out through a side door and wandered along the garden, which was terraced into flat areas of grass or flowers, down with the lie of the land. Someone had planned it skilfully, planting the salt-resistant, warm climate shrubs that grew only in south Cornwall and shrivelled in the rest of the country's winter. The grounds must have been ravishing in their prime, but it seemed to be a long time since pruning and renewal had been properly done so the camellias and magnolias had grown leggy and sparsely covered, and even ignorant Tess, who had never had or even wanted a garden of her own, could see where branches should have been cut or borders weeded.

She aimed towards the sea, passing some cottages where other people were arriving with cases and ruck-sacks, throwing open windows, exclaiming, flinging their belongings on to the path and grass in an ecstasy of freedom from urban wariness. At a picnic table outside a converted tractor shed two women sat with gritty pottery mugs taking snapshots of each other. "Isn't it gorgeous?" one cried and Tess enthused appropriately back.

She had seen several curious little structures on the valley sides, and turned aside to look at one, a small summerhouse, built of overlapping planks, enclosed on three sides and roofed but open to the view, with nothing inside except a built-in bench. These must be the painting huts mentioned in the brochure. Tess sat on the bench, where one would be sheltered from wind and

174

rain. Very snug, she thought, looking down to the tiny empty harbour and triangle of yellow sand. Looking across the valley she saw another painting hut was occupied by a burly woman in a red smock, who looked up, grinned and waved her paintbrush in a friendly way.

Deciding to go down to the beach another day, Tess turned back. The grass was roughly mown in a path between higher growth, so Tess followed it up and round until she came on an outhouse.

No, correction; this was not an outhouse but *the* outhouse, the very one she had seen in photographs, where Luisa Weiss had died.

The structure, once a barn, had been converted into a studio long ago, so the new roof had come by now to match the older slates that hung in overlapping rows on one wall. The others had been built of huge granite boulders, the stone on which it stood so it looked as though it had grown out of the ground itself. A space, once presumably the barnyard, was marked out by granite mushrooms. A wooden dovecote stood there, and white pigeons were pecking over the cobbled ground. A former cider press and a container that had once been a feeding trough contained drooping fuchsias just coming into multicoloured flower. An old wooden bench, sun-bleached and roughened with lichen, stood against the wall below a stone-arched window. Coming closer, Tess saw there was a plaque set into the wall beside the blue-painted plank door. It was slate, carved in elegant italic script, and read: "Remember Luisa Victoria Considine Weiss, writer, 1947-1970. Dear mother of Scarlett and Saffron and wife of Raymond. Requiescat in pace."

The name "Raymond" and the word "wife" were more to be guessed than read because someone had apparently attacked the inscription with a chisel, leaving a scar on its sombre greyness.

Tess turned the iron ring handle and opened the door. It squeaked loudly. Inside the air was cool and still, the only sound the gentle murmur of the doves in the yard. The light was dim in here and there was no sign of lamps or switches to illuminate the large space, its floor polished black slates, its walls whitewashed, furnished with a long table, on which there was a pottery jug of mauve lilacs and rhododendrons. A dozen easels and some folding stools were leaning against the end wall.

Tess went in and looked up. The pitched roof, made of unstained wooden planks, was supported by horizontal oak beams, old, darkened wood with gouges from historic chisels and rusty nails and hooks. The beams were about eight feet from the floor. Tess jumped with an outstretched arm and found she could touch one with the tips of her fingers. This one? she wondered; and then leapt to scrape her fingertips against the others.

"This is the place, in case you're wondering," a chilly voice remarked behind her. Saffron Weiss was standing in the open doorway.

"I'm so sorry," Tess said without thinking. Sorry for trespassing, sorry for the girl and her dead mother, sorry because this place was sad. She added, "I met her once."

Taken by surprise, Saffron spoke like a child. "Who?"

"Your mother."

"You can't have."

"She was pregnant with you."

"You're making it up."

"No. I was thirteen, it was at a conference in Oxford. I was there by accident . . ." Tess told Saffron about that life-changing experience and her lasting memory of the vibrant, inspirational woman. "I thought she was absolutely wonderful, I've never forgotten her."

"I never knew her."

"I know."

"I was here, in this very place, looking at her, lying there actually watching when she . . ." Saffron choked off her own words.

Tess put her arms round the girl's shoulders and felt deep shudders shaking her narrow frame. She seems much younger than twenty-five, Tess thought. She said in a soothing voice, "You couldn't have seen her, Saffron, not really, not at two months old."

"What do you know about it? Who do you think you are? Are you one of those women, feminists? Sneaking in here and nosing in things that aren't any of your business, poking your nose in where it's not wanted, spoiling our things, we should be prosecuting you for trespass and criminal damage instead of treating you like a guest."

It took Tess a moment to work out what the girl was talking about. "The inscription outside?"

"Trying to get rid of my father's name, writing him out of the story."

"I'm nothing to do with that, Saffron, I promise you, I don't know anything about it. What happened?"

"They keep doing it, those *wimmin* — every time we have the thing repaired or have a new one made, they come here to spoil it, and in the churchyard on her grave, desecrating it, they won't admit Daddy was part of her life, they think it was all his fault, as though he'd driven her to do it — of all people! As though he ever could! He's such a good man, my father, so kind and gentle, and he's had such a hard time, it makes me sick. Sick!"

Luisa Weiss was frequently described as a victim of male supremacy in general and in particular oppression by her husband Raymond. It must hurt her family to keep reading that. "It's going a bit far to deface the memorial," Tess agreed.

"A bit far! My poor daddy, he's suffered so much more than anyone deserves to, with his wife leaving him the way she did. My mother. Killing herself."

It was like an echo. Who else had spoken in that tone? Petronella Williams. Two young women, indignant, hurt, bewildered. And deceived.

"I wonder if she did kill herself," Tess said. The words were out of her mouth before her brain registered she was going to say them, before she even knew herself she thought them.

Momentarily sharing the identical surprise, the two women stared at each other in silence. Then Saffron said in a very soft voice, "What did you say?"

"I just can't help wondering if someone else was involved."

"If you knew how I long for that," the girl cried. "If only somebody else had done it, if it hadn't been her that chose to leave me!"

It suddenly seemed impossible to talk about this, standing in the very place where Luisa died. I'd have

**178**

burnt the place down, Tess thought, but Saffron twitched at the flowers, glancing upwards with automatic reverence, and Tess realised this was a shrine to her. Was that table the spot from which Luisa had stepped into her darkness?

"I have this picture in my mind," Tess said slowly. She forgot who she was speaking to as she concentrated on making precise an image that had been vague and undefined, that she hardly knew she had conceived until the words came into her head. "It's because the baby — you, Saffron — had that cut on its, that is, your forehead." Saffron pushed her fringe upwards with one hand while the forefinger of the other traced the almost invisible mark between the eyebrows. Tess went on, "If there had been someone else there, somebody who came here when your father was out —"

"Stop it," Saffron cried, "don't talk about it!" She ran out of the door into the yard, where a flock of white doves took off noisily at her approach. Tess, following slowly, saw her stop suddenly, hands clenched and shoulders rigid. Then the girl turned round and said, her voice trembling, "Dad once said he thought there was a murderer. But my sister said he was just trying to make it seem better for us, as though she hadn't been bored to death by us after all."

A musical but loud bell chimed insistently over the valley. "Supper time, we've got to go," Saffron said.

"I'm coming," Tess said. "We can talk about this later."

"How can you? I don't want to talk about it."

"But perhaps —"

"No. Not ever. I won't," said Saffron Weiss.

179

# CHAPTER
# TWELVE

As Desmond tidied his flat and packed the one bag he was taking with him, he tried to make up his mind as to what he ought to do.

Back in the days when he had been an ambitious police officer in south London, Constable Desmond Kennedy had once worked with a Sergeant Rogerson. The woman police constable who had come round after the fire in Tess's flat had mentioned a Detective Inspector Rogerson from Notting Dale. Desmond wondered whether it was the same man. Not a bad guy; he had at least tried to conceal his disgust after that ill-fated Gay Pride march, unlike other former colleagues who immediately treated Desmond as a pariah.

As so often before, Desmond told himself he'd lost nothing. The comforts of candour were definitely greater than the reassurance of professional acceptance. He got along fine without the macho bigots who behaved as though he consisted only of a walking sexuality, as though his skills and intellect and sympathy, valued up until that moment, were all negated by that one aspect of his life.

As even more often before Desmond reminded himself that it made no difference. His illness was diagnosed not long after he left the force, so he would have had to go for one reason if not another. None the less, the memory of those uncomfortable weeks still rankled and Desmond had steered clear of cops ever since he stopped being one.

There. That was the flat done. Fridge empty and the door prevented from closing with a folded tea towel. Cooker clean, bedding folded, ornaments packed into crates, personal papers stuffed into black refuse sacks and out waiting for the dustmen. Library books returned. Bills paid. Gas off. Covered in a chilly sweat, Desmond went in to wash. He wiped over the bathroom again before dressing in the comfortable travelling clothes he had left on the bed, shorts and a polo shirt under a track suit, training shoes on his feet, flipflops in his bag, and a peaked cap pulled down over his forehead to hide the betraying black sarcoma, the mark of Cain.

Desmond had left out a ready-made salad for his last light snack before the night flight. On his desk lay some blank paper and correspondence cards.

Who had he to write to? A card to Tess Redpath, another to the lifeguard at the Ealing baths.

And was he going to get in touch with Rogerson?

Why not, after all? If he was derided or despised, it would be out of his earshot.

I'll gamble, he thought. If he's in, I'll say something. If not, not.

He rang, and Rogerson was in and even sounded pleased to hear Desmond's voice. Where was he living, what was he doing, why didn't they go for a drink?

"I'm going away tonight," Desmond said.

"Well, when you're back, what do you say — now we're neighbours again."

"Sure," Desmond said. "When I get back."

"You told my girl you had something to tell me."

"An idea, no more."

"You always were an ideas man."

"One of your officers had a robbery and query arson in Arundel Gardens last month. It was in my building, as it happened."

"I saw the report. Nasty business."

"Are you getting anywhere with it?"

"Slowly slowly. You got anything for us?"

"A tenuous connection. But I wanted to mention it before I leave. It just might tie up with something else — the Williams death in the Isle of Man."

"The Pet's mother, do you mean?"

"That's the one."

"I can't trespass on that. Why do you mention it — don't you think it was the right verdict?"

Desmond's light voice went through the details.

"Bit thin," Rogerson said.

"I'm not asking you to do anything about it," Desmond said coldly. "Merely, to satisfy my conscience, to note, if you will, please, that I have reported the facts."

# CHAPTER
# THIRTEEN

Tess couldn't wait to get herself out of Cornwall when she was young. Excitement and fulfilment were waiting up there in the real world, and she simply couldn't understand why other people chose to be "away from it all". So it was with amazement that she woke up on the third morning at Thalassa and realised she had spent the time in a kind of stupor, neglecting and even forgetting the real reason for being there.

Or no, she thought, that isn't quite true. I came to find out more about Luisa's history and thought I'd need to win her family's confidence to do so. And now I've won their confidence and I can't bring myself to ask the questions.

The instant rapport Tess had felt with Raymond all those years ago had revived on the first evening, when, sitting at the end of the long pine table, he'd charmed and encouraged his guests, while Saffron kept as far as possible from Tess.

She had not yet felt able to raise the subject of Luisa's putative suicide again. It would spoil everything. Later, she kept telling herself, soon.

Perhaps every single one of the guests, or at least every single female one of them, felt she'd made a special relationship with Raymond. But had he sought them all out in their painting huts during the next two days, as he had sought out Tess? Had he taken them all for cliff walks? Did he imperceptibly steer the others to the chair next to his own?

Tess told herself not to be bamboozled. She mustn't be taken in by a host's professional manners. But she was irresistibly flattered and charmed too. Raymond was both interesting and interested. Kind. Funny. They got on so well together. How could Tess possibly spoil things by probing and asking, using suggestion and suppression to winkle confidences out of him?

Tess had done that in the Isle of Man. It had been easy as pie, she'd extracted confidences from Petronella like taking sweeties from a blind baby, Tess thought, in words commonly used in her childhood. To Petronella and the Blagdens Tess had recited her cover story without a qualm, hardly conscious let alone caring that it was all a lie. She'd felt pleased with herself for producing the words with such smooth professionalism. She'd been grown-up and histrionic, behaving like the best detectives and spies — and journalists.

Thinking about it now Tess no longer felt she had been professional or grown-up. Niggles of shame squirmed within her. She had a vision of herself in the Methodist Chapel in St Austell, aged about ten, in a flowered dress with new white shoes, when a hell-fire preacher anathematised liars. "Tell the truth and shame the devil," he shouted and she'd promised, "I will, I always will." It had felt like role playing, not lying, when she had spoken to Petronella Williams and wormed confidences out of her. Reliving the deceit now, Tess thought there had been something in Jacques's strictures about the media after all, perhaps it was a dirty trade. She would certainly feel dirty if she lied to Raymond, it would spoil everything.

She went to the dining-room, where hot drinks, cold food and the daily papers were laid out, and sat down with coffee and toast to read the *Guardian*, where she found a picture of Jacques and Sibyl. Jacques had been promoted to a senior NATO appointment. Oh my God, Tess thought. It was him. It was all on account of that diskette. He got it back and then he felt safe to — how could he? Burglary! Arson! I won't let him get away — No. Take a break, girl. He'll be shifting himself as it is, for fear I'll work it out, wondering what I'll do. Sleep on it. Work out what's best to do. Don't leap in.

She turned to the tabloid section and a leisurely account of the disaster at Tarrant's Crossing, with fewer eye-catching pictures than the *Argus* magazine's glossy pages, using words to indicate the atmosphere of a tragedy dating from the days when people were left alone to do their own thing on their own property; an American's home was his castle. Even if there had been suspicions about the goings-on at the old ranch, nobody would have wanted to interfere. As it happened, anyone who did know a whole lot of people were living there simply assumed they were in a hippie commune. We keep out of each other's business round here, one farmer had said later; we're neighbourly but we don't interfere. Neighbourly was a relative term. The speaker's own place was nearly twenty miles from the next one, which had once been a ranch known as Tarrant's Crossing till it was bought up by folk from the north. It was Nowheresville, until the day some time in October 1965 when it burnt to the ground. Nobody could be sure which day, or how it had happened, or who were the men, women and children whose charred bodies were found there. At least some of their identities had perished with them.

One victim only could be described by the neighbours, the young man who had the commune's dealings with the outside world. John Doe, which nobody believed was his name, was weird, according to the traders in the nearest town, Eloy. A bartender said he had a wild temper and a woman shopkeeper said he was scary. He had been arrested once on a charge of murder, when he was alleged to have shot dead a man who had argued with him in a bar, but an unbreakable alibi was given by other people from the commune at Tarrant's Crossing who swore he'd been with them all night.

And that was it. Some names of victims were listed, people whose families had known they were in the commune, but nobody ever seemed to have left it alive.

Tess felt an absent-minded spurt of loyalty to the *Argus*. This is all scissors and paste and pretension, we did it better, she thought; then she remembered she did not want the *Argus* to be better, she wanted it to be in deep trouble, and sack all its editorial staff, disgraced and unemployable, and fold in irredeemable debt. And then she realised she simply didn't care. It's over, done with. No need to say "Be nice", she realised, there was no need for ill wishes now. She had forgiven and almost

186

forgotten them all even before Ilona turned up at Thalassa the previous evening having tracked Tess down and given her no chance to be chilly or reproachful by starting right in on the apologies herself. She admitted she'd been a bad friend, disloyal, unsympathetic, *unforgivable.*

"But you will forgive me, Tessie, won't you, my job was on the line." No longer. Ilona was pregnant. Her boyfriend was setting up an independent production company and she was going to work with him. She had stuck it out at the *Argus* long enough to get her paid maternity leave but had no intention of returning to her job. "I couldn't have stood Carne much longer in any case, I mean — is he creepy or what!"

"But why did you come here?" Tess had asked, amazed to find Ilona esconced in the drawing-room.

"To speak to you. Well, Tess, you must admit you haven't been returning my calls so when I finally got through to a human being — your niece, was it? — and she said you were down here I thought I'd just come and give you this myself and face you."

"Face me? I mean, it's lovely to see you, Ilona, it always is, but what on earth do you mean?"

"I wanted to say I was sorry for not being nice when they gave you the push."

"Oh listen, that's so sweet of you, thank you so much, and coming all this way too, but don't worry, I understood how difficult it was. Really."

"I've found out lots more about Carne to tell you, and I picked this up to bring you 'cos I knew none of that lot would ever send it on."

The envelope was addressed in Amanda Slowe's primitive handwriting to Tess at the *Argus*; inside, with a covering note saying she had found the page stuck in a paperback book, was a rough draft of Peter Slowe's story.

Aged eleven, he had been out playing on the cliffs and saw a man with staring eyes take out a sharp knife and cut some rope off Peter's grandad's boat. The man frightened him so much he never dared say a word to anyone. It was the day Luisa Weiss died, and that was why it stuck in his mind, because of all the fuss, with policemen asking round in the neighbourhood if anyone had seen anything suspicious and appeals for information on TV.

Peter Slowe, too scared to speak, had just run home. Then he kept quiet for so long he eventually forgot about it. Then he was reminded of Luisa Weiss's name by seeing it in the press and it all came back to him, and he realised the man who scared him might have had something to do with her death.

Rope. The rope with which Luisa hanged herself had been identified. A fisherman — Peter Slowe's grandfather — had noticed that a length of the same blue nylon cord had been cut from a coil on his boat, but nobody had ever been able to work out how Luisa had got it, because the fishing boat had been pulled on to a beach three miles away from Thalassa. The fisherman had not been out for a few days and admitted he was not sure when he had last noticed the complete coil of rope so the assumption was that Luisa had made preparations in advance for her last action.

Ilona's insistent voice interrupted Tess's thoughts. "Do listen, Tessie, that can't be as interesting as hearing about Carne."

"Sorry, Ilona, what were you saying?"

"The thing is once I knew I'd be leaving I wasn't worried any more — what could he do to me?"

"Something pretty nasty, actually."

"He'd just have chucked me out a bit sooner if anyone had found me which they didn't. I had lots of chances to scan his files. His office is on a completely different system from the rest of the *Argus*, it's wired into Carneco Canada and I wasn't supposed to have access but I'm a computer whizz. He didn't know that when he hired me," she added with great self-satisfaction. "He thought he was getting a dumb blonde."

Tess had thought the same thing when she first met Ilona in her leotard, bouncing up and down in an aerobic frenzy. As they got into the habit of meeting for lunch every month or so, Tess had come to appreciate Ilona's optimistic, can-do brightness. Tess said, "So what did you find out about Carne?"

"It was a question of piecing bits of information together. Bank accounts and the dates they were opened, passport numbers and the place of issue, letters, bills, old law suits . . . it's amazing how much information you can get out of a man's own computer files if you happen to be his personal assistant, so-called. He shouldn't have underestimated me," Ilona had added.

"Morning, Tess." Here was Ilona, in complete dumb blonde mode, wearing white jeans and a tight shirt that left several inches of midriff bare, a green jewel in her belly button, white thongs on her feet and long nails painted the exact colour of the Golden Delicious apple she began to peel. Tess greeted her affectionately. It was the deed of a friend to have followed Tess down here for the sake of warming the coolness between them.

Alfred Rutter came into the room, made for the coffee, poured a cup and gulped it in one continuous movement. Only then did he look across at the two women and, spreading his arms in a capacious gesture, shout (for he always communicated at the top of his bass voice), "Good morning, good morning, anyone for painting?" Rutter's own pictures were huge, brilliantly coloured and thick with gobbets of paint. The canvas he was working on at Thalassa, a portrait of Saffron Weiss, pale tones against a velvety green background, was as bristly as a hedgehog. There was no need to like his art to be inspired by him into making one's own. Tess had astonished herself by filling nearly a whole sketchbook with drawings and watercolours of Thalassa. Under Alfred's encouragement she worked quickly, with increasing enjoyment and almost — not quite — well enough to be willing to let others see what she had already learnt to do.

"To your stations, girls, chop chop," Alfred exhorted.

But Ilona wanted to talk to Tess again. "I've got to get it all off my chest." She teetered down the garden on her high heels to share the bench in Tess's painting hut. While Tess made passes at her paper with a soft pencil, Ilona picked paint blisters off the boards of the hut and talked more about F.B. Carne, by whom she was still enthralled.

**190**

He wasn't Indian or Mexican, as it turned out, but Canadian born and Jewish bred. "He's from Toronto," Ilona said, almost with indignation. "God knows why that's got to be a secret. Ferdinand Kahn, he was born. Changed the spelling when he got his second passport."

He had gone to the United States and opened a bank account with very little money in it in New York, in 1963. Within three years he had become a millionaire though Ilona had not been able to find out where the money came from. He returned to Canada and bought his first newspaper in Ontario in 1966. After that —

"Stop," Tess said. "Let me think. Something came into my head but . . . wait a minute." She gazed blankly out to sea. Nothing. "Never mind, it'll come back to me." Ilona went on with her story of F.B. Carne's rise to riches but Tess had been distracted. It seemed irrelevant here. Do I care any more? she wondered, and realised she wouldn't go back to the *Argus* if Hamish Beck and Carne himself came along that very cinder path on their knees to ask her. I don't need it, she thought, the job, living in London, it all seems somehow irrelevant. Do I actually want to go back to London? For her it was a heretical idea.

"So he bought the *Argus* and there we are," Ilona finished triumphantly. "Tess?"

"Mmm."

"Have you been listening?"

"Yes, of course."

"You haven't. You're thinking about something completely different."

"No, but Alfred's having a painting class in the studio."

"Oh my God," Ilona squeaked. "What's that?"

She sprang to her feet trembling. Tess said, "It's only a creepy-crawly, here, let me . . ."

"God, I hate the country," Ilona said. "I'll be glad to get back to town, won't you?"

"I wouldn't mind staying here for ever, actually."

"Ah. The gorgeous Raymond."

"Don't be silly. Are you coming?"

Ilona came, but she couldn't see much point in it. Tess had a lovely time splodging acrylic paint around as crudely and happily as a primary school kid. Later she sat on the beach and skimmed pebbles into the sea while Raymond scraped a boat. That evening she went to supper in Honeysuckle with a silent, smiling etcher and a watercolourist who was an academic folklorist and eager to tell other people about piskies, though in fact most of the conversation was about the Weiss family. Saffron was a dear girl. Scarlett was what you might call hard-boiled and hadn't been able to shake the dust of home off her feet fast enough. She would never speak of Luisa whose memory she hated and resented and whose message she despised. Scarlett didn't want anything whatever to do with Thalassa, Cornwall or, above all, political feminism and the cult of her mother. Raymond was lovely, charming but sad. He should have found another wife years ago.

Her interest quickened, Tess asked, "Why ever didn't he?" and was told there had been ladies in residence during some summers, but none seemed to stick. "Once bitten, twice shy," the etcher suddenly said before relapsing into silence.

Thalassa's gentle pace and lack of pressure were very seductive. On the third day Tess woke to sunshine again, and looked out of the window to see that new blossoms had burst — rose-coloured hawthorn and chestnut candles, elderflower and rowan. The sea was calm and blue and the smell, the very essence of freshness, seemed to be summoning her outside. Going down for breakfast in a room furnished in the original "Liberty style" she thought she would take herself out to sit in a painting hut listening to birds and buzzes, removed out of this world into a temporary haven. She could live like this. She could sell the flat.

"Letters." Saffron came into the dining-room with a bundle of mail and sorted it into piles on the dark oak sideboard. "Dad, me, Olly and Jane, Dad, Miss — there's nobody here called Redpath."

"That's mine," Tess said.

"Is it? Why — sorry. Nothing to do with me."

It was a card from Desmond, and Lara, having been given it to address, had put in a covering note. "We're having a wonderful time, hope you are too, lots and lots of love." The message was encircled with crosses and circles, kisses and hugs.

Desmond wrote that he was going away to the Red Sea. "I won't be here when you come home. Good luck with your quest, and with everything else."

The Red Sea, good luck with . . . I won't be here when . . . The back of Tess's hand jerked up against her lips in an unconscious gesture of dismay. Tess ran up to her room to rummage in her purse and down to the telephone in the hall. She jerked her phonecard into the slot.

"Biddy, is that you? Oh, Lara. Hallo, darling, it's Tess. Listen, have you seen Desmond?"

"Not since the night before last, he brought me something up to address for you. I posted it yesterday, didn't you get it?"

"Yes, but I'm a bit worried about him."

"I know, he's got Aids, hasn't he?"

"How do you — well anyway, Lara, can I speak to your mum?"

"She's in the bath, shall I get her?" As Lara spoke, Tess heard her own front door bell ring.

"It's OK, Lara, just see who's at the door first."

The sounds of Notting Hill came down the telephone line. Traffic, groaning brakes from black cabs, a heavy lorry, a police siren. Lara's radio, the Capital Radio disc jockey belting out artificial excitement. Music with a heavy beat. Lara's rubber soles squeaked over the floor from which charred and sodden carpets had been lifted.

Tess heard Lara say, "Hi, I'm on the phone." Then the receiver was replaced and there was nothing but the telephone buzz. Tess felt a momentary anxiety, it wasn't like Lara to be rude to her, but Biddy was there, nothing could be wrong — and here was Raymond. He had followed Saffron into the hall, where they stood looking at a package the postman had brought.

"I was expecting something bigger than that," Saffron said. "When they said papers I thought they meant boxes full."

194

"I think the trustees sorted most of the documents," Raymond said.

"I'm not sure I really want to see what's inside."

"Leave it for a bit, just put it away for the time being and we'll look together later on. Tess, d'you want to come with me? I've got to go to Penzance."

Joyfully Tess ran for her bag, leapt into Raymond's old and battered Volvo, watched his brown, knobbled hands on the wheel and gearstick. She was intensely aware of his physical presence at her side, in her mind outlining his sun-darkened neck and forearms and the shape of flesh and bones that disappeared under the faded blue shirt. His skin would be warm to the touch, like his handshake. His lips . . .

He began to talk about the landscape. Then they compared living in towns to living in the country. Then they talked about where they had grown up. Raymond hadn't realised Tess was Cornish herself but he knew St Austell well. Tess thought she could visualise the exact house in South Kensington where Raymond's family lived. Then Raymond said Saffron had told him Tess once met Luisa, and Tess said she'd only seen her, and seen him on that occasion too, reminding him about the women's liberation conference.

Raymond told her about the book appearing next week, the final collection of Luisa's writings, not her best, a bit of a scraping of the barrel, but there would be a market for it. They always ploughed all the royalties back into Thalassa which, God knew, needed them. Tess was just saying she was looking forward to reading the book when Raymond suddenly gasped and banged his clenched fist on the steering wheel. In a tone of voice that made Tess cringe he said, "Now I remember where we met before. Damn it, you're a journalist, aren't you?"

He pulled the car into the side of the lane, stopped and turned to stare at Tess with such a chilly expression that quite unconsciously she put up her hand to shield her eyes. "What are you doing at Thalassa? Are you spying on us? And what's your name? You aren't really called Trevail."

Tess clasped her shaking hands tightly together in her lap. Her voice sounded thin in her ears as she said, "Redpath. Tess Redpath."

"I ought to put you out of the car this minute."

They were on the coast road Tess had come along the other day, with hedges on both sides. A horn sounded from behind. Tess said, "Park somewhere, Raymond, let me explain."

She watched his beaked, grim profile as he drove slowly on and then swung the car into a field gateway. There were liver spots on his hands and he had left a tuft of unshaved grey stubble on his chin. His mouth was tightened into a straight line. Tess wanted to whimper like a dog at his anger. She said, "Raymond, listen. Will you listen? Please?"

He nodded, not looking at her. "Say your piece. But I'll say this first. I don't allow reporters or any other media types at Thalassa, you've done enough damage over the years to me and my daughters and my property. No doubt you know that already, or you wouldn't have oiled your way in there in disguise. I must say, I was quite taken in. I didn't take you for a liar."

"I was. I'm not now." Tess's voice was trembling. She felt for the door handle. "Can we get out? I feel a bit . . ."

Grim-faced, he followed her along a narrow path beside a hay field towards the cliff top. Standing at its edge with the swirling high tide two hundred feet below, Tess said, "It's true I came here to find out about Luisa, I did want to write about her but I won't now, I can't. Couldn't. Everything's different now. These three days, I've just been painting and thinking, it's been so lovely. I've got to know you. You've been so . . . well, anyway, what I mean is I'm sorry to have come on false pretences but please let me stay because I'm not going to do the story. I couldn't ever write a word about your wife now, not when you've been so . . ."

"What were you going to write? What did you come here to see? Another exposé of Raymond Weiss as male chauvinist pig? Another rant about neglected Luisa driven to despair?"

"Not that."

"I don't believe you."

"I don't think she was driven to despair. I don't think she committed suicide. I think she was murdered."

He turned away, shading his eyes. Then he took hold of Tess's arm above the elbow, holding hard enough to hurt, and pushed her in front of him along the narrow, aromatic path, to a cluster of rocky outcrops rising on the cliff top from a swathe of bluebells and young bracken. The scent was swooning sweet. "Sit down." She sat down. "Tell me what you mean. Why do you think she was killed?"

Tess had not fully analysed her own thought processes

until this moment. Putting them into words for the first time was an act of discovery as well as explanation. Her voice was low and halting and Raymond stood above her like a stone statue, motionless, listening, his head bent and eyes on the ground.

"First of all, I just couldn't imagine her doing it. She was so vital. And she loved the little girl so much, even I could see that and I was only a kid myself. She wouldn't have left her, or the baby."

"That's soggy. Impertinent, too. What gives you the right to judge her?"

"I have no right," Tess said humbly. She looked up into Raymond's face with a sort of despair. He hates me, she thought, I've hurt him. Raymond's hand, hanging at his side, was shaking. Greatly daring, Tess put her own on his, feeling the dry skin with terrified delight, waiting for him to snatch himself away. And then he turned his hand, so they were palm to palm, fingers within fingers.

"I wouldn't have thought it of you, Tess. Cheating me."

"I haven't cheated, not from the moment I arrived and saw you. I did come here to spy, it's true, but then I couldn't bring myself to do it. Not on you."

"Not on me?" He pulled her up to stand, and looked into her eyes. His were as blue as the sea behind him. Tall though she was, he was taller, grave, inquiring. He said, "I feel like a teenager."

Tess felt a jet of joy shoot through her as he tentatively put his arms round her, pulled her towards him, put his warm lips on her face, her neck, her lips.

198

A while later he drew away to look into her face. "Tess?" he murmured. "Are we too old for this game?"

Aeons later, or minutes, Tess remembered to reply.

Later still an inquisitive dog was followed by two mountain bike riders in skin-tight gear and hard hats.

"Lucky they came by or we might have stayed here till we grew moss," Raymond said. Tess returned to the real world, but oh! how different it seemed. Straightening her clothes she looked at him cautiously and found he was looking at her in the same way. Was he already regretting it? Did he think she was?

"Tess?"

"Mmm."

"Sit down here. Not too close, or I'll be distracted again." Even as he spoke his arm stretched across the gap. In the end they nestled as close together as rush hour travellers, in this different, beautiful, sunny loneliness. "Listen, we've got to concentrate."

"Yes, Raymond," she said, pleased by the sound of his name on her lips.

"Tell me again why you came."

"But it's gone, the reason. I couldn't possibly —"

"No, I know you won't write it now. But what were you going to write? About poor Luisa?"

She turned her eyes away from him to settle on an oil tanker creeping up the English Channel on the horizon. "Luisa. Yes. Well, the thing is . . . I don't know how to say it to you."

"Oh, I can take it," Raymond said. "It's twenty-five years ago, though I did feel utterly miserable for years, missing her for myself and the girls and feeling guilty, I really began to think those women were right and I'd been so selfish and unobservant that I'd driven her to suicide myself, but you can't brood for ever. I just wish it hadn't had such a disastrous effect on the girls, they reacted in quite different ways but you can see the result. Scarlett's got as far away from us all as she can and despises everything her mother stood for and Saffron's scared to go further from home than Penzance. I did my best but nobody could be normal knowing their mother killed herself rather than stay with them. None of us can."

"It may not have been suicide, you know."

"Oh Tess. It's nice of you to make that suggestion but the police were satisfied, and the coroner. There can't be any doubt really."

"But nobody knew about the rope."

"What d'you mean?" Raymond asked.

"They thought she'd got it in advance, planned what to do, but there was someone else near Thalassa that day, a man who cut the rope off a coil on a fishing boat. I know the police found where it had come from and thought Luisa must have gone there another day, but they were wrong. Someone saw it happen."

"Someone saw . . ." Raymond's voice trailed away. Then, drawing away from Tess, he said, "I know nothing about that."

Tess explained about the late Peter Slowe and added, "Don't you see, if someone came with the equipment he might have . . ." She found she couldn't utter the brutal words.

Raymond said, "I used to pray for it to have been

murder. To have been able to believe she hadn't been so desperate to escape from me, to forgive myself for not perceiving her despair. If I could have remembered her as the person I loved who wouldn't ever have hurt me like that. My Luisa, the Luisa I thought I knew, loved the children so much she'd have lain down under a fast train for their sakes."

"I thought she must have felt that way," Tess said. "The cut on the baby's face . . . Peter Slowe said the man he saw had a sharp knife, he threatened him with it. She'd have done anything to save them, wouldn't she?"

They stared into each other's faces, each with the same hideous vision in their minds.

The stranger takes the white bundle from the mother's arms. Sensing her anxiety, the infant cries so that the reflex flow of milk prickles upwards in the mother's breasts. He flicks out the sharp, pointed blade. He puts it against the child's soft skin . . . and the mother would do anything, absolutely anything at all, she would die to save her baby. She will knot the rope at his command, she will put it over a beam, she will climb on the table and put it round her neck. And jump? When the crimson bead pops out on the tiny forehead, when the red line lengthens and the blood drips down on the white shawl — yes. Yes, she will jump.

His mouth in a rictus of horror, Raymond put his head in his hands and groaned, the words coming hoarse and desperate from the depths, "Who? Why? Luisa!"

# CHAPTER
# FOURTEEN

If they went back to Thalassa Raymond would immediately be set upon with requests and comments. They had far too many things to say to each other for that. Equally, they both suddenly felt they could not go on talking about Luisa's hideous death; or at least, not immediately. They drove across the peninsula towards the north coast and St Ives, telling each other sweet nothings interspersed with the exchange of sensible information. Tess felt as though she had bathed in the fires of rejuvenation, like Rider Haggard's She. She didn't need to look at herself in a mirror to know she was glowing, healthy and pretty. Her eyes saw colours more vividly, the taste in her mouth was fresh and sweet, her skin had become like a conductor of electric sensation, so even brushing against the car door sent a ripple of delicious sensation through her veins.

I'm starting a new life, she thought, but it felt costly natural. The battered car was as familiar as the man driving it, and she could have been travelling in his passenger seat like this for years, it seemed so right and proper for them to be side by side. His mind must have been running along the same lines. As the car came over the hill, and they saw the expanse of fields and uncultivated hillside falling gently away towards the Atlantic, Raymond said,

"You won't go away, will you? You'll stay here?"

"As long as you'll have me," she replied without hesitating.

She would sell the flat. She didn't need a new job on some superficial, snide magazine, Hamish and Valerie and the rest could take a running jump. Tess would forget struggle and unequal competition. And Jacques? I might even let him get away with it after all, I don't need revenge. Forget him, once and for all. This is what I need, this and Raymond, she thought, breathing in the unpolluted air.

They had been making for St Ives, but realised they did not want to sit on opposite sides of a restaurant table so Raymond bought apples and Cornish pasties in a village shop.

He said, "Best if we're not overheard, there's lots of people know me round here." So they sat with their backs against the ancient stones of West Penwith and forced themselves to concentrate on the unhappy dead.

"It wasn't just Luisa, you see," Tess said. "I've been awfully slow in realising it. But I thought Jill Williams had copied her, you see. That's what we were supposed to think."

Raymond seldom read the papers and never followed the news. Tess had to explain not only about Jill Williams's death, but about Petronella and her prince. She slid lightly over her own involvement. Then she realised that lying about her own lies would be little better than the deception she had intended to practise on

Raymond himself, and shamefacedly confessed the deception she had used on Petronella, whereby she had found out that Jill Williams and Luisa had once known each other and travelled together in America.

"I'm sure I've never even heard of the woman. Of course I know Luisa went to the States when she was at college though it was before I met her, but she didn't really talk about it. Jill — what would she have been called then?"

"I don't know. I had thought you might have known something."

"I don't, though. But Tess, students travelling round always meet lots of different people, it doesn't mean you have anything to do with them later. Are you really sure there's a connection?"

"It was something Desmond said. He's my neighbour in London, he was a cop once so he was able to get a copy of the police report about Luisa's death. Oh Raymond, I'm sorry, I shouldn't —"

"It's all right. Go on."

"Honestly? I don't want to hurt you."

"Really."

"Desmond noticed something else. Luisa died very soon after *Into Captivity* appeared, which means it was just after she first had her picture in the papers and appeared on TV. And that's what happened to Jill Williams. She'd led a terribly secretive life, it was like she was scared of anyone seeing her picture. She actually threw Petronella's camera into the sea when she tried to take a photo of her. And then Petronella got engaged and Jill couldn't avoid the publicity that went with it. Her name and picture were in the papers and on TV. So it could be when she told Petronella her engagement would be the death of her she really meant it. Could she have thought having her picture published would be the death of her?"

"She might have been hiding out, in fact?"

"She could have gone to the Isle of Man to go to ground. Her neighbours certainly all said she was pretty reclusive."

"But why? What was it all about?"

"I'm thinking aloud," Tess said. "What if something happened when Luisa and Jill were together, which means when they went to America that time? What if they knew someone was going to come after them? What if they kept clear on purpose after they came home? I know Jill was pregnant and then she was in hospital with post-natal depression, so they could have lost contact quite naturally, but they may have had a reason for it. Perhaps someone really did come after both of them, one after another, as soon as they poked their heads above the parapet."

"But Tess, you said Jill Williams killed herself. There was a suicide verdict."

"Like Luisa."

"You don't think . . .?"

"Jill Williams had a dog. A long-haired, red, miniature dachshund and she loved it as much as she ever loved anything, much more than she loved Petronella by the sound of it. And when she was found, the dog had a cut on its head. A sharp long cut. Like Luisa's baby. Like Saffron."

"Don't, Tess, I can't bear it," Raymond said, holding one hand up in a warding-off gesture, pulling Tess towards him with the other. "Let's not talk about it now."

They wanted to think about themselves, or rather, each about the other. Their minds were full of needful, delightful inquiries and confidences. Their childhood, families, other loves; their work, enthusiasms, hatreds.

"It sounds ridiculous," Raymond said, "but I feel as though I'd never loved anyone before, as though this is the first day of the rest of my life."

"Love?" Tess repeated. "I never really knew the meaning of the word before."

But death nagged at them. Luisa and Jill Williams were not the only ones.

The editor of the *Argus* magazine had died in the middle of collecting facts about Luisa. Peter Slowe rang to offer her information about something he remembered. Moira died that very night, mugged in the deserted office car-park, and Peter Slowe himself was killed before he could tell the tale again. If Moira had not scribbled down his telephone number and Tess had not happened to try it, his memory of a man with a knife would have been extinguished.

Four deaths.

"There can't be a connection," Raymond protested. "It's all too unlikely."

"I think there must be," Tess replied.

Later on they lay entwined on the ground, panting, replete. "At our age!" Tess exclaimed, laughing, and

Raymond pushed himself into a sitting position and looked down at her anxiously.

"But we aren't the same age. I'm far too old for you. You could be my —"

She put her finger across his lips. She liked the touch of them, smooth and full, and she liked the discovery of his innocence, not that he was virginal, of course, but he was obviously inexperienced, for it was as though he didn't quite know what to do except for the one thing he needed to do for himself, and though Tess was filled with delight it was a more emotional than physical satisfaction. But oh, how wonderful it would be to show him, leisurely and lovingly, to have pleasure increasing every time and new discoveries to make. Lying now with her head on his chest she thought how she'd once joked about men who were no good in bed, who didn't know which button to press or couldn't be bothered to turn her on. Tess would never have believed she'd fall for an older, ignorant, clumsy man. But fall she had. I'm really in love, she thought joyously, it's never felt like this before.

"Oh God, there's someone coming," Raymond said, jumping to his feet and pulling at his shirt.

"It doesn't matter, don't worry about it."

"That's the generation gap. In my day we did worry."

A man smoking a pipe with a tall, crooked stick and a collie slinking at his heel. "Why, it's Ray. Howdo, nice day."

"Good afternoon, Trevor."

The man nodded, gave Tess a knowing look and went on up the hill.

"It'll be all over West Penwith, Raymond Weiss with a woman up on Carn Galva," Raymond groaned. "You can't do anything without someone seeing you."

"Do you think anyone else saw the man with the knife, then, apart from Peter Slowe?"

"Nobody saw anyone in the valley that day, apart from the usual, you know, like the post van. And one of the Mormons, they were always coming round."

"Mormons?"

"It was a joke in the neighbourhood, people used to say they had to spend a year selling religion before they were allowed to settle down in Salt Lake City with their multiple wives. They were nice clean-looking chaps, in suits."

"It was a Jehovah's Witness, in Dunkloss." Tess tried to remember what the woman had said, the fat neighbour whose son had gone round to stop Jill Williams's dog barking. "She told the Jehovah's Witness there was no point in calling at Jill's house because she wouldn't talk to him, but suppose he did call there, suppose . . ."

"I can't really bring myself to think about it."

They walked down the hill closely together. Raymond had not locked the car — he said he never did, it was so old nobody would steal it — and he held the door open for Tess. She ducked under his arm. "Do we have to go to the police?"

He said, "They wouldn't thank us. All this supposition, guesswork, instinct. When Luisa died I tried to persuade them to investigate it more but they would have it she'd done it herself, and what with looking after the girls and trying to calm Luisa's mother down and run

Thalassa — I just gave up. Maybe if I'd been firmer about it they might have found some evidence, but as it was . . ."

"Do you want to talk to anyone else about it? Saffron? Scarlett?"

"I think it would only upset them."

# CHAPTER
# FIFTEEN

Consuelo Esteban quickly reached the conclusion that moving to London had been a mistake. She hated the climate and distrusted the food and was perfectly miserable in the apartment she and Juan Pedro had taken in Notting Hill for the year he would be working in the London office. The flat had been guaranteed quiet and comfortable by the landlord and the district sounded glamorous from afar; the glossy magazines they read to learn about England described it as a centre of cultural life, full of Bohemian writers and artists and a café society which, Consuelo thought, would make her feel at home. But she had not met any writers or artists and the cafés, though full, were exclusive. Nobody spoke to strangers.

Consuelo was lonely and bored. Juan Pedro's office was too far away for him to come home for lunch, as in Madrid he did, like everyone else in that civilised society. She thought the streets were dirty, the shops dingy and the weather grim. Rain at the end of May was an insult. The lectures about fine art she'd signed on for were boring. Consuelo was miserable.

To make everything worse, the rented flat in Arundel Gardens, even with the fire damage repaired, was still far from the luxurious and well-equipped haven the agents had promised. It compared pitifully with the Estebans' own home in a modern suburb of Madrid, which was futuristic and (thanks to an illegal immigrant from Zaire) spotless. This dump was not even peaceful. As though the constant traffic noise was not enough to endure, the last few days had been made hideous by offensive music coming from another apartment in the building. Radio music, interrupted sometimes by the blessedly lower blur of a disc jockey's patter, but always resumed, at more or less excessive volume.

All day. All night. Alone, because Juan Pedro was away in Leicester, or Leeds or perhaps Liverpool; Consuelo knew nothing of English geography. The pounding, rhythmic beat thudded through the building like a road mender's hammer. Voiced screeches and wails penetrated the walls.

Consuelo went out and spent money; shoes, a new bag, flowers, a striped sweater. Half the day gone. Then she set off again to take the 23 bus, sitting on the upper deck following on its slow, stately course past Paddington, Edgware Road, along Oxford Street and Regent Street, Piccadilly, the Strand, and back again. Then she went to the pictures but her English wasn't good enough to understand the film. Then she felt forced back to the flat and the rumpus was still going on.

"*Joder*! Fuck!" she shouted as she came in through the street door and even from there heard it loud and clear. Before climbing the stairs she knocked at the front door of the ground-floor flat where a polite, ill man lived on his own. No answer. She went out on to the pavement wondering if she could see through his windows, but saw the old wooden shutters which unfolded across the windows were all closed. Had he been driven away by the noise? But he was a friend of the woman upstairs, an unsmart, overweight mess of a female, with unrefined, pink features and a hairstyle and clothes with which no sane woman could ever let herself be seen in public. Her carelessness had already caused a fire in the building. Now the woman's lack of consideration for anyone else had become quite intolerable.

Opening her own door Consuelo gave her usual automatic, satisfied glance in the glass above the hall table, licked her finger and smoothed a black eyebrow without even realising she was doing so. Then she climbed on to the kitchen table with the broom and banged its handle against the ceiling. Some plaster fell on to the floor. Not my problem, she thought; serve the landlord right for not making it clear to us the place was uninhabitable. Bang, bang, bang.

Nothing. No footsteps, no diminution in sound. Bang, bang. Consuelo attacked the ceiling with a fury fanned by the heavy metal sounds she was now forced to hear. "Shut up, shut up," she yelled.

Nothing. No reaction.

She's gone away, Consuelo thought, gone on holiday and left the radio blaring away. It could go on for weeks. It is unendurable, I shall go mad.

Juan Pedro rang to say he would have to stay away for another night and Consuelo blasted his ears with a tirade of indignation and blame. How could he expect her to live like this, why had he dumped her in this dreadful place and left her all alone, what right had he to treat her like a chattel? He thought she was a thing to be put down and picked up when it was convenient. A thing with stone ears.

Shouting through her voice Juan Pedro eventually made her hear. If the neighbours didn't answer their door bells or telephones, then of course she should ring the landlord. Or the agents. Or even the police. No, he said, of course Consuelo couldn't possibly be expected to put up with it, he was only sorry he could not get back this evening to look after her, poor little pigeon; his darling; *querida*. A little soothed by Juan Pedro's amorous sympathy, Consuelo went into the sitting-room to search for the landlord's telephone number.

While she was looking someone came to her own door. Howard Irons from the house next door. Could she help him, his children couldn't sleep with the music coming through the party wall and Miss Redpath wasn't answering her phone.

Consuelo threw herself into his arms, though only metaphorically as he backed nervously into the hall when she approached.

Together they bewailed and accused. No consideration, the way people behaved nowadays, there should be a law against it. In Madrid there was a law against it.

Inspired, the neighbour remembered there was a law against it in London too, something to do with decibels and the tort of nuisance. "I shall ring the council," he said firmly.

"Oh do it from here, please, do it now, let me listen," Consuelo cried.

"Oh my God it's the Sex Pistols."

"Sex . . .?"

"A group. A band. Listen, isn't it frightful? She must have gone quite mad."

"Or bad, she has gone. Or at the least, deaf."

"I can't stand this racket, let me look in your phone book, Kensington Council, no, it's called Kensington and Chelsea, isn't it. Hornton Street . . . environmental protection, do you think we want, or housing?"

Consuelo, standing very close, said in her passionate contralto, "It matters not, my friend. We require merely authority."

Authority took a long time to come. It was evening before a bashful, bearded official turned up to measure the noise nuisance with an electronic gadget. "But it is not the extent, the volume only," Consuelo pleaded. "It is that it does not stop. All day, all night, ceaseless."

"Neighbour mediation might be called for here."

"I'm not waiting for any mediation. In fact I'll break in if you won't," said Mr Irons.

"Me? Break in? I couldn't do that, I'm not authorised," the official said.

"But what are we to do?"

"It's a case for the police," the official decided.

There was a long wait for the police too; and all the while, the local pop radio station poured out multidecibels. Juan Pedro rang. Howard Irons's wife rang. The landlord did not ring. Howard Irons and Consuelo drank some glasses of Fine Cortado sherry and shared a bottle of Marques de Caceres, the best Spanish wine the local shop could offer, with olives for which Consuelo felt bound to apologise.

A couple of policemen came at the time the Ironses usually went to bed and the Estebans usually had dinner. Consuelo and Howard followed to watch.

Their knocks unanswered, the two young men with rather dismaying ease broke down the locked front door of the top flat.

The noise surged out even more loudly as the door opened.

"Hello, anyone here?"

Consuelo made to push past the policemen to get into the room it was coming from. One of them put up his arm to block her passage. "Something's been going on here, look at this."

"It was the fire, this mess. The woman was careless about this too, and there was a fire in the building, it is now since some many days."

"About a fortnight," Howard Irons said.

"It is the day I move in here," Consuelo said.

"It smells like it and more," the policeman said.

"Go on, go on, I implore you, the owner is not here."

"Hallo?" he called again, and then moved forward on the temporary covering of polythene sheeting that had been laid over the charred floorboards. He paused, his broad shoulders filling the gap of the open sitting-room door.

"What is it, why do you not . . .?"

Then the man turned and came back to the door where Howard Irons and Consuelo stood. "I'm going to have to ask you to go downstairs to your own flat for a while, madam, please."

Consuelo was a small, narrow woman and even in her spiky heels she was able to nip under the officer's arm and towards the sound. "I *will* turn it off at last," she said through the Opium-impregnated handkerchief she held clamped to her nose.

The sitting-room door opened away from the wall of the room, so from the hall it was only possible to see the straight line along the wall and to the window over the communal garden.

The blaring radio, plugged into a wall socket, was on the further window-sill.

As she reached it Consuelo glanced to her side, into the main part of the room. It was hardly furnished because so much had been destroyed in the fire or been removed after it. The floor in here was also sheeted in polythene. That was why blood had not dripped through the floor and through the ceiling of Consuelo's flat.

The blood had flowed like a gushing tap, spreading freely and wide. Had it ceased to flow because it congealed? Or because there was no more to come? Or because the dead heart ceased to pump it out of her neighbour's body? Poor Miss Redpath, poor woman.

Woman?

Consuelo was unconscious that she had vomited a projectile of bile from her mouth, or that she had been grabbed and steered out of the room, or that one policeman was chiding her, the other speaking into his radio, and Howard Irons was asking her what she'd seen.

"What is it, what's in there, what's happened, why didn't you turn the music off?"

"Woman?" Consuelo muttered. "*Mujer? Non, no era una mujer, era una hija joven*, a young girl. Rapine, murder, God help us, murder. In our house."

# CHAPTER
# SIXTEEN

"I really shouldn't be looking at this without Scarlett here," Saffron said, holding the sheaf of stiff pages. The paper had been in a dark place since it was written, so was not discoloured or stained. Only the pale ink and soft outlines of a manual tyewriter betrayed the fact that the document dated from a pre-electronic age.

"I thought Scarlett wasn't interested," Raymond said.

"But it's all so personal, you'd have thought —"

"You won't want me here then," Tess said, anxious to maintain her friendly relationship with Raymond's daughter.

Saffron began, "Well, if you wouldn't mind —"

"Darling, I'll leave you to it as well, if you think it's as private as all that," Raymond said.

"But Daddy —"

"No secrets between Tess and me," he said in an unusually decisive tone.

"No, Raymond, I don't want to make Saffron —"

"What's the point anyway? I'll only tell you everything afterwards," he said with an intimate smile.

Saffron, so far, had accepted the new relationship between her father and apple green Tess without any sign of resentment. Looking from one to the other, she said,

"You stay, Tess, if that's how Daddy feels about it. It's got to be old history, after all."

"Well, if you're sure, Saffron. Chuck me out if you change your mind."

"'Statement of Luisa Victoria Considine to Kenneth Hardman, Solicitor to the Supreme Court, 23 November 1965.' But Daddy, it's before you were even married."

"Old Hardman's been dead for years, he must have been pretty ancient even in 1965," Raymond Weiss said.

"But why ever was Mummy making a statement then? She must have been younger than I am now," Saffron wondered.

"I've no idea. Read on and see."

"'I make this statement of my own volition and in my own words knowing full well that it may be used in evidence in legal proceedings, or in evidence against me. I do so on the express understanding that the said statement will be kept under confidential seal by Wootton Hardman Ltd until twenty-five years after my decease unless certain circumstances, to be specified below, should arise.'"

"At that time she must have expected to live for many years. This wasn't supposed to be read till some time in the next century," Raymond said.

"Listen, this is obviously confidential family stuff, you don't want me to hear it," Tess made herself say.

"You're family now," Raymond said. "Sit down."

"Did Mummy ever tell you about this, Daddy?" Saffron asked.

"Not a sausage."

"Just say the minute you want me to go away," Tess said.

"The next page is where it really starts being in her own words," Raymond, who had been reading silently on, observed.

"Did she dictate it, do you think?" Tess asked.

"No, look, don't you recognise the typeface, Saffy, it's the same as all the manuscripts and her diaries. Luisa typed this out on her old Imperial herself, and then she and old Hardman initialled every page."

Saffron read aloud:

"Statement of Luisa Victoria Considine

"At the end of the summer term of 1965, which had been my third term at Corsham Art School, my mother, Mrs Imogen Ellice, arranged for me to travel to the United States and visit her cousins by marriage, Mr and Mrs Gerald Ellice, in New York and then go with them to their estate on Long Island for the summer. I arrived there on June 23rd.

"On July 2nd, Mrs Gerald Ellice, my cousin Sadie, fell seriously ill, having had a stroke. Cousin Gerald said I would have to return to England at once though I did not want to go back so soon. However he was anxious for me to leave, which I could understand as it was inconvenient to have me in the way when the apartment was turned upside down with nurses round-the-clock and the Ellices' daughter, who lived in Atlanta, needing her bedroom which I was using. So I decided to tell the Ellices I was going home but I did not ring to tell my mother so, for although she would have been scandalised and worried if she had known, I had made up my mind to stay in America and travel round on my own.

"Cousin Gerald drove me to Idlewild airport where I said goodbye to him and went inside, but as soon as he had gone I returned to the taxi rank and was taken to the Greyhound bus terminal downtown. I had enough money because my mother, not wanting me to be a charge on the Ellices, had given me enough travellers' cheques to last the ten weeks I was supposed to be away. I cashed two and bought a bus ticket which allowed me to travel anywhere in the country for the next two months. I set off that very afternoon for Washington DC."

"But girls just didn't *do* that kind of thing in 1965," Raymond exclaimed. "Travelling round the States all alone on a Greyhound bus — it was unheard of."

"She must already have been very self-assured," Tess remarked.

Saffron said, "We always knew Mummy was different, though, didn't we?

"I found a YWCA to stay in for two nights in Washington before going on south to Baltimore because in the Y I had met someone who told me of a family who would give me a job there as an au pair girl. I then lived in Baltimore for three weeks looking after the two small children of a urologist at Johns

Hopkins Medical School. While I was there I was introduced by my employers to an English girl called Gillian Betteridge, who was a third year student at the Slade School of Art. She had been in Baltimore for one semester on an exchange scholarship. We got on well, especially as we both wanted to be artists, so we decided to travel round the country together. I helped Gillian to buy her Greyhound bus ticket because she had no financial help from her foster family who, she told me, had lost interest in her once she was eighteen."

"It was Jill Williams!" Tess said softly. "So they really did meet in America."

"Mr Hardman has told me to list the places we visited on our journey and witnesses who would support it, but I have lost the diary I kept of our travels. We usually managed to find Ys to stay in, or cheap motels; a couple of times we were taken home and put up by people we met on the bus. Even complete strangers were incredibly hospitable. We never settled on a plan, but just zigzagged round at random as the bus timetable dictated since we tried to travel at night so as to save the cost of accommodation. Some of the places we stopped over at were San Antonio, Houston, a place in Louisiana called Tangipahoa, Denver, Salt Lake City and Phoenix, Arizona.

"We had agreed we wanted to see the Grand Canyon and the Rockies, and then get over to the west coast and hang round in Hollywood and San Francisco. But by the time we got to Arizona I was finding Gillian very irritating. We did not have much in common, apart from both being English art students. She was a foster child, estranged from the people who brought her up, who lived somewhere in the Midlands. She had been to a local grammar school and thought I was a snob in the way I behaved and for having been to public school and talking with a posh accent. St Paul's being a day school, I had not much experience of sharing a bedroom, let alone a bed, which we often had to do though always with a pillow between us."

"Luisa had never even heard of lesbians when we got married," Raymond said.
"Oh Dad!"
"No, honestly. Girls hadn't, in the mid-sixties."

"Gillian thought I was prudish and body-shy, whereas I found her embarrassingly uninhibited. I have no doubt I annoyed her just as much as she was beginning to annoy me, and perhaps, like me, she was trying to think of a polite way of saying we should continue separately, but I hesitated to leave her because I knew she could not have afforded to continue the journey without me there to help out. And we were both tired after so many uncomfortable journeys and broken nights. I was even beginning to think I might just give up and go home, because once I had got over being excited by the strangeness and foreignness, everything had become very predictable. Wherever we went in America there seemed to be the identical places in which to eat the identical food, and everyone we spoke to said the same things and asked the same questions. So I was feeling jaded and depressed, I could see Gillian was too, and we seemed to disagree and have coolnesses between us more and more.

"After Phoenix, where we had quarrelled and bickered about almost everything, I was determined that I really would do something, so I planned to break it to Gillian that I had had enough at the next stopover, which was going to be a night in some motel in Tucson.

"That day the Greyhound broke down. We had left very early, so I went to sleep in the seat, and was woken up by an almighty bang from underneath the chassis and then the bus stopped with a great jerk that shot me forward into the seat in front, giving me a headache which lasted for days. Gillian, who was sitting next to me, had been awake, so she managed to brace herself and was all right, though quite a lot of the other people in the bus, which had not been anywhere near full, were moaning a bit. But nobody was seriously hurt, they were just making a fuss.

"We seemed to be miles from anywhere, on a long straight empty road in the desert, but the driver came round and said a town was up ahead and if he could not stop a car or truck to take a message he would get up there himself to phone for help.

"We waited round for a long time. The other passengers were complaining a lot and it was incredibly hot whether we were in the sun or inside the bus so in the end I thought I would set off towards the town anyway and asked the driver to pick me up again when he caught up. I quite hoped Gillian would not want to come but she did. We both left our bags on the bus. I had my purse but not my passport as we went off together walking along the road.

"It was hotter and drier than I had ever imagined and by the time we had been walking for three-quarters of an hour I had a huge blister, Gillian was badly sunburnt and we were gasping with thirst. But the town was not all that far away, for we reached it by midday, and I have never seen anything more welcome than the Howard Johnson's diner on the highway.

"First we each used the rest room and drank lots of Coca Cola and then we told the bartender about the stranded bus so he could call the breakdown truck. There were not many people in the diner, but one was a tall young man with fair hair who came over because he had heard us talking and realised we were English. He was English too. He told us he was called Christopher Williams, Kit for short. He had been playing in a tennis tournament in California, representing his college, and just like us had decided not to fly back with his mates but to travel back slowly across America. He had hitch-hiked this far, and was expecting to pick up another lift.

"We sat there for ages, it was such a relief to have someone else to talk to as well as Gillian that even she seemed less infuriating. Kit told us about the people he had met playing tennis and the places he had seen. He had a new camera of a kind I had never seen, called a Polaroid, which developed the pictures on the spot, and we each took turns taking photographs of the other two together. Kit had some paper and envelopes so he sent his family one of the snaps and I sent one to my father, knowing he would never speak to my mother to let her know I was not with the Ellices any more. Gillian did not do the same because she said nobody would be interested.

"I liked Kit Williams very much but Mr Hardman has told me to emphasise that I was not then or at any time in love with him.

"Mummy's style wasn't anywhere near so dry in her books, do you suppose that Mr Hardman went over every word?" Saffron said.

"It is a bit like a school essay," Tess agreed.

"I expect old Hardman edited her first draft, Luisa never wrote like this," Raymond said. "He turned it into a legal document. But, for heaven's sake, why?"

"You read now, Daddy. It's making me feel sort of funny."

"Have a drink, Saffron, here's some water," Tess said.

"I don't mean thirsty. Nervous. Apprehensive. I'm scared of what's coming next."

Raymond pulled the folder towards him, less affected by this voice from the past than Saffron was. Under the table his leg was pressed against Tess's but she was obscurely embarrassed by the combination of his former and new love, and nervous of intruding on the intimacies obviously still to come, so she casually rose and moved over to the window and stood facing the stupendous view, with her back to the chaotic little room which was the Weisses' retreat from paying guests.

Raymond's tone was deep, harmonious and even authoritative. He read on.

"Kit Williams said why did not the three of us go on together, and we were discussing which direction to take when we were joined at the table by a man of about thirty wearing formal clothes unlike anyone else in the diner. He had on a dark suit, white shirt, striped tie and polished shoes. His skin was very tanned, his hair black in a very short crew cut, his eyes large and light brown. I am confident I would recognise him again. He carried a briefcase from which he took some religious tracts. He said everyone called him Junior so we should too. We said our names were Gilly and Kit and Lulu —

"She never let anyone call her Lulu," Raymond interpolated. "Never, when I knew her.

"— and he told us about a revolution in his life and how he had Found God and become part of the great family of believers. He had been a sinner and very unhappy, but now he was redeemed.

"He was very attractive and amusing, and told lots

of jokes and anecdotes, and although I did not feel very comfortable with his subject, I was quite impressed all the same, and found myself listening and agreeing more than I would have expected of myself, because at school and college I had a reputation for always disputing and answering back.

"After a while I realised that both Gillian and Kit were even more impressed by Junior than I was, they were hanging on his words. I made myself ask some questions because I did not want him to think I was a pushover like they were, and he answered me so cleverly and sensibly that I could not argue with him at all, especially as my companions were shushing me and saying I should not interrupt. Junior was interested in us all and wanted to know where we had come from and what our families were like and when they expected us home and how much longer we would be travelling round America. I told him all about my mother and stepfather and my father's place in Cornwall, and that they all thought I was safely with relations, and Kit, who said he had been to Eton and his people lived in a place in Herefordshire, said nobody was expecting him home for months. Gillian said she was alone in the world and entirely her own mistress.

"Junior insisted on buying us a meal which we had in the diner, and afterwards when there was no sign of the Greyhound bus we all admitted we were feeling very sleepy, having had such an early start to the day, although I later suspected Junior had put some sedative in our food. He suggested we should go back with him to his ranch, which he said was not far away, where his kinfolk would be happy to offer us hospitality. We agreed, and told the bartender we would collect our stuff later if the bus driver left it with him when he came by.

"Junior's car was outside the diner and its seats were so soft and deep that we all fell asleep while he drove. We must have travelled quite a long way, for the sun had almost set when he woke us by saying, 'Here we are.'

"We were driving along a dirt track. The desert and the cactuses and stones and distant mountains all looked pink in the setting sunlight. I do not know how long it had been since Junior turned off the highway.

"It became dark very quickly and there were no lights in the desert as far as I could see out of the car windows. I caught sight of a high wire fence and began to feel nervous, wondering where we were being taken to. Then we slowed down at some high gates in another fence, which seemed to open automatically, for I did not see anyone nearby. Kit Williams asked, 'Where on earth are we?' and Junior said, 'Nearly home.' Then he stopped the car at a gate in a high stone wall. He said, 'Here we are, come right in. Come and join the kinfolk.'"

"Oh my God."
"Tess? What is it?" Raymond said.
"Now I know where they were. The Kinfolk!"
"What does it mean?"

"It means they were at Tarrant's Crossing."

"What! Luisa at . . . ? It's not possible, she'd have told me!" Raymond knew the full implications of that name.

Saffron didn't. "What are you talking about, what do you mean? I've never heard of —"

"Read on, please read on," Tess urged. Raymond steadied his voice and hands and continued.

"There were lots of people in the house when we arrived that evening, and at first we just thought they were all Junior's family. Everyone was introduced by their Christian names or nicknames. I remember Hank, Chuck, Kiddo, Beth, Norbert, Amy, Martha, Lisbet, Carole, Walt, Ikey, Pete, Mo and Simeon, but there were many others. I never heard anyone's surname and I do not think Gillian and I ever gave ours. There was a children's house, which I never went into, and some of the women were pregnant.

"It was only the next day that we understood the word Kinfolk did not refer to Junior's relations. It meant the people who had come to join the community of believers.

"I will not describe my first impressions of the ranch because they were deceptive. It took me some days to understand that we were in a religious community of people who followed, obeyed and even worshipped the leader, who was known as Swami. I do not know his real name.

"Junior was one of the brethren too. His task was to go out into the highways and byways and spread the word. He told us he wanted to influence the world for the good."

"Wait a moment," Tess said.

"What is it?"

"That phrase, influencing the world for the good, where does that come from?"

"I don't know."

"I'm sure I came across it not so long ago, goodness knows where though. Never mind, sorry I interrupted, do go on."

"I learnt he also carried out any of the community's practical dealings with the outside world, for although the ranch was a very long way from any other habitation and almost entirely self-sufficient, with its own water supply which we pumped by hand, there were still local taxes and charges and so on that had to be paid. I do not think the ranch was on the telephone. I believe Junior (whose real name I do not know) was the community's treasurer.

"There were about sixty other people living there, all of them members of the Kinfolk and most young to middle-aged, both men and women and nearly all American although I met one Mexican, one French-woman and a Lebanese married couple. Nobody was black.

"Except for Swami himself, the Kinfolk slept in dormitories, ate in a refectory and worked at running the house and land, mostly growing food. There were rosters for duties. At first I was set to canning beans for the winter stores and Gillian became a cleaner. As far as I know Kit worked in the fields. I did not object to working, being quite glad to stay in one place for a while after so much travelling round, but we did not find out very much about the other Kinfolk, because there was a rule of almost invariable silence, called Tongue Guard. We were permitted to talk to each other only at the evening meal, before Swami spoke to us. Swami had lived in a lamasery in Tibet, where he had found enlightenment.

"I admit that I believed Swami to be a remarkable person but my companions actually believed he was a superior being who had been granted superhuman revelations and powers. I was afraid to admit to being less dazzled by Swami than the other Kinfolk. There may have been some others who were un-convinced but I did not know of any. I cannot explain why I was not completely bowled over by him like everyone else, though perhaps it is worth mentioning here that I was an unsuitable subject for hypnosis when we had an experiment at school.

"The days were like I supposed they would be in a convent and for a while, although the life was phys-ically exhausting, I found it restful, after being on the road, like going on a retreat.

"It was not until we had been at the ranch for three or four days that I began to realise what we had got ourselves into and by then Gillian had been duped to such an extent that she believed herself to be in paradise. I know now it would not have been easy for me to get away at that point, and it might actually have been impossible, because the compound was enclosed by the two high fences I had glimpsed on the way in and guarded by Kinfolk against intruders. I understood later that they had guns. I now know I would not have been allowed to get away but I never even tried because I did not feel I could go without Gillian and she would not consider leaving when I whispered the suggestion to her in the communal shower room.

"We were the most recent arrivals and I eventually realised that everyone else had been with the Kinfolk long enough to have been very effectively brainwashed, even those who had once come there as casually and unintentionally as we had. I gathered that some members had been there for several years. They had lost all contact with their families. When I discovered that I began to be frightened that we would somehow be stuck there too. I began to understand I was a prisoner.

"There did not seem to be a single person on the ranch, except for me, who was observing what went on in any way rather than throwing themselves into participating wholeheartedly. Gillian told me the moment she had surrendered her soul to Swami had been the greatest relief of her life, like putting down a heavy burden. As far as I could see Kit had become an ardent disciple of Swami's too, though I never had a chance to speak to him alone.

"In retrospect I can see that I too was bemused to some extent, for I had agreed without any hesitation to hand over all my money. I later discovered that people newly adopted into the family always paid their way by depositing everything they possessed in the Kinfolk's funds; and one or two of those I talked to had once been rich, and said it was their greatest joy to have passed the burden on.

"I now realise Swami used hypnotic powers; but I also believe some sedative or hallucinatory drugs were routinely put into the communal dinner pot. Otherwise I cannot understand how I could have taken the ceremonies we attended so calmly and even, after the first one, joined in. Nevertheless, I am now deeply regretful and ashamed of the part I played in the rituals enacted at Tarrant's Crossing, as I later discovered the ranch was called.

"Mr Hardman has told me not to go into details about what went on there though I am haunted by my experiences and long to put them into words, but Mr Hardman says this is not the place to describe —"

"Raymond? Tess?"

"Not just now."

"Hallo, are you in there? Can I come in?"

Raymond dragged himself into the present day as Ilona Spivak came into the room. He said, "It's a bad moment, Ilona, I'm so sorry, can it wait for half an hour?"

Saffron was still far away and long ago. She muttered, "We've got to finish this, Daddy, don't stop now."

But a young woman came into the room behind Ilona.

234

She was a police constable in uniform, black tights, navy skirt, festooned with equipment, and with a muffled squawk emitted by the speaker hooked on her shoulder.

Raymond said, "Annie Hicks! My dear girl, your mother told me you'd joined the force, it's good to see you."

"Good morning, Mr Weiss, thank you. Are you Miss Redpath?"

"Yes."

"May I have a word with you?"

"Of course, fire ahead."

"In private, please, madam."

Tess felt the blood draining from her own cheeks. Raymond gripped her arm and pushed her down on to a chair.

In a husky rasp, Tess asked, "What is it? What's the matter? Is it Lara? Biddy? Has something happened?"

# CHAPTER
# SEVENTEEN

Tess was required to get to London as quickly as possible. The police drove her with blue light flashing to Newquay airport, where she just caught a scheduled flight and was escorted to the last available seat on it. She was met at Heathrow by a synthetically sympathetic civilian from Notting Dale police station.

This journey hardly registered on her mind at all. She moved in a stupor. The voice snarling inside her head was not one she recognised, not the Tess who always told herself to be nice. She was possessed by a warped, vicious alien, whose hideous thoughts seemed natural because the order of life had been turned upside down. Somewhere in her mind was an incubus telling her so. It made no difference to the scheme of things, women and children were born, and lived, and died and were forgotten, why should Biddy and Lara be exempt? Because they were Tess's family? What did Tess need a family for? She was self-sufficient, wasn't she? Surfacing momentarily, as the coffee from a paper cup scalded her gullet, she told herself this was self-protection. If she let loneliness or lost love into her head now she would go mad. She would pull the world down about herself. How could these people be going about their daily business, be laughing or eating or snoring, jaws dropped, heads cocked against the plane seat, when Biddy, calm, kind, protective, affectionate Biddy was . . . No. Measure Biddy against the countless armies of the dead. A grain of sand, no more. Weigh Lara against the children killed in wars, raped, shovelled into gas chambers or mass graves. What was so special about this child, that she should have been immune? The earth would still turn on its axis without her. Tess sat taut and still as she was moved insensibly towards London, and welcomed horrors into her mind, to drown the other, unthinkable horror.

Raymond behaved with a dynamism Saffron had never seen and did not much like. He swept random belongings into a suitcase, leapt into the old Volvo and set off eastwards at speed, arriving in Arundel Gardens only a couple of hours after Tess had been faced with the polythene-shrouded devastation in her flat. By that time the photographers and reporters had gone and the two bodies had been taken away to a mortuary.

Tess, meanwhile, had been escorted down to the police station. She was trying to force her fogged mind into working out where her brother-in-law could be and where Paul, her nephew, was. Someone had to tell them.

Malcolm had rung Biddy and left her a message on Tess's answering machine. The police had removed it from Tess's flat and played it to her.

First she heard her own voice from the day before, which was the day after her last words with Lara had been cut short by a ring at the door bell, the day, she was told, after the innocent Lara, leading the caller into the sitting-room, had turned and faced the gun that killed her. The day after Biddy, without pulling the plug out, had got out of the bath, presumably called out to ask who was there, and in her turn been shot dead. Her body, draped in a towel, was lying across the side of the bath. The towel, the bathmat, the floor and the soapy water were all drenched in her blood.

Tess shuddered at the sound of her own strange, cheerful voice. "I'm having a marvellous time," it said. "There's someone you've got to meet. I can't wait to tell you, both of you, I'm so happy, are you out somewhere having fun? Give me a call here the minute you get in, the number's 01736 —"

She said helplessly, "I wanted them to know about Raymond. Raymond Weiss. In Cornwall. Our . . . That's how you found me, isn't it? You must have used the phone number."

The messages played inexorably on.

The builders: a delay in delivery of the parquet floor she had chosen, they wouldn't be there till next week.

The surgery: Tess was due for a smear at the Well Women clinic.

The Samaritans: could Tess possibly help out again, they had lots of people off sick.

"I once trained as a Samaritan but I don't have a regular time, I just fill in when they are short," she explained pointlessly to the two officers who were rehearing the tape with her.

"This is the one we want you to hear, madam," one said.

238

Malcolm's voice. "Hi Bids, hi Lara, how's my two best girls? I'm at home now, AOK here, Ma's settled in fine, they don't need me and Kurt says I'm due a few days so I'm off sailing with the chaps. See you next week, take care."

The officer said, "Where does Mr Trevail sail, do you know?"

Tess had not the faintest idea. "I didn't even know he did sail. But I'm sure he hasn't got a boat of his own, Biddy would have . . ." Her sister's name on her lips felt like a sudden wound in her head, as though the gun that took Lara's and Biddy's lives had pierced her too. From the moment she had heard of the crime, Tess had been frozen into calm. Now, suddenly, her control melted and she screamed the names of her sister and her beloved niece, a gut-wrenched emission of agony and misery from a mouth open in a black hole of despair. Her hands tore at her clothes, pulling them, wrenching them into tatters. Some atavistic instinct directed her hands to her hair. She began to tug and tear at it. Somewhere there were voices and footsteps but she was impervious to them. And then a stab at her upper arm, and merciful oblivion.

Temporary oblivion. Malcolm needed to be told. The police needed the bodies identified. The next of kin must do it, Biddy's husband, Lara's father. Paul was too young. He hadn't been told.

Lara was too young, she shrieked, but no sound came out.

But nobody could find Malcolm. They couldn't wait,

they had to be sure who the girl and the woman were, whose blood-drained bodies had lain on the floor of Tess's home.

Tess had never seen a dead person before.

Tess must do it.

Tess must be driven to the mortuary and put on a gown and a mask and rubber boots and be guided with a hand on her arm across the cold tiles to the high tables each with a green mound laid out on it and it was Tess who must look and keep looking as an attendant pulled the green covering back, folding it a little way to hide as much as could be hidden while letting her see enough to be sure what, who —

The skin waxy, yellowed, the chicken pox pits enhanced but lines of ageing smoothed, the protruding tooth still biting the lower lip, the first pale brown liver spot on the white forehead. It was Biddy. My sister, she thought, my only — A tight grip on her arm, just above the elbow, a hand in hers.

He's done this before. He saw his wife like this, Raymond saw Luisa. He's strong, he survived. I can't look, I can't see my own darling girl

The cloth was pulled back. A bandage had been tied over the forehead, high white swathes of cloth. Concealment, not cure. Underneath — no.

The part of her face you can see is peaceful. White, calm, like an alabaster statue, the regular lips smoothed into a sculptured neutrality, heavy white lids closed over her eyes with the blackened lashes moon-shaped on the cheeks.

She's not dead, she's asleep, Tess told herself. Lara's not dead.

"Is this Lara Trevail? You needn't speak, Miss Redpath, a nod will do."

Raymond's voice, awed, appalled. "It could be you lying there, she's so like you. It could be Tess."

"It's my — it's Lara, my baby, my . . . !"

Over Tess's hiccups and gasps, Inspector Rogerson spoke to Raymond.

"We believe the girl was taken for her aunt. The perpetrator thought it was Miss Redpath."

"And Biddy Trevail?"

"Came in when she heard the noise and killed to keep her quiet. That's the way it looks to us."

# CHAPTER
# EIGHTEEN

The whine of hatred was in Tess's ears when she came round from the sedative. Her head was instantly clear, her brain felt keen and icy cold, as though the events she had experienced had been in a memorably cathartic film. All emotion was spent.

Her family, Biddy and Lara, had been shot dead, killed, left lying in their own blood in Tess's home. She had seen the traces of the crime. She had looked on their bodies. But not a twinge of human sorrow stirred in her. It was a tale told by a stranger, about strangers, to a stranger — herself, the new, onlooking Tess, now woken and sitting up, looking round, as unsurprised by her strange surroundings as she was unmoved by human feelings. Instead she heard the snarl which had filled her mind on the journey to London. Two people more or less, it said, what's the difference? The world didn't need them. You won't miss them. You hardly ever saw them. What do you need a sister and a niece for?

No "Be nice, Tess" came. The heartless, unfeeling cynic she had spent a lifetime suppressing had taken over. Forced at last to admit into her consciousness the impermissible underside, she had woken from a dream into the nightmare which turned out to be real life, full of blood, hate, revenge, destruction.

She was in a strange bed, in a room impersonally furnished in beige and cream like a three star hotel. The window was covered by a close-fitting metallic blind. She could not be bothered to raise it and look out.

She saw she was wearing men's pyjamas, pale blue poplin. Their packaging was in the waste-paper basket beside the glass-topped coffee table. They had come from Peter Jones.

The bathroom contained everything one could possibly need, all in new, unopened boxes. Tess used the lavatory. She saw her period had started. A box of tampons had been provided. Clean your teeth, the voice nagged, brush your hair. Obeying, Tess looked at the stranger in the mirror, gaunt and diminished, no longer a Dutch doll. Lara had wished to look pale and interesting, Tess recalled without a twinge.

When she came out of the bathroom Raymond was waiting. He had brought a tray with a vacuum jug of coffee and some rolls and some individual packs of milk and butter. Isn't he old, the voice said. He has wattles and wrinkles, there is an ugly mole on his neck, his eyes are fading.

He looked at her cautiously, wondering, she could tell, whether to sweep her into the cradle of his arms, but she made a movement which immediately deterred him. He said, "You slept a long time."

"What time is it now?"

"Mid-morning. When you feel up to it they want to talk to you."

"Who?" Tess asked indifferently.

"The police. Detective Inspector Rogerson."

"Is he here? What is this, some hotel?"

"No, they call it a safe house. We're in Surrey. It's a hide-out of some sort."

Like a serpent stirring under the muddy bottom of the sea a familiar emotion pushed at Tess's conscious mind. Fear? No, indifference. She would stay indifferent.

"Why?" she said.

"They think you aren't safe."

Safe, safe, what does safe matter? You're expendable too, the inner voice mocked. Who needs you?

"Are you all right?" Raymond asked.

"Fine."

"You haven't drunk your coffee. Look, I've put sugar in, your blood sugar must be low."

"I'm fine."

"Tess..." She moved backwards, away from his intimate gaze and reaching hands. No hurt showed in his face. He said steadily, "I wanted you to know what they seem to be thinking."

She sat on the side of the bed, clasping her hands tightly in her lap, her eyes fixed somewhere in the middle distance but her ear cocked to hear what he had to say. He moved backwards to the built-in unit, desk or dressing-table, and put his hands out to grip its surface. She saw his knuckles whiten. He was nervous and tense. Well, she thought, and so?

"Inspector Rogerson had a letter from Desmond Kennedy."

"Desmond," she murmured as though the name meant

244

nothing to her. But it did. Her gay neighbour. Fag, queer, homo, nancy boy. What had Jacques called him? Poofter. The poofter was probably dead by this time, she thought coldly, he's taken his galloping Aids to a warm and distant sea and drowned himself. But he was your friend, a subversive whisper murmured. And so? asked the snarling incubus, so what? Friends die. In another five years, less, in five months it would seem as though he had never been. No loss. Nobody was any loss.

"Kennedy drew Rogerson's attention to similarities between my Luisa's suicide and Jill Williams's, just as you pointed out to me yourself. They were interested in that already because the Isle of Man police have reopened the Jill Williams case, the suicide verdict isn't satisfactory. Something to do with scientific tests that weren't available when Luisa died, chemical analysis of the rope fibres, I think they said but I couldn't care less about the details, only the results."

Why's he telling me this, what does it matter? she thought. Dead and gone, all those women, four of them, all dead and gone and soon forgotten.

Raymond sat beside her on the bed, but Tess remained rigid and unyielding. She remembered she had thought she loved him. She knew she had promised to stay with him for ever. Who had that woman been, the soft, anxious to please, easily pleased Tess Redpath who told herself she was experiencing love? That woman had been killed too, like all the others, Luisa, Jill, Biddy, Lara. Someone else, long suppressed, had come to life in her place, a realist who saw things plain, not sicklied over with a pale cast of sentimentality. The Tess who

245

had thought there must be niceness, love and kindness in the world had gone. Ugliness was truth.

He had taken her hand in his. The skin on his hand was loose, spotted with large brown freckles, with brindled hairs on the back of his fingers. His grasp was warm but she did not find it comforting. He said, "We didn't have time to talk about — I don't know what you think about religion. There's a vicar ready to come and talk to you if it would help."

Once upon a time Tess had been a Methodist. After that she'd been what her mother called a Christmas Christian. She said indifferently, "No thanks."

"Mightn't it be some sort of comfort?"

"Comfort? To pray to a deity who . . ." The thought bored her. She did not finish the sentence.

"Luisa was brought up a Catholic. After she died I tried to keep it up for the girls' sake, but I found I couldn't either. I'll tell them you don't want it."

Soggy, she thought, wet, useless. What's he for?

He echoed her thought. "I know I'm not being much use, Tess, but you know I'm here for you."

"I'll manage."

"You'll be numb, just now, I remember it. Then you'll be furious, don't be surprised when you're so angry you can't speak or think or anything. After that you'll feel ashamed because you are alive and they aren't. And sick. And terrified, panic-struck. But I'll be there, I'll help you. And if there's to be a press conference, best for it to be now while you feel somehow frozen and separate from it all. Do you think you're up to it?"

"Me?"

"You and Malcolm together. Your nephew Paul's been sent to Malcolm's parents."

"Why?"

"To protect him from —"

"No. Why me at a press conference?"

"They want you to appeal for witnesses to come forward, you might jog a memory, there might be some-one who noticed a stranger going into your house."

"Rogerson's told you to sell me the idea, has he?" she said.

"My dear one. Tess. Listen, I know what you're going through, I understand how you feel. Nothing I can do is going to help, I realise that, though anything you want, you only have to say. I . . ." He paused, and added very softly, "I've been there myself."

He hasn't, the voice jeered, he couldn't have, he's soggy, soft-centred, he doesn't understand. He's a loser. He's battened on to his wife's memory, lived off her for years, he's a second-rater.

After a pause in the internal dialogue, her own voice sounded in her head. It said, "So are you." Aloud, Tess said, "I'll do the press conference."

"But you've got to be very brave, and speak to Roger-son first. He's downstairs, waiting for you. He has so many questions, things only you can answer, even though you were in Cornwall when . . . when it hap-pened."

"I was speaking to Lara at the very moment her killer came, which no doubt the itemised telephone records will prove," Tess said coldly.

"Oh my dear girl, I'm so —"

"I'll need my clothes."

Her clothes were in the wardrobe, hung there by whoever it was that had undressed her and put her to bed. Tess put them on, the denim jeans, blue chambray shirt and herringbone tweed jacket she had chosen on a morning — yesterday morning — when she had leapt from her bed full of enthusiasm for the day to come and happiness about the day that had passed. That Tess was dead. She had been killed too.

Tess had seen all this before, on television. She had watched as desperate people bared their souls. She remembered their clothes, their shaking voices, but not what they said. It was all just entertainment, of a kind.

Tess was not a desperate person. She was calm and controlled. What did it matter? What did anything matter?

The room was at Notting Dale police station, to which they were driven in a police car with motor-cycle outriders. Tess supposed anyone watching would think she was a dangerous criminal.

The table, on a low dais, was covered with a green baize cloth. Why was it always green? The air was stale, tainted by old smoke and humanity. There was a carafe of slightly scummy water and two thick glasses. There was a pad of paper and a sharp pencil. What was she expected to write? There was a fringe of little oblong tape recorders and microphones on stands covering the full length of the table, the black snouts pointing towards her like the muzzles of a pack of questing hounds. Four television cameras were mounted on tall tripods, with ducking, dodging men peering first at her and then through their viewfinders. The windowless, low-ceilinged room was full of moulded grey plastic chairs, nearly all occupied, most of them by men. At the back, their eyes scanning to and fro across the audience, stood police officers. It was thought the killer might try to get in as a reporter. Press passes had been scrupulously scrutinised, weapons checks made.

There were four chairs at the table. A woman police constable sat beside Tess, no doubt with smelling salts at the ready. But she wouldn't need those. This was another ritual, as the inquest and funeral would be, meaningless, pointless exercises to be endured. Once upon a time that other woman who had been called Tess would have been nervous in front of this critical audience, and devoured by anxiety and vanity at the thought of her face on the screen. She'd have made the car stop so she could buy make-up and insisted on having her hair done. None of it meant anything now. They could take her as she was or leave her, like it or lump it.

Which was more than Malcolm could. He sat on Inspector Rogerson's other side, a stout man collapsed in upon himself. His eyes were bloodshot and swollen and although he had shaved, patches of grey stubble still showed on his glistening face. Someone had combed the straggles of sandy hair sideways across the dome of his skull. His trembling hand plucked continuously at the open collar of his green polo shirt. His face was blank. He was so heavily sedated that his only greeting to Tess had been to fall, heavily and weeping, into her embrace. He could hardly speak. Tess would do the talking.

She looked at the waiting reporters. Few were bothering to note the words of Rogerson's statement. They were waiting for the meat of the interview, the bereaved family's shaky, heartfelt appeal. The words had been written out for her in large print on a card the WPC slid in front of Tess. "If anyone saw anything, anything at all, that might give a clue . . ." She read them aloud in a flat monotone. Then she listened to her interrogators.

The first few were the routine questions addressed to everyone else who had ever sat in this place. Were there any suspects? Don't say his name in public, for God's sake! Rogerson had exclaimed, when Tess mentioned Jacques. So she pretended there were no suspects. What could have been the motive? Was it true that Tess Redpath's flat had been burgled shortly before, should the police have supplied protection after that, had the authorities slipped up?

Then came the sensational stuff. Was it the case that Tess Redpath had found out something about Petronella Williams which might have been the motive for the attacks intended to be on her? That was the ITN reporter. He didn't mention Petronella's powerful new protectors. He didn't need to. Everyone knew what he meant. Had the prince's family tried to rub Tess out because of something she knew?

Rogerson had told her to play her cards close to her chest. What did he mean? What cards? Tess answered the question, ignoring the meaningful, sexless pressure on her left thigh.

She thought, They wanted me to go public so I bloody well will. "I know one thing about Jill Williams. She was in hiding most of her life because she was afraid the same thing would happen to her as had happened twenty-five years earlier to her one-time friend Luisa Weiss, she'd be murdered. She was right to be afraid. The moment they appeared in public and had their pictures in the media, they were both rubbed out."

Uproar. Then out of the competitive clamour of calls and queries came one she could understand. "What did it have to do with you, Tess? Why did you turn into a target?"

Rogerson had asked the same question. It was one to which the answer had come to her without thought, as though it had always been waiting. "It was because of the piece about Jill and Luisa with my by-line in the *Sentinel*. I said I knew what the connection was."

"What was it?"

"Tess!"

"Tess, over here, the *Evening —*"

"What did you know?"

"Where did Luisa meet Jill?"

"Does Petronella know?"

"Did Petronella tell you?"

"Who's doing all this?"

Why ask me? How should I know? Floundering in the wave of curiosity, Tess felt like a piece of floating debris, buffeted and tossed around, without understanding or will or interest. She was no more than a target, a passive block. *They* understood, *they* planned, *they* decided — whoever they were. Other people settled what must happen to Tess, what had happened to her family, but she had no say in the matter, or clues or explanations or volition.

"How should I know?" she muttered.

Rogerson's angry, powerful voice topped the chorus. "That's enough, folks, that'll do for today, no more questions."

The WPC had already gripped Tess's arm painfully above the elbow, trying to shut her up. "Time to go," she said.

On the way to the door a man stepped in front of Tess, darting under an arm to hug her and kiss her cheeks. He ignored Rogerson's dismissive gesture and the two uniformed officers who stepped beside him, isolating Tess and himself in a corner of privacy.

"Tessie, I'm so sorry, we all are, everyone sent their sympathy." It was Archie Frazer. Tess had forgotten the *Argus*'s crime reporter would be there. Realising an old friend had been watching shook her composure, as though the old Tess was waiting to burst through her new hard shell.

"Thanks, Archie, that's kind."

"Is there anything I can do for you? Come and crash out at my place, if you like, as you can't use —"

"No, I won't be staying in London, I'll go home to Cornwall, it's safe there," she said. She did not know she had made that decision until she heard her own voice.

# CHAPTER
# NINETEEN

"I saw you on TV," Saffron said. She was hovering awkwardly in the small kitchen, alternately sitting on the leatherette stool and getting up to stare out of the window over the sink, which looked on to a garden already, in so few days, shaggy and neglected. The nicely fitted kitchen, all blond wood and sky blue formica, seemed degraded too, in spite of Tess's cleaning and tidying. It ought not to be difficult to reproduce Biddy's meticulous housewifery but somehow one kept noticing that her touch was missing. Not that it mattered. Paul had gone to stay with his maternal grandparents and had so far refused to enter his motherless home for a single minute. Malcolm was there but he didn't want anything from the kitchen. Slumped on the sofa in front of the sports channel, he spent his time getting quietly drunk. Meanwhile Tess's mother had made one of those rapid descents into further dislocation which, they had been warned, were characteristic of Alzheimer's patients. Lena Redpath did not know that her elder daughter and only granddaughter were dead. She had become oblivious to the fact that they had ever lived.

I don't know what I'm doing here, Tess thought. Malcolm, not yet silenced by his first whisky, made it abundantly clear he blamed Tess — as though she didn't blame herself. Her flat, her enemy, her responsibility. He didn't want her there, he wouldn't let her touch Biddy's things or Lara's, so she was sleeping in Paul's chaotic room and keeping clear of her brother-in-law. But where else ought she to be?

I suppose I'll think of something soon, she told herself. After the inquest. And the funeral. She could not bring herself to think of either, and in any case both were to be delayed until some authority said they could go ahead. Until then they were all in limbo. But where was limbo?

At Thalassa, according to Raymond. "Even if you've changed your mind about me, about us, it's still your refuge. We're waiting for you."

This morning, day three of the new Tess's dark new life, Saffron, shy but determined, had appeared on the doorstep. Still dressed in droopy informality, she was carrying a florist's formal bouquet of unnaturally fluorescent orange carnations and could not look Tess in the eye. None the less she followed her into the kitchen and accepted a mug of Nescafé without milk because Tess had forgotten to buy any. "You could have something to eat," Tess said vaguely. Indeed there was a wide choice of things to eat, because neighbours and sympathisers had been delivering offerings, usually in person, but often just leaving them on the doorstep — casseroles and pies, biscuits and cakes. On the first day the encamped reporters had been glad of them, but media interest had moved elsewhere by now. Some late-comers had laid polythene-wrapped flowers in the street against the picket fence, among them one pale blue teddy bear. Tess wanted someone to clear the lot away because whenever Malcolm's bleary eyes fell on them he let out an animal-like wail of agony.

Saffron could see him through the open serving hatch, a great, grey man slumped in front of American football. A dirty sweat shirt had ridden up over his belly. His feet were bare. The low, stained table was covered with cans and dirty glasses. Tess had tried to clear them away but he had glared and cursed.

Saffron averted her eyes and made herself meet Tess's. Saffron was dismayed to see the change in her. She looked, to Saffron, all mourning mauve, and her face, which a few days before had seemed so bright and animated, was stodgily blank. Then, Saffron could quite see why Raymond had fallen for Tess. Now the only emotion she could provoke was pity.

"Actually," Saffron said, "I came to take you back to Thalassa, I've got the Volvo."

"I suppose that's your father's idea."

"He would like you to come, yes, but it's not only that. Please come. I've got something to show you, Tess, Dad wants you to see it before we give it to the police, I've discovered what this is all about."

## Statement of Luisa Victoria Considine, continued

The fourth evening we were at the ranch was Sunday. Swami conducted a long service which was religious but not Christian. Males and females sat on opposite sides of the room. Children sat at the front.

A group of musicians played guitars and drums, to which we sang. Something akin to incense, which was sweet but different from the one I am familiar with in church, made me feel woozy. I now realise I was inhaling a mind-altering drug.

Swami preached, speaking, shouting and intoning for a long time but it did not feel too long. Everyone there had entered a trance-like state, in which Swami seemed to be a holy prophet, perhaps even a god.

I believed Swami had made me understand I was a sinner and Junior had sought me out on the highways and byways to save me. But my sins were very terrible. I knew I must be punished and abase myself before I would be fit for Swami to touch with the long nail of his little finger.

We were punished in the presence of the Kinfolk. With his own sacred hand Swami chastised me and when I cried out he told me the sound would expel the devil within me. He beat me with a three-foot paddle, and Junior held a microphone to my lips as I screamed. The Kinfolk echoed my cries.

I could say much more about this. It is an indelible memory. But Mr Hardman has told me to delete the details of Swami's discipline since they are not relevant.

During the week after my first punishment I was ill and weak, but I had to work in the fields all the same. I believed the harsh regime was saving my soul, and Swami was cruel to be kind. I was determined to be cured of my wickedness and former sins but at the same time with a small part of my mind I was angry and resentful, and hated Swami for what he was doing to me.

It was the following week that the women examined me to see if I was fit to be summoned to Swami's chamber. Mr Hardman has told me to confirm I was a virgin before this time.

The other women saw that I was washed and scented, they brushed my hair for an hour and shaved all my body hair, even from my arms. Gillian and I were the youngest of the women, and during the next weeks Swami chose one of us, or sometimes both of us at once, almost every night. Once, when we were both unclean, one of the children was sent to satisfy him, and when she began to scream the Kinfolk sang loud enough to drown the sound.

I lost count of the time we had been at the ranch, but we must have been there for about six weeks before I began to come to my senses. It was on a day when my morning porridge cup fell off the table before I had eaten anything and I was punished immediately. I now realise the communal porridge must always have been drugged because that day, although my back was painful from the chastisement, my mind was properly clear for the first time, and even when I went to Swami, he felt like an ordinary man and not a god. Suddenly I was amazed at myself for having submitted to him and his monstrous regime for all this time, and terrified by what was happening to me. I was afraid I had completely lost my will and powers of self-determination and would stay at the ranch for ever, like the other Kinfolk, deluded and betrayed by a man who, however charismatic, repelled me now. Before that I had taken for granted he was above any mortal moral code. I suddenly understood, as well, that the pointless, painful rules we had to obey wore our critical faculties down. The Kinfolk had lost all self-respect. But now I found I could remember my family, to whom I had not given a thought for weeks, and realised I had to get away before it was too late, and I must get Gillian away too, although as far as I knew she had no desire to leave Swami and the ranch.

But the ranch was fenced in, the gate was guarded, I had lost my money and passport, I did not know where we were or who to ring for help if I could reach a telephone, and I was so weakened by the diet, and the tension, and the chastisements, I knew I would not be able to walk very far, while the nearest help might be miles and miles away.

That day I tried to speak to Gillian, but she refused to listen to me and I did not dare to press on for fear she would tell on me to the Kinfolk. Then I tried to find Kit, and saw him in the distance with the other men, but his face was dazed and stupefied and he did not seem to know me. I felt very alone.

For the next few days I managed to pretend to eat the porridge but not in fact to eat it. If anyone had suspected me, the deception would have been easy to discover but I was careful not to let anything show in my face or behaviour. I tried to keep a good eye out for some way of escaping.

I realised Junior was my only hope because he was the only person who ever seemed to leave the compound, but I was careful to avoid him for fear he would have seen what I was thinking.

I thought a lot about the ranch at that time and since and have come to the conclusion that Swami really did believe himself to be a celestial being, as he claimed, and was deluded, not just plain wicked, even when he abused young children. In fact I do not even think he was consciously a confidence trickster or a fraud, rather I am convinced Swami was sincere. Wrong and criminal, but nevertheless sincere.

Swami called Junior his son, and I believe this was more than an expression, for I could see a physical likeness between them, although Swami was fat and old. Their eyes were the same colour, and their heads, Swami's bald and Junior's crewcut, both the same high-domed, almost pointed shape.

I am certain Junior did not believe in his father but cynically manipulated him and all the people who became Kinfolk, knowing exactly what he was doing when he enticed people to the ranch. He was very persuasive. I also think he had some kind of hypnotic ability, not as powerful as Swami's but enough to influence many people. I remember how his amber eyes, so like Swami's own, stared at mine and then Gillian's and Kit's, that morning at the diner. Once his victims were in the ranch, he always ensured they were kept drugged and under Swami's spell. Thinking about it now, in retrospect, I realise Junior took considerable pleasure in seeing other people being degraded or hurt and enjoyed having power over us.

I realised some of the Kinfolk had been well off or even rich. One elderly woman, it came to me suddenly, was a famous oil heiress whose picture I had often seen. All these people had given everything they possessed to the Kinfolk, which meant they had put their wealth in Junior's control and at his disposal.

Once I had realised what a mess I was in, it became dreadfully difficult to hide my fear and anxiety, but I knew I had to pretend to be contented and play along with the Kinfolk's requirements. I had seen the graves where "late kin" were buried, and did not want to end up in one myself.

I was frightened of Junior and would not have put it past him to dispose of dissident Kinfolk to stop them escaping to tell the world what was going on at the ranch. I was terrified of being imprisoned there for the rest of my life, especially as Swami seemed to be getting more and more manic, increasingly possessed by his self-deception, as the days went by. In retrospect I realise he too must have been taking drugs, though whether it was his choice to do so or Junior fed them to him I simply do not know. He seemed to be having hallucinations, for his preaching now embraced fires, eruptions, floods and holocausts in a maniacal vision of some kind of

Judgement Day. He kept saying the ranch was threatened from outside by hosts of enemies. I was even more frightened when he said we must live together or die together. I realised then that I must find a way out quickly.

At about that time I was put on new duties outdoors, clearing a new area of land for planting. It was overgrown with great, tough cactuses and I had to be issued with sharp tools — they must have thought I was trustworthy by that time. It was hard and painful work, I was covered with cuts and scratches. When they went septic I could not stop one of the Kinfolk smearing them with jelly from another kind of cactus, but they did seem to heal quickly.

One day, I was handed the machete and pail by a Kinfolk who was even more than usually dopey, so I was able to sneak a pair of strong cutters under my gown. That was the first thing I had independently done though I had thought plenty, and it made me feel stronger to have taken even that tiny action on my own initiative. That day I hid the cutters in the cactus field. The next time Junior drove off, I managed to sneak further down the rough ground towards the fence and began trying to cut through the linked wire. I struggled, secretly, and at odd moments, for days, whenever I could, always returning meekly to the house and meekly going to Swami and letting him do what he wanted to me, and pretending all the time to be moving round in an obedient daze. I did not know how I would get myself and Gillian away but I was determined to manage it somehow.

I worked out later that we had been with the Kinfolk for two and a half months when everything finally blew up. The prayer meetings were becoming longer and more ardent than ever, the shouting and crying and chastising more violent, coupled with repeated assurances that we were all going to God, soon we would be in heaven. I did not realise the exact significance of these assertions.

One day, which I now know was October 29th, Swami summoned the Kinfolk in the late afternoon. We came in from the outdoor work, hot and tired, but everyone else seemed full of the usual enthusiasm for the old man. He was in the hall, seated on his platform, with the usual flaming torches around his chair. There was also a strong smell of kerosene both in that room and in the rest of the ranch house.

I had diarrhoea and went out again to the toilets, so then, luckily, I had to sit at the back. Gillian was nearby. I looked for Kit among the men, and eventually found him, but his face had become blank and expressionless and he had made no sign of knowing me or Gillian for weeks. He did not look unhappy.

I felt apprehensive and ill at ease, for I had the feeling the assembled Kinfolk were on tenterhooks, as though they knew there would be some specially awesome happening that day. Swami's oratory seemed wilder and more insistent than ever, and all the Kinfolk moaned and swayed in rapture as he declaimed about death and eternity. Suddenly

Swami grasped two of the flaming torches, swung them round above his head and threw them. One landed among the women at the front, who began to scream, agonised screams such as I had never heard and hope I will never hear again, as their dresses and hair caught fire. The other torch ignited the floor matting, which must have been soaked with the kerosene I had smelt.

I realised the whole place would go up in flames. I accept I must have known even then that I should have tried to put the fire out, because I was one of the only people there who was thinking straight, and at the very least I ought to have rescued the children or died in the attempt. I have no excuse for not trying to do so. I can only say I reacted entirely on impulse, desperate to escape at last, but I shall always feel sorry for my dreadful cowardice, and I do not think even absolution, which I have been given, will ever take the feelings of guilt and remorse away.

I ran to where Gillian was standing stock still, not trying to help or get away, just paralysed like the other people, and I grabbed her by the wrist and forced her to run away with me out of the assembly hall, out of the building, across the yard, through the fields, through the cactus patch, to the fence where I had started cutting the wires. Desperately I attacked the remaining strands. Gillian stood there like a lump of stone. I shrieked at her to help and make some effort, but she waited to be pushed or pulled by me. All her initiative had gone.

I do not know how long it took before I had made a hole big enough for me to push Gillian through ahead of me, and then crawl under myself. I was concentrating so hard on escaping that the sound of the conflagration turned into a sort of background noise, but now, I have it in my mind all the time. Even from that distance, one could hear the screams.

At last we were on the far side of the fence. I seized Gillian's arm again and made her run with me across the sand and stone of the desert. When I turned to look back I suddenly realised there was an automobile moving in the compound, and for a moment thought Junior had brought it to take people to safety, and was about to go back and help him get people out, but then I saw his car was not stopping, he drove straight by and towards the gate. I was afraid he was coming for us, and dragged Gillian behind a clump of prickly pears, and as we crouched there, he drove straight off and away.

We stayed hiding there, I was trying to think what to do and work out what had happened. Looking back, I took in the full horror of what was happening.

The ranch house was blazing. I saw someone run out with her clothes on fire. She fell to the ground and rolled to try to put the fire out, but then lay twitching and then still. We saw trees ignite, suddenly like a struck match. We saw cactuses burning. Even from that distance I could feel the extra heat. It took a long time before all the sounds died away and then the silence seemed horrible, because we knew that everyone was dead.

We lay low, clinging together for warmth and comfort in the icy night. My hands were raw from cutting the fence and Gillian kept trying to be sick, but we had not had anything to eat or drink for hours. I later understood Gillian was nauseous because she was pregnant. As soon as it was light enough to see we began to walk towards the rising sun, and while we walked I worked out what to say and coached Gillian in the story to which we must both stick.

I had several reasons for not wanting to tell the truth.

Firstly, because I was ashamed, and did not want my family and friends and newspaper readers to know I had been bamboozled and raped in a madman's commune. Even more, I could not bear anyone to know I had left children and other victims to die. There might not have been anything I could do to save them, but I should have tried.

But my main reason for wanting to escape from Arizona and the United States without being identified was this: I realised that Junior, whose real name I still do not know, thought he was the sole survivor of the Kinfolk.

I was then, and am still, afraid of his trying to silence the only witnesses alive.

We spent a second night in the open, and by morning were deeply chilled and completely dehydrated. Jill had slumped into virtual uncon-sciousness. I do not think we could have walked any further or even survived much longer but after sun-rise I heard a pick-up truck and managed to stand up and attract the driver's attention. He was a naturalist from Eloy who'd been watching the wildlife with a night sight. Neither of us could say much even after he had poured liquid down our throats, but I claimed we were English tourists whose car crashed into a deep canyon, and we had wandered in the desert for forty-eight hours. We said Kit Williams had been the driver and we were certain he was dead. My story was accepted, for other people had been lost after going into the desert without proper equip-ment. An attempt was made to find the wrecked car and Kit's body, but we were eventually told it was impossible and we must just hope someone would stumble on them some day.

Tarrant's Crossing itself, as I later learnt the Kin-folk's ranch was called, was so remote that nobody discovered the disaster had happened for nearly three weeks, and by then Gillian Betteridge and I had been repatriated to England, when it made a great sensation and the newspapers were full of it for weeks because the ranch had been entirely burnt to the ground and everyone inside had perished.

I know that the man we called Junior escaped from the ranch that day. I do not know his real name, or his whereabouts, or his true relationship with the man known as Swami. I believe he thinks he is the only survivor and the only person alive who knows what went on at Tarrant's Crossing. I have no doubt he has taken possession of the money and property new members made over to the Kinfolk. I am sure I would recognise him again.

I am aware that Gillian Betteridge has claimed her pregnancy is by Kit Williams. I have no proof that it is not true.

Neither Gillian Betteridge nor I have given evidence about the events at Tarrant's Crossing, either in America or Great Britain. Mr Hardman advised it is my duty to come forward as a witness, but also warned me of the legal and social consequences. Pending my doing so I have made this notarised statement.

Mr Hardman has given me an assurance that it will be kept in confidence till twenty-five years after my death unless or until the man I knew as "Junior" comes to trial.

Signed

Luisa Victoria Considine, 12 December 1965.

Witnessed by Kenneth Hardman, Solicitor to the Supreme Court.

Vera Pinter, Shorthand typist.

# CHAPTER
# TWENTY

She sat alone except for Raymond's silent dog Rufus, which lay close to her, whether at his command or not she did not know.

Down below, the sea, choppy today, with white flecks on a steel grey expanse and no ships in sight. Near by, the sloping, grassy ground, its green scattered with boulders, clumps of gorse and heather, and at ground level tiny plants. Without moving from her painting-hut she could see violets, harebells, daisies, thrift, spurge and four other varieties she could not name.

That stone was granite and quartz. That smell was of wild thyme. That bird was a magpie, that sound the hoot of a distant buoy. The identifications were a solace, a reminder of order and patterns in a fragmented world. Tess's internal armour of loathing and disgust was cracking now. Other ideas came pushing through, though she couldn't think straight and everything was muddled together: there was still the dreadful bleak indifference and cynicism of the first two days, now increasingly mixed with uncomplicated grief for Biddy and Lara, fear for herself, and a remembrance, perhaps a resurgence, of the love-at-first-sight she had felt for Raymond; appreciation of the scene before her, relief at having some peace and privacy; plus a cold, intellectual realisation slowly firming up in her mind, of what must actually have happened to Lara, and Biddy, and Jill Williams, and Luisa, and why. When she had worked it all out she would tell the police. They had interrogated her in London and in Cornwall, suspicious, even hostile men had asked useless questions, but they were no further on, she had heard, none of the responses to her televised appeal had produced useful information. A week on, the story was not even in the news any more. Soon it would be forgotten — though not by Saffron.

Tess had not voiced it to Raymond or Saffron, who, having known none of the victims personally, was fired as much by intellectual curiosity as emotion. That morning she had been going on about it again.

"I've worked it out, Tess, it's all the Williamses' fault, don't you agree? Jill Williams must have murdered Mummy to stop her telling who her baby's father really was, and lay low all her life so Petronella would always think it had been Kit. And Petronella's family — I don't suppose they'd have looked after her if they'd known." She was silent for a moment, and then went on, "Or what about the prince's security men? Maybe they killed Jill to stop anyone discovering the truth about Petronella."

Tess found herself reacting slowly these days, and was one idea in retard when she said, "Jill was shut away in a mental hospital for years after Petronella was born. Petronella must have been getting on for five when Luisa died."

"Are you saying she did it as soon as she came out?

And then committed suicide out of remorse?" Saffron said.

Tess was about to answer when a wave of grey disgust swept over her. She felt like someone just keeping afloat having come, lungs bursting, to the surface. She took gasps of the air of conversation and company, but the dirty water of alienation kept suddenly swamping her. It was Raymond who answered Saffron.

"No, darling, we think the same person killed your mother and Jill Williams, and poor Tess's family too. They thought poor little Lara was Tess."

Then he had noticed Tess's face, and stopped, and gestured at Saffron. The dense, still quiet of Thalassa descended again.

All the painting guests had gone when they got there. No reporters or photographers seemed to be staking the place out. Tess's sluggish mind registered they had no reason to connect her with Raymond; and of all the deaths the police were now investigating, Luisa's, being so long ago, must seem far less worth covering than the others. Than Lara's, or Biddy's, or Petronella's mother's.

Tess had told Inspector Rogerson about Moira, the *Argus* editor who had been mugged just when she was looking into Luisa's death, and about Peter Slowe, who was killed before he could tell what he knew about it. But Rogerson had not added those bits of information to his public presentation, and he had told her not to mention it either. Not that she wanted to.

Raymond and Saffron had chosen an upstairs room for Tess this time. It was a room for their own guests rather than course participants, had a high, soft bed with a flowered eiderdown, old mahogany furniture faded by the strong light into a straw colour, and curtains and covers on which only the ghost of a bright chintz could be discerned. It was a comforting, comfortable space, very different in style from Tess's own flat and from the Trevails' house, so she was not pestered by reminders of other bedrooms in other homes. And it was more homely than the guest rooms at the Blagdens', where not an inch was left untitivated.

Tess had slept better here. Not well, with nightmares haunting even her sedated mind, but better. In the morning it became just possible to believe that she might live again, though never normally. Whatever normally had meant. There was no going back to her false state of immunity, when she had not supposed the dramas and tragedies which were an assistant editor's raw material had any application to her own humdrum life.

Raymond sat at his kitchen table grasping a stoneware mug. His silent presence seemed reassuring. Tess's eyes fixed on his strong, steady hands. The telephone rang in the hall and Saffron went out.

"Daddy, it's for you."

"Yes," he said, and "No," and "If it's really necessary." He and Saffron were needed in Camborne, he explained and drew Saffron outside the room, but Tess heard his whisper. The police needed a statement from them at their county headquarters.

They want to confirm an alibi for me, she thought drearily. They think I could have gone to London and done that to my family.

She heard Saffron whisper urgently, "But Daddy, I thought we were supposed to be keeping her safe," and Raymond murmur, "The police must think it's OK to leave her, otherwise they wouldn't have told us to come."

But Raymond would not go until he had settled Tess in her painting hut. Paints, book, tray with a vacuum flask and tin of biscuits, binoculars. "Will you be all right on your own?" he asked anxiously. "Rufus can stay with you and we'll be as quick as we can."

Tess was relieved to be alone, and said so.

"Right, well you shouldn't be disturbed here." But he came back five minutes later with a portable cassette player and a selection of tapes. Momentarily Tess wondered whether to thank him anyway. Then she admitted she derived no pleasure from music. No more lies, she thought.

All those lies. Her own deceits, her pretences, her "cover stories". How she'd been punished! But other people had suffered more for her sins. What would the old preacher have said? Was it indeed all Tess's fault? Malcolm had believed it was. But Raymond said she should not blame herself. That would be like saying rape was the victim's fault for being there.

It hadn't been Lara's fault for being there. It hadn't been her fault she told a stranger on the telephone that Tess was still investigating Luisa's death and had come up with something interesting. Nor had it been her fault that that someone had come to kill Tess and killed Lara because she was there in Tess's place.

Poor girl, poor little girl. For the first time Tess's eyes filled with uncomplicated, natural tears.

"Tess, my dear . . ." Raymond's voice was filled with concern.

"She was going to be a wonderful woman one day, a top person. It should have been me."

"She must have been a lovely girl, Tess, I don't doubt it, but so are you, she wouldn't have wanted —"

"It doesn't matter, I accepted years ago that I was never going to get to the top or be best at anything. Most people don't, you know. But Lara would. I hoped she would."

Raymond cleared his throat several times and when he spoke it was with an unfamiliar hesitation in his voice.

"I've got a confession to make."

"A confession?" Her hands flew to her mouth. "You didn't . . . !" Tess's voice was so appalled that Raymond was taken aback.

"What's wrong?"

"Luisa . . . you don't mean . . . ?"

"Tess! You can't suppose . . . No. I'm talking about something quite else. Something private. Luisa's papers, the unfinished work and the diaries, I want to tell you —"

"The ones that are coming out this month? Her new book?"

"I wrote it."

"What? I know you had to do a lot of editing, but —"

"I wrote it all. I used the pink foolscap paper she liked and the old typewriter she always wrote on, I even found some of her own carbon paper. One or two of the pieces

I just expanded, notes she'd made herself, but I invented the rest, I imitated her style. I forged it."

"But why?" Tess demanded. "I don't understand."

"For the money. We need the money for Thalassa, we aren't making enough to keep it going, it was the only way I could think of to get some influx of cash, a decent advance, an American sale. That's why."

Tess said, "What makes you tell me so now?"

"I don't want to go on pretending. In comparison with these dreadful things, how can I carry on a petty deception, just for money? I want to be honest so you'd know what I am. You seemed to think I was special, but I'm very ordinary, very uncreative and I've lived off Luisa's genius all these years."

"Didn't anyone guess?"

"Not that I know of, and I don't think anyone could prove it, all that happens is people say I'm scraping the barrel to publish odds and ends she never intended to be read by anyone else. But I want you to know what I really am."

It didn't seem to matter much, but in so far as she cared, Tess was glad to know that Raymond was imperfect too. As he went up the slope towards the house she watched his lean back and stooping shoulders with a resurgence of an earlier emotion, love crossed with relief at finding love. She had a flash of realisation that she was going to get over it, stay here, be with Raymond and be all right.

A fitful gleam of sun came from behind the sullen clouds. Tess, who had been bone tired since arriving at Thalassa, leaned her face back in the warmth and descended into a guilty, haunted doze full of random memories. Lara's bedroom, meeting Ilona in the steam room at the Porchester baths, her mother's degeneration, Archie Frazer, her desk at the *Argus*.

She woke with a start, a voice in her mind. Lara's voice? For an instant before it dissipated she saw everything. Panting, she realised, I do know who it was, if only I could think it through. It's all there, in my subconscious. I've got all the information. Think, Tess, think.

The outlines of a figure coalesced in her mind. Junior, from the Kinfolk, their only survivor, with his high-domed, crew-cut head and his amber eyes. Petronella's amber eyes, staring into the fire at the Blagdens', her charisma, Junior's charisma. Swami as Luisa described him, mesmerising all those people into self-abnegation. If Petronella was really Swami's child, it made her Junior's sister. Junior, who had escaped from the carnage at Tarrant's Crossing, believing he was the only person left alive who knew what had gone on there, the inheritor of the deluded Kinfolk's wealth.

Junior must have thought he was safe once all of them were dead. He could start a new life as a rich man. Then Luisa wrote a book which sold all over the world. Her picture was in papers from Penzance to Peru. Luisa, last seen by Junior in the ranch. Luisa, who could give him away.

Tess pushed aside the tartan rug Raymond had tucked round her knees and got up to walk the hundred yards up the valley to the studio where Luisa had died. Its door was propped open with a three-legged stone bowl, so she went in.

Junior had come to Thalassa and found Luisa alone with the baby. No, that wasn't right, of course he'd been sure she would be alone with the baby, because he had rung with a made-up message to get Raymond to go out to Penzance.

Something anxious stirred at the back of Tess's mind. She hoped Raymond would come back soon.

Don't be silly, she admonished herself, nothing's going to happen here, the police wouldn't have called him away if they hadn't been sure it was all right.

Had Luisa come into the converted barn to write or paint, had she walked aimlessly down the garden as mothers do with wailing babies, where did Junior find her? Had she recognised him at once, did she know he meant trouble, did she understand why?

It was here, in this whitewashed shed. Standing under the rough-cut wood of the fatal beam, Tess faced the half-open door and tried to visualise Junior with his coil of stolen rope.

The sight was vivid in her mind's eye. Then a shadow blocked the shaft of light, a tall shadow, the shadow of a man. The dog barked furiously and lurched forward. "Raymond?" Tess said. "Is that you?" And Junior himself came in through the door.

# CHAPTER
# TWENTY-ONE

Junior.

Or Senior; in his late fifties, by this time.

He was a short, burly figure dressed in clothes to deter casual interest. With dark glasses on, and a red and white bobble hat, plus jeans, training shoes, a loose sweat shirt with its collar zipped and turned up over the neatly pointed grey beard and carrying a small green rucksack, he would have been unremarkable and unrecognisable. Coming along the coastal footpath and up the valley, he was just another hiker.

But now he was holding the hat and shades. His brown-skinned, fleshy face was revealed, with its fringe of beard and newly cut hair round an almost pointed scalp and yellow eyes.

The dog launched himself at the man, a whirlpool of glossy black. Ferdinand B. Carne directed his gaze at the animal and raised his finger. Rufus was immediately silent, flattened into a black stripe on the ground beside the man.

I knew all along, came the instantaneous thought. It was all there, Tess realised, the information unrecognised but hanging over me. Who else could it be?

The dread proprietor was really Junior. Junior had

become the *Argus*'s proprietor. Junior, once known as John Doe, was F.B. Carne or Khan or Kahn.

In a parody of office manners he said, "Ms Redpath. Good-day to you."

Tess stood in a kind of paralysis while a stream of events rushed in front of her with the speed of a drowning person's life history.

That last day at the *Argus*. He'd asked what she was working on and she mentioned new material about Luisa Weiss in the same conversation as the deaths at Tarrant's Crossing. He must have understood her to mean she knew things she shouldn't know. That was why he lost his temper and made Hamish get rid of her and then made sure she'd never get another job where she would use the information he thought she had.

It was he who had come upon Moira in the office when she was there alone catching up with her work. Moira had told him what she had heard from Peter Slowe: exciting new details about a man on the cliff path with a rope on the day Luisa Weiss died. Poor Peter Slowe. And poor Moira. No wonder Bert, sleeping rough in the *Argus* car-park, had not seen anyone who didn't belong there. He'd only seen the proprietor himself.

It was Carne, all the time, it had always been Carne. He'd come here to kill Luisa. He'd gone to the Isle of Man to kill Jill Williams. He'd intended to silence Tess in her turn but it was Lara, not Tess, he'd found in her flat.

How did he know she was here? His own chief crime reporter Archie Frazer told him. How had he — but of course. It had not been the police who summoned Raymond to Camborne that morning.

This remorseless, pitiless man was a mass murderer. Victims littered his tracks.

Far, far away something screamed through Tess's abstraction. Run, escape, get away. But a heavy, soggy inertia occupied her conscious mind and weighted down her limbs. She felt as passive as the quelled dog Rufus.

He was staring into her soul. His tiger eyes, large, unblinking, black-fringed, held her gaze. He was speaking. What was he saying? His voice was very gentle. He sounded reassuring. Gentle. Kind. He was not to be feared. The words were calm and soothing. He wanted her to do something. He wanted her to come with him, walk nearer to him across the floor and take his strong hand and go beside him to the sea, to the cliff top, the high cliff over the sea, out of this place, come, Tess, come . . .

Tess's feet stirred sluggishly on the stone-flagged floor, one edging forward, then the other shuffling in front of it, as she was drawn inexorably towards Ferdinand B. Came.

A distant sound momentarily interrupted the concentration he'd induced. A flash of rebellion briefly stopped movement, as Luisa's face flashed before her, a vibrant, defiant Luisa, the star who inspired the thirteen-year-old Tess. Another voice was shrieking inside her head. She dragged her eyes from his, but the white walls and solid furniture seemed shadowy and insubstantial. He was the only real thing there and the magnet of his gaze dragged hers back towards him.

What was that noise? A rattle, a roar, overhead now, closer, louder. He grabbed her hand and took her out of the studio into the cobbled yard. Shockingly low, immediately above them a blue and white helicopter was hovering. It trembled like a giant dragonfly. A man was leaning sideways out of its open door shouting. Shouting.

Startled into awareness, Tess tried to snatch her wrist out of Carne's grasp, but he tightened his hand.

A voice boomed from the sky, louder than the rotor blades, filling the air with terror. She could not take the words in. What was happening, what was going on? Her mind was freed into her own intellectual control, but it only uselessly repeated, "I don't understand. This can't be happening. This isn't real!"

She felt a hard pressure on her temple. He was holding a gun. It was pressed against her head.

For a brief instant there was stillness. Her body understood before her brain did. First she felt her legs weaken, bowels loosen, and hot urine trickling out and down her thighs, then she understood she was his hostage. He was going to shoot her as he'd shot Biddy and — yes, she realised, he wiped out my Lara, he'll kill me.

Resignation took brief hold. It was only fair. Tess had no right to live with Lara dead.

But then a furious refusal swept passivity away. It's not — I won't — NO!

If Tess had thought about what she was doing she would not have risked his pressure on the trigger; better be a hostage than a corpse. But her reaction had no intellectual input. Instinct forced her to escape and she twisted herself down and sideways, wrenching at his grasp.

He did fire the gun. But in the very instant she collapsed from the searing, slashing agony, she felt the weight of his body fall on to her. She was whining like a fox in a trap but he was silent, a heavy weight. A dead weight.

Blinded by her own blood gushing from a gash across her scalp, Tess did not see the police marksman approach in combat position, nor was she aware of the others who followed him, flooding into the sunny courtyard in their incongruous battle gear. But she felt it and screamed when they moved him away and touched her, And by the time she was lifted on to a stretcher, kind unconsciousness had supervened.

Thalassa was dotted with mementoes of mortality. Inscrutable granite standing stones from distant antiquity, a pagan graveyard excavated by Luisa's grandfather, carved slate memorials to nameless mariners who had died on the cove's vicious rocks, the war memorial with the names of nine local boys, the plaque commemorating Luisa herself, the deathly studio itself. In every one of the cottages generations of residents had breathed their last and at least two Considines had died in their beds. There were dead birds and spiders, dying flowers, stumps of diseased elm trees. In the midst of life we are in death. Tess remembered the old preacher of her childhood saying so, his tone as solemn as the words. Even Raymond's bookcases had been a reminder, being full of the murder mysteries which used to be his favourite reading, but he'd noticed Tess noticing them and the next time she went into the long sitting-room the shelves had been emptied.

She would recover. Gradually her grief would mitigate, terror and trauma would pass, the wound in her scalp would heal. One day, she could sense it would be soon, she would love Raymond again. They were well suited, two low-flyers together. It was good to be somewhere that had hardly changed for years, in a community where remarks about any individual were preceded by a run-down of his ancestors. She needed the security of a long view, after her former job's short-termism.

Meanwhile Raymond was looking after her but Tess had moved into the cottage called Honeysuckle. She needed to keep a little distance, at least for the time being. Ilona had very kindly come to stay with her — "What else are friends for?" — and like all other friends and enemies, even Jacques, who had written cautiously but sympathetically from Brussels, told Tess to "give it time".

Tess's own flat was on the market, and she did not care whether it was as a wreck ripe for development and with exciting associations, or a house of horror. She would never bring herself to enter the building or the street or even the neighbourhood again. It would be haunted by its dead. Biddy, Lara, even Desmond Kennedy. He had fulfilled his own prediction, anticipating his death from Aids by swimming out into the warm blue waters of the Red Sea and never coming back. Behind him in London he left a scrupulously ordered apartment and a will leaving everything to the London Lighthouse charity.

The estate agents had rung that morning with a couple of offers for Tess's flat. The money was not much by London standards, but would buy a lot of property in west Cornwall. Tess was going to use it to pay Scarlett Weiss off. It was the least she could do for Saffron, who had saved her life. Raymond would without question have gone all the way to Camborne that day, nearly an hour's drive, to discover nobody at the police head-quarters had spoken to him. It was Saffron who realised they should have checked and insisted on stopping at a call box, and Saffron whose passionate arguments had convinced the authorities there was trouble at Thalassa.

Already the life Tess had led for years seemed vague and insubstantial. She could not imagine why she'd given a damn for the *Argus* or her social life, or for Jacques. He'd sent flowers, a showy bouquet, its card signed in a florist's backward sloping writing, with the single letter J. She momentarily wondered how long he would manage to keep his anonymous distance from the affair, and could not be bothered to care.

Tess played childish games with Ilona, Monopoly and rummy, and strolled on the cliffs with Raymond or Saffron and tried not to think.

Now Ilona was asking questions again, delicately probing. Tess felt her mind skittering nervously away.

Death talk had been the stuff of Tess's working life, for newspaper people lived on it. War, assassination, plane crashes, domestic murders — such had been her raw material, but she had no experience to guide her now. On the far side of the divide between the press and the public, she did not know what words to use or thoughts to think. She was unrehearsed for tragedy.

The hammering headache was poised to come back, but if she kept her head very still she could keep it at bay. The doctors, who earlier had congratulated her on a narrow escape, told her she should be feeling all right by now and it was time to cut down on the painkillers and sleeping pills, take some exercise, look to the future.

Carne's life had been saved by heroic surgery. As soon as he regained consciousness he had been charged with the murders of Biddy and Lara Trevail, Peter Slowe and Moira Hill Dexter, and moved to a prison hospital. The charge sheet did not mention Luisa Weiss or Jill Williams; Ilona had heard from someone at the *Argus* that the Crown Prosecution Service was not convinced of his responsibility for their deaths, and anyway could never make a jury believe in it. But Luisa's so-called suicide and the events at Tarrant's Crossing were expected to be part of the evidence, which meant that all the most dramatic details were *sub judice* and could not be reported or discussed in public, at least not within the jurisdiction, though nothing could silence the American media.

In private, frenzied negotiations were taking place and questions being asked. Immediately Carne was sentenced a flood of books and articles would appear. And the new production company set up by Ilona Spivak and her partner had won a commission to make a drama-documentary for BBC2. Ilona had mentioned it as soon as she arrived. "I won't do it if you mind, Tessie. Do you mind?"

"I don't really want to talk about it."

"It's up to you, I won't press you, but someone will be doing it whatever happens. They've already started."

Tess had not wanted to read the press coverage, least of all what it said about her. But, like her tongue on a sensitive tooth, she had not been able to stop her eyes falling on her own name, the adjectives applied to it, the regrettably recognisable photographs.

Raymond, although he had suffered such intrusion so often and for so long, could not bear it for Tess. It had been she, quoting an old, familiar justification, who had been forced to calm him down. "Once you've let journalists in, even if it's only once and you think their nosiness is contained, you have lost the right to complain. You can't agree to an interview and then limit the content. Either you never answer a single question or welcome a single printed compliment, or you've lost your arguments for privacy."

"But you never did."

"Yes, I was interviewed for a women's magazine, years ago. It was just the once, but that was only because nobody else was interested, I'd have loved to be famous. At least, I thought I would, then."

"There ought to be some way of controlling it."

"There isn't, not really. Letting the media into your life, you've caught a tiger by the tail."

Having changed sides, Tess knew what she was up against. She could not stop other people writing about, enacting and observing her own personal experiences.

Once, years ago, she had stood by as an experienced crime reporter persuaded a murderer's wife to sell her story exclusively to the *Argus*, using the arguments Ilona did not need to spell out.

"At least you know we'll be on your side," Ilona had said, and then did not mention the subject for a few days. At last, cautiously, like someone trying to draw near to a wild animal, she had begun to speak about it, and when Tess did not bite her head off, brought out her notes and working papers.

"Of course we can't say Petsy wasn't really Kit Williams's daughter, not in so many words, 'cos we couldn't ever prove it unless she co-operates with tests and you can't see her doing that, can you? She must be terrified the prince'll back out of marrying her as it is. But I did hear they were going to nip off and tie the knot quickly, just in case. I think it's a shame. Don't you think a state wedding would make things seem better?"

Now that she at last felt Tess was up to it, Ilona had been talk talk talking all morning. She talked about people. What must they have thought, why did they do this, what made them say that?

Tell me about Raymond, she urged, what did he say, what does he do, what's he like in bed? The question, perfectly acceptable in the past and part of the normal exchange between Tess and her female friends, now seemed unanswerable. Tess could not possibly tell Ilona what Raymond did or liked, it would be a betrayal; and in realising that, Tess realised it was the first time she had ever known such exclusive confidence with any man.

286

Ilona, like a badly trained reporter, kept asking what Tess felt. "What did it feel like when you first saw him?" she would demand. And now, emboldened by Tess's return to real life, she asked, "Describe how it felt the moment Carne came through the door." Tess knew that such questions would be the inevitable aftermath, sooner or later. In the past she had often despatched reporters to ask them. Ilona, who had been a good friend, had the right to the first answers, but Tess, who had never been very perceptive or sensitive about other people's reactions, did not want to describe her own, and all the less because the only emotions she could remember ever feeling in her whole life were grief and shock. Anyway, she couldn't begin to imagine what Luisa must have thought, or Moira, or Carne himself, and didn't care, either, least of all about him.

But Ilona was a people person herself, she always said, and on she went with her pop psychology: Carne's overpowering father, his peculiar upbringing, incapable of love, long trained for influencing people, unable to believe they were as important as he was.

"He never had a friend, there's not been a single person to say they were fond of him. He just built up his empire, money, businesses, newspapers, observed the social forms, kept himself to himself. You wouldn't have thought it was possible to be so secretive and get away with it, these days, but he did. A great, looming, unidentified, powerful presence, that's what we'll show. A lonely, secretive nutter who simply got rid of anyone who was inconvenient. I bet he had many more victims, if only we knew who they were."

Even the *Western Morning News*, a regional paper, and the only one Tess was now prepared to read, had forced before her eyes far more than she had ever wanted to know about Carne. What did she care that he'd had a peculiar childhood? The story was that he'd been trailed round Canada from Hicksville to dump with a travelling circus because his father was a self-styled Indian fakir. His mother, it turned out, had committed suicide. Hanged herself with a clothes line when Junior was only four years old.

Well, so what? Did that excuse megalomania and murder? Did that justify conning idiots out of their money at Tarrant's Crossing and — as it now turned out there had been — previous, smaller communes in other parts of North America before that?

No, it didn't. Nor did it explain his growing up as a power freak and loner. He'd never married or, as far as the snoops could find out, had a relationship with woman, man or animal. Other people were never real to him. Tess didn't want to know. The very thought of him polluted this place. She said wearily, "Do we have to go on talking about him?"

"Oh poor Tess, there's me rabbiting on when you're so miserable. It's just, this is such a chance for us, to have an inside story in our first production."

"I know, I want it to be a success for you, Ilona, I know how important it is."

"You are sweet."

"How will you tackle it?" Tess made herself inquire.

"We're thinking of doing the whole programme through your eyes, actually, Tess, the innocent onlooker drawn in by accident. We might go backwards, start when Carne comes in on you in the studio here, some scenic shots of this place, the beach, the view, Luisa's barn, and then what happened in your flat — sorry, I won't mention that again, sorry, sorry, and the talk you had with Petronella in that guest house, and the day Carne got you sacked from the *Argus* — or do you think that might be better at the beginning after all?"

"Whatever you think best."

"We'll have to work it out. Or maybe we'd better use flashbacks after all. We've had a brilliant offer from an actor for Carne's part, and we've already got lots of ideas for who to do you, unless you want to decide, you know I won't do anything without your say-so, Tessie, I want to make sure you like what we make of it."

I'm sure I won't, Tess thought. She cringed from the whole idea of seeing herself portrayed in a drama-documentary, and although she knew someone else would do it, if Ilona didn't, all the same she didn't want television cameras at Thalassa and script writers putting words in her mouth.

What was it she'd heard Jason Spedding say, that last morning at work? That someone — it must have been poor, undepicted Jill Williams — might as well be a savage who believed photographs stole her soul. As Ilona — so kind, so concerned, always such a good mate — spoke, Tess could see herself becoming something else in her friend's mind, the object of research and invention, an artificial construct.

"We want to use Luisa's studio as the main back-ground," Ilona said. "We might call the piece something to do with it. The house of death . . . the studio of death . . . the barn . . ."

Tess thought, as she'd thought the first time she saw the place, they should have burnt it down. Ilona burbled on about development money, schedules, publicity, agents, while Tess's mind filled with flames. Not the nightmare conflagration which haunted Jill Williams and Luisa, not the holocausts and immolation that filled their private art and verse, but cleansing, healing, cauterising fire.

Tinder, she thought. Petrol, dry straw and kindling. A funeral pyre for the lies of the past, for Luisa, for Biddy and Lara. That is what Raymond must do for me. It's what I shall do for Saffron. We shall burn the place down together.

And Ilona's programme?

No. Not Ilona, not anyone else. No inventions or projections, no trespassing.

If my story is to be told, Tess decided, it will have to be told by me.

ISIS publish a wide range of books in large print, from fiction to biography. A full list of titles is available free of charge from the address below. Alternatively, contact your local library for details of their collection of ISIS large print books.

Details of ISIS complete and unabridged audio books are also available.

Any suggestions for books you would like to see in large print or audio are always welcome.

7 Centremead
Osney Mead
Oxford OX2 0ES
(01865) 250333

# GENERAL FICTION

KINGSLEY AMIS
**Biographer's Moustache**

JUDY ASTLEY
**Seven for a Secret**
**Just For the Summer**

BERYL BAINBRIDGE
**An Awfully Big Adventure**
**Every Man For Himself**

JULIAN BARNES
**Cross Channel**

H. E. BATES
**A Crown Of Wild Myrtle**

CHARLOTTE BINGHAM
**At Home**

JOHN BRAINE
**Room at the Top**

ANITA BROOKNER
**Incidents in the Rue Laugier**

GEORGE MACKAY BROWN
**Beside the Ocean of Time**

ANTHONY BURGESS
**A Dead Man in Deptford**

ANGELA CARTER
**Shadow Dance**

THOMAS H. COOK
**Breakheart Hill**

# GENERAL FICTION

CATHERINE COOKSON
**The Branded Man**

LES DAWSON
**The Blade and the Passion**

KATHLEEN DAYUS
**April Showers**

JUDE DEVEREAUX
**The Heiress**

LAWRENCE DURRELL
**White Eagles Over Serbia**

DOROTHY EDEN
**Crow Hollow**

HOWARD FAST
**The Bridge Builder's Story**

RUMER GODDEN
**An Episode of Sparrows**

WILLIAM GOLDING
**The Double Tongue**

PATRICIA GREEN, CHARLES COLLINGWOOD
& HEIDI NIKLAUS
**The Book of The Archers**

KATE GRENVILLE
**Dark Places**

JOHN HADFIELD
**Love on a Branch Line**

# GENERAL FICTION

SUSAN HILL
**The Albatross and Other Stories**
**The Bird of Night**
**A Bit of Singing and Dancing**
**A Change For the Better**
**I'm the King of the Castle**
**In the Springtime of the Year**

JANETTE TURNER HOSPITAL
**Oyster**

ANGELA HUTH
**Nowhere Girl**
**South of the Lights**
**Such Visitors**
**Virginia Fly is Drowning**

JAN KARON
**At Home in Mitford**

GARRISON KEILLOR
**The Book of Guys**

THOMAS KENEALLY
**A River Town**

DORIS LESSING
**Love Again**

PENELOPE LIVELY
**Heat Wave**

LARRY MCMURTRY
**The Late Child**

# GENERAL FICTION

DAVID MALOUF
**Remembering Babylon**

GABRIEL GARCÍA MÁRQUEZ
**Of Love and Other Demons**

DAPHNE DU MAURIER
**Rule Britannia**

CHRISTOPHER MONGER
**The Englishman Who Went Up a Hill and Came
Down a Mountain**

L. M. MONTGOMERY
**Anne of the Island**

IRIS MURDOCH
**Jackson's Dilemma**

DAVID NOBBS
**The Legacy of Reginald Perrin**

PATRICK O'BRIAN
**The Commodore**

UNA-MARY PARKER
**False Promises**
**Taking Control**

JILL PATON WALSH
**Knowledge of Angels**
**A Piece of Justice**

MARJORIE QUARTON
**One Dog, His Man and His Trials**

# GENERAL FICTION

Douglas Reeman
**A Dawn Like Thunder**

Jean Rhys
**After Leaving Mr Mackenzie**
**Good Morning, Midnight**
**Sleep It Off, Lady**
**Smile, Please**
**Tigers are Better-Looking**
**Voyage in the Dark**

Harold Robbins
**The Raiders**

Jennifer Rowe
**Stranglehold**

Mary Selby
**A Wing and a Prayer**

Mary Sheepshanks
**A Price For Everything**

Jane Smiley
**Moo**

Muriel Spark
**Reality and Dreams**

Susanna Tamaro
**Follow Your Heart**

Leslie Thomas
**Virgin Soldiers**